WHAT'S REAL

WHAT'S REAL

Daaimah S. Poole

Kensington Publishing Corp.
http://www.kensingtonbooks.com

DAFINA BOOKS are published by

Kensington Publishing Corp.
850 Third Avenue
New York, NY 10022

First Dafina trade paperback printing: May 2005
First Dafina mass market printing: November 2006

10 9 8 7 6 5 4 3 2 1

Printed in the United States of America

Acknowledgments

Thank you Allah for this blessing.

Okay, first and foremost I want to say thank you to everyone who has picked up, read, or told someone about *Yo Yo Love* and *Got A Man*. I appreciate the e-mails, letters, and love from everyone. I would like to thank all my family and friends for your continued support. All the readers, book clubs, African-American bookstores, Culture Plus, and A & B book distributors.

To my family: my dad, Auzzie; my mom, Robin; my boys, Hamid and Ahsan; my sisters, Daaiyah, Nadirah, and Najah; my step-mom, Pulcheria; my grandmother Dolores Dandridge, and the rest of my family—thank you so much; I love you all. Thank you to Alvin Cooke, the Dandridges, Pooles, Wertzses, friends and anybody I forgot to mention.

Thanks to Karen E. Quinones Miller (*Ida B.*) for always being there. Shawna Grundy (*Gotta Have It*), Nikki Turner (*The Glamorous Life*), Allison Hobbs (*Insatiable*), Camille Miller, Fatimah Lane, Bruce Seiber and Nancy Grant.

Special thanks to my agent, Shashana Crichton. I would also like to thank everyone at Kensington Publishing: Karen Thomas, Nicole Bruce, Jessica McClean, and Lydia Stein.

For everyone who wants to write, pick up a pen and get started. Dreams do come true.

Thanks for the love,

Daaimah

Chapter One

Janelle Martin

"**S**o that's it? I can't say anything to you? You're going to go be a groupie for the weekend," Sean said.

"I'm not a groupie!" I yelled into the phone at work.

"Any girls who follow rappers and athletes out of town are groupies!" Sean yelled back at me.

"First of all, I'm not following anyone. Second, I don't have to explain shit to you. You know what it is. Why don't you just say you don't want me to go?"

"Okay, I don't want you to go," he said remorsefully.

"I can't do that, Sean. I already paid for everything and took off from work. I'll see you when I get back. And as far as I remember, we are not together like that."

"Whatever, Nellie. If I really was a hater I wouldn't have given you money to go," he said.

"You didn't contribute that much. Bye, Sean," I said and hung up. Men always want to be all up on you when they know somebody else wants you or you're going out with your friends. If I was staying in the house doing nothing and asking him to go somewhere, Sean would give me fifty reasons why he couldn't go. But since I'm going away he wants to act like he can't live without me. I don't owe Sean shit. He is not even my man. He has a lot of nerve asking me not to go on my trip. Sean is just my dog. We go to clubs and the movies together. He breaks me off when I need some. And he is there when I need somebody to talk to about my problems with a guy I'm dating. I've known Sean since high school. He was a senior and I was a junior. He used to like me, but at that time I didn't date high school boys, so he wasn't my type. We ran into each other at Pegasus Nightclub a couple of years ago. We were out of school and Sean looked good and had matured. We got together that night and it has been on ever since. I like Sean, but we could never be a couple, because he is somebody that is in transition. Transition, meaning he has great potential but has not tapped it yet. He's twenty-five, hasn't finished college, never had a job more than three months, but he says he's going to be a millionaire by thirty. I wonder how. He's cute and dresses stylishly. He was into button-down shirts, blazers, and ripped jeans before they were trendy. He is always superclean. I guess he is borderline metro sexual. He is funny, makes me laugh, and has goals, but he has no money. If he had the world, he would give it to me. But that's the problem, he ain't got no fucking money. He has visions for the future and a lot of good ideas, but no way to see them through. Our relationship is open, he can see who he wants and vice versa. We both try not to catch feelings when we talk to other people. We have talked about being exclusive, but we decided against it. Sometimes it's hard, because like I said, he is my dog as well as my lover. I wish I would not go on vacation for his ass. I didn't get mad at him when he went to All-Star Weekend in Los Angeles.

I need a vacation from Sean, my job, and my family too! My mother and two brothers, Taron and Jamal, moved in on me about seven months ago. They were *supposed* to be staying with me for only a couple of months until my mom saved enough for another apartment or she found a job. Neither has happened and I am stuck with them. The public relations firm she worked at for eighteen years laid her off. She was a couple of years away from retirement. They were supposed to give her a pension, but instead they filed for bankruptcy and didn't give my mom anything. She lost her apartment and her car was repoed. My one-bedroom apartment looks like a hurricane hit it because of them. I come home and there will be shoes, socks, and clothes all over the floor. My brothers leave the toilet seat up and don't flush it. Taron is eight, Jamal is ten, and they are more than a handful.

My mother cooks and won't wash the pots she burns. And she burns everything, even rice. Then she tries to doctor the rice up with butter and seasoned salt like you can't taste the burnt. As quickly as I clean up, they dirty up. I have stepped on race cars and tripped over balls. I am losing my damn mind. It's so bad in my house that I'm ready to leave, but I don't have anywhere else to go.

My bills are kicking my butt. Everything is on the verge of being cut off. My electric is so high from my brothers staring at the damn X-box game all day. My cable bill is three hundred dollars from them ordering the same movies over and over again. My mother doesn't click over when she's on the other line and then she doesn't give me my messages until two days later. I really am about to scream. I want to kick them out so bad. But it's my mom and brothers, so I can't. So I let them stay and I deal with it.

I work at the Pique, a clothing store in the Gallery Mall in downtown Philly. I'm frustrated with my job because I am the assistant manager. I do everything the manager, Joan, should do. I do the payroll, inventory, dressing the mannequins, hiring, and firing. I close the store at night because Joan never has the time because she is too busy prancing her fat ass to Aunt Annie's Pretzels at the other end of the mall. I have been in retail since I was about fifteen and it is getting on my nerves. I started out at the Gap; then I came here.

I hate closing the store at the end of the night. Every time

I close, I have to make sure all the clothes are put back, hung up, and all the hangers are straight and lined up. I hate cleaning out the dressing rooms. I also have to make sure the money is right and check all the employees' bags to see if anybody tried to take home some free gifts from the store. The only good thing about working here is my 15 percent discount and being able to get first pick on any size 8 that comes in.

It was almost closing time and there were still like twenty people in line. It was only me and the new girl, Shana, working. She's a young girl who comes in after her classes at Community College. She's like nineteen and a little ditzy but cool. Only problem with her is she doesn't know what the hell she's doing. Every other minute she has a void. So I have to clean up her mistakes all night.

I was doing a return when Shana nudged me in the arm and said, "Janelle, that girl just put something in her bag!" I looked up to see what Shana was talking about. I saw the girl. It was now time to play security guard too! I walked over to a few feet from the petite girl who seemed to be helping herself to different color tank tops. Her bag was bulky. I watched her for a moment, then decided to approach her. First, I peeked at her through the jean rack and that's when I noticed she had a baby stroller with her and no baby. Underneath the stroller was almost a whole rack of our jean shorts and cargo pants. I walked behind her and said, "What's in your bag?"

"What? Nothing's in my bag!" the girl said as she turned around, startled and her eyes wide open.

"Well, let me see for myself," I said as I tried to take the bag from the girl.

"No, get off my shit!" she yelled as she gave me attitude and tried to snatch the bag back from me. Customers were coming over to see what was going on. I could tell the girl was becoming embarrassed because of the crowd forming. I grabbed the bag again and it split open. Everything fell out. There were about a dozen shirts and aluminum foil on the floor. She looked down at the stuff and then up at me. Then I said, "Come with me."

She followed and said, "I got kids. Please don't call the cops on me." I kept walking to the front of the store. I felt sorry for the girl, but I had to call the cops. The aluminum foil let me know she knew exactly what she was doing. She was not a rookie. See, the foil deters our sensor system from going off. I grabbed the stroller and the rest of the merchandise. I asked the girl her name and was about to call the cops. Instead of obliging she ran out of the store. Shana called mall security. That was senseless because they were slow. They came about five minutes after she left. I didn't bother chasing her. For what? They were not paying me enough for that shit.

After all that drama we rang everybody up and emptied the store. It was a quarter to eight, the end of the evening finally here. I told Shana to hurry up and lock the door. As soon as she did a girl knocked on the door and asked if she could come in. I decided to let her in because she said that she only wanted to get one thing and technically we were not supposed to lock the door until five of eight. I said, "Okay, let her in." Ten minutes later when I looked up, she was still shopping and trying clothes on. I told her that we were closing and she came out of the dressing room, said sorry, and paid for her things. Shana let her out and another woman tried to ask if she could come in. Nope, it was time to go home, I thought. I shook my head no. The woman said, "Please" and put her hands together like she was praying. I was tired and the store had to get clean. So I shook my head no again. She gave me an angry face and then said, "Your sign says you close at eight o'clock and it's only seven fifty-five."

I looked back at her and said, "We're closed!" She put her middle finger up and walked away.

"Why didn't you let her in?" Shana asked.

"You saw what happened when we let the last one in. She didn't want to leave. They know what time the mall closes. I have to count these drawers and get this place ready for tomorrow." I went into the dressing room and found empty hangers and clothes everywhere. It kills me the way people trash dressing rooms. They try things on and just leave them on the floor without thinking about putting them back on the hangers. I guess if I didn't work in retail I wouldn't care either. Shana began vacuuming and I went around inspecting the racks. We didn't finish cleaning the store until close to nine. I dropped Shana off at the subway, then went to the bank and made our deposit. I was so tired I couldn't wait until tomorrow. I was getting on my plane and heading on my vacation to Miami. A three-day weekend was what I needed. No ringing up anybody, no chasing people, no cleaning. I might even meet somebody down there. I heard all the men be down there looking good. I might get one and then I can drop Sean. My cousin Natalie and her friend Tanya are leaving today. I wish I could go with them, but I couldn't take off Thursday and Friday. They needed me at the store because Joan wouldn't come in.

My uncle Teddy was going to drop me off at the airport so I wouldn't have to catch a cab or the bus. He is my mother's brother and always helps me and my mom out. We are very close. He helped my mom raise me. He never had any kids of his own. My mom said she doesn't think he could have any. My real dad, Randy, was never there. I saw him every once in a while when he came to town. Randy just sent the child support check in the mail every other week. When my mother married my brothers' father, my uncle Teddy was more of a father than their real dad, taking them to basketball games and jogging with them. Their father and my mom were married for ten years. They just got divorced about three months ago, but have been separated for six years. He don't do shit for my brothers and only lives about six blocks from my apartment.

I really can't afford to go on this trip, but I need to go. I basically begged and borrowed to go. It's a sad situation when you're calculating your bills and you're broke. But it's even sadder to know when you get your next check you're still going to be broke. I calculated I'm going to be broke three more paychecks until I pay everybody back who sponsored me to go on this trip. My uncle Teddy gave me money. Sean gave me a few dollars and my mom even chipped in and she doesn't have any money. When you're broke you learn how to make money stretch by any means necessary. I alternate months on paying bills. One month electric gets paid the next month the phone. It usually works. My car is another story. It is always breaking down. If it's not the alternator it's the brakes, fuel pump or a tune-up. It is always something and it always will be. That's why I'm not worried about spending bill money to go on my trip.

At least I'm going on vacation. Philadelphia International Airport, here I come. I can't wait to get on the plane, sit on the beach, and drink a frozen lime margarita with a salt rim and forget all my worries.

Chapter Two

Tanya Lewis

Last night I had a dream that Barry was still alive. He looked exactly the same way I remember. Same deep chocolate skin, tall, and a closely shaved brown bald head. He was on the run and I was with him. We were hiding out at a motel. We were lying in the bed talking when we heard banging on the door. Then I heard, "Open up! Police!" and then more banging on the door. We put on our clothes and escaped through the bathroom window. Barry kept saying, "Don't call anybody, we got to keep a low profile. You can't let anyone know where we are." We checked in to another motel. We stayed inside about twenty-two hours of the day. We didn't want anybody to know what we looked like in case the cops came around asking questions. "Don't let anybody know where we at," he repeated.

We went to the movies in my dream and I remember I couldn't concentrate. I thought the police were going to find us. I was worried that they were going to lock Barry up. Seeing and feeling Barry felt so real. Then I remember touching his face and saying, "Barry, you are dead. How did you come back to life?" He looked at me.

Then that very moment I awoke. They say that when you dream about a dead person, that's his way of making contact with you. If that's true, Barry must know how much I miss him and how I think about him every day. How I wish I could have told him good-bye before he was murdered. Barry's little brother Moe shot him in the head. They were both high, counting their money. Moe was playing with a silver revolver. He was always pulling out his old-ass gun on someone and pointing it. He picked up the gun and acted like he was going to shoot Barry and the gun accidentally went off. At least that's Moe's version of what went down. The police said Moe killed Barry over three thousand dollars and some crack.

That was six years ago, but it still feels like yesterday. Moe got twenty-five years. He has to serve at least fifteen before he is up for parole. Barry was my baby, the love of my life. We had been together since the eighth grade. His grandmom went to my grandmom's church. We were inseparable. Barry's grandmom would always drag him to church with her so he would stay out of trouble, and I would see him there. We started talking at church functions and picnics. One day we both played sick from church and went to the neighborhood carnival.

Me and Barry were sixteen when our son, Davon, was born. When I got pregnant, I had to drop out of school because I was always sick. After I had Davon I didn't bother to go back. At the time, Barry was in juvie for dealing. His whole time in we remained close and in love. We wrote each other every day and I would bring the baby up for visits every weekend. He promised he wouldn't fuck up while he was in there and got to come home early to me and Davon. When he got home, he made up for being away from me and Davon by moving us out of my grandmom's house and buying me a car. I didn't even know how to drive. He would hustle, steal, or do whatever it took to hold me down. Barry was so good to me. We had our daughter, Deja, two years after Davon.

One night when we were at dinner, Barry was ready to steal a Louis Vuitton bag for me, when we had money on us.

I said, "Bey, I like her bag." He asked me if I wanted him to steal it for me. He said, "I can get it as soon as she walks out." I told him I didn't want it that bad.

The next day he got a booster to get the same bag for me. Some people said that Barry was a thug and that he would steal from anybody and got what he deserved. But I know he had a good heart. He was a good man; his grandmom brought him up good. Moe sometimes asks me to bring my kids up to the prison to see him. The nerve of him, knowing what he did. He is the reason Barry isn't here, whether it was an accident or not. I just can't do it.

After he was murdered, I couldn't make it on my own. I couldn't keep my apartment up and dress nice too. I never had to take care of myself. Barry used to treat me like his little princess; he would help me take care of the kids. He did everything for me. Welfare was not enough to pay my rent. I had two kids. Davon was three and Deja was just turning one. So I ended up moving back in with my grandmom and we have been here ever since. I get a welfare check and with that money I try to pay my grandmom and get food. My grandmom took care of me most of my life. Now she is helping me take care of my kids. Our clothes money and shit like that I get from niggas or doing some kind of hustle. I don't boost. That shit is corny and not enough money in it for me. I don't have time to steal clothes and then try to sell them. I might do a credit card or check scam here or there, but nothing major. And when I do that I don't touch the shit myself because that's federal time and I'm not trying to go to jail.

Davon is now nine and Deja is seven. Deja is in second and Davon's in the fourth grade. I was packing my bag when Deja ran into the room and said, "Mommy, we coming with you today?"

"No, baby, Mommy is going out of town." I pressed her Afro puff on her ponytail in and continued packing.

"Tanya, you need to take them kids with you. You never take them anywhere," my grandmother lectured as she stood in the doorway of my room with her hand on her hip. She had her rollers in her hair and a red flowered housecoat on. My grandmother looks good for her age. She's almost sixty. Henrietta is a woman that can hold her own. She doesn't take shit from people and she will tell you about yourself.

"Mom-Mom, leave me alone. I'll take them somewhere when I get back. I'm going to Miami with Natalie and her cousin," I said as I tried to finish packing.

"Tanya, you ain't right! You just like your mother."

"Mom-Mom, you tripping. Leave me alone, I'm trying to pack," I said as I folded my turquoise bathing suit and placed it in my suitcase.

"I'm not tripping. You are wrong. You had fun making them, not me," she said. Then she looked up toward the ceiling and said, "Lord, I don't know why people think they can just leave their kids on me. Your mother did it. You're doing it and I guess in ten years your daughter will do it too."

"Mom-Mom, you know we love you. You know I'm nothing like your daughter Saundra. Davon and Deja are not going to leave their kids on you, because they are not having kids early. I'm going to send them to college and they are going to have good jobs," I said as I went to hug her. She backed away from me and said, "Don't try to butter me up. How you got money to go on a trip to Miami when you didn't even give me any money this month?"

Just when I was about to answer her question, my ride beeped his horn.

"I got to go, Mom-Mom. We'll talk when I get back," I said. I gave Deja a hug and kissed her and my grandmother good-bye. Walei, my ride, was outside. He is this African guy who loves to be mistreated, especially by me. I had met him walking down the street about two months ago. He rode past me and beeped his horn. I kept walking, so he put his car in reverse to talk to me, but another car was coming. So he went around the block. When he came back he jumped out of his car and said, "You are an attractive lady. Are you married?" I told him no. Then he said my skin was radiant and he had never seen anyone as beautiful as me. I have been in his pocket ever since. You would never know he was African until he opened his mouth. He has a thick accent. He treats me good and gives up the money. He bought me a Christian Dior bag. We go to fine restaurants all the time. He wants to show me off and I haven't even kissed him. He's like the only guy I can get money out of without having sex. I'm his showpiece and he is my moneyman. Walei even paid for my trip. He asked me if he could go and of course, I laughed at him. Walei is a student at the University of Pennsylvania. He is studying engineering or some shit like that. He's about to graduate after he takes his summer classes. He comes from Lagos, Nigeria. He said it's just like New York City and one day he is going to take me home to meet his family. I think not. I'm not going to no Africa. For what? So I can get stuck? Please.

Chapter Three

Natalie Martin-Grant

I wanted to get my hair braided for my mini vacation. I didn't want to be looking a mess with big puffy hair. I wanted to be able to get into the pool, to jet ski, and still look cute. I do not have time to even think about doing my thick hair in hot, humid weather. A girl at my son's day care told me about a girl that did braids in her apartment building. She said that the girl, Heather, was fast, good, and cheap. Three things I needed. I called Heather and she said that she couldn't squeeze me in until Thursday, which was the day of my trip. My flight would leave at 5:00 p.m. and I wanted to be at the airport by 3:00 p.m. I had to get there two hours in advance because of the security check. I asked if I could come real early. She said I could come any time while her kids was at school. So we agreed on ten.

I arrived at her apartment, and I swear, the roaches answered the door. As soon as I knocked, one crawled down the door. I could smell a nasty mix of funk and roach spray. She opened the door wearing a dingy white bra and bright purple tights with white bleach stains on them. Her bones were sticking out of her ribs. She looked like a walking skeleton and had a cigarette dangling from her mouth.

"How you doing? You Natalie?" she asked as she opened

the door. "I thought you was my old man. I forgot I told you to come this morning," she said as I walked inside her apartment. She asked me what kind of hair I bought as she threw dirty clothes off her sofa onto the floor.

"I just bought the 1B Beverly Johnson," I answered. She told me that was cool and asked me if I had a comb. I pulled one out of my pocketbook and then she asked me how I wanted my hair braided. I told her straight back with two layers and a design. Then she told me to have a seat on the floor. She took a pillow off her sofa and put it on the floor for me to sit on. It was so uncomfortable and her floor was very dirty. There were dirty shoe tracks and juice spills. While she was braiding my hair, I was swatting flies that flew by me. Her house would be the perfect setting for a Raid commercial. I wanted to kick myself for being cheap and not just going to a braiding shop to get my hair done professionally. Then I saw a mouse run across the kitchen floor and jump into the trash bag. She must have been used to seeing mice, because she didn't budge. I screamed, "It's a mouse" and jumped off the pillow.

She said, "Oh, don't worry about that mouse. He ain't coming over here." To reassure me she went and let her cat out of the bathroom. I sat back down. I wanted to get up and leave, but I needed my hair done. She was pulling my edges so tight. I felt like she was doing it on purpose. Then she asked me if I was tender-headed and told me to sit still and lean my head toward her. Then someone knocked on her door. It was her old man. He was a *real* old man too. He was about fifty and smelled like liquor. He sat down on the sofa next to her.

"Butch, where my cigarette money?" she asked. He dug in his pockets and gave her a few dollars. She put the money in her dirty bra. He was sipping on something in a brown bag. She took a swig and I was totally disgusted. Then they offered me some. I declined and tried to just watch television, but I didn't feel right. Finally after an hour and a half she was done. I needed some aspirins because my head was hurting. I paid her, said thank you, and walked to my car. Before I got back in my car I shook my clothes off to make sure I didn't take any of her friends with me. I had saved about fifty dollars by going to her. However, the next time I'm not going to be cheap and will go to the African braiding shop. It might cost more, but at least there are no rats and roaches running around. And you get in and out without the extra drama. I checked myself out in my rearview mirror. I smoothed down the hair that outlined my face. I had to admit, she could braid some hair. Even if her house was a hot mess.

It was just about noon. I needed to see if I could find a black skirt to go with a black and white shirt I had for my trip. When I arrived at the mall I went into the small-girl store. I took about five skirts into the dressing room with me. None of them fit. One wouldn't go over my hips, the other wouldn't zip, and I think I busted one of the others. I put that skirt at the bottom of the pile when I gave them back to the salesgirl and hoped she didn't notice. I had no luck in that store. *They do not cut their sizes right. Everything runs too small. These clothes are cut for a white girl with no hips. I got hips and butt,* I thought. *This is some bullshit, huh? I'm getting real tired of not being able to wear anything. I'm going with my girls to the beach and I can't find anything to wear.* What was I going to do? I needed a skirt badly! So I had to do the ultimate. The ultimate was to enter the big-girl store. I had *never, ever* in my life bought anything out of the big-girl store. I am small at the top and big on the bottom. My stomach is perfect when I hold it in. When I don't, that is another story. I am a 14 and in between sizes. Okay, maybe I am a 16, but I can fit some 14s. Anyway, I have been working out since I had my baby and trying to go back to a 14, maybe even 12. I was always a borderline big girl. Now, today, I was officially a big girl. I moped into Ashley Stewart in the mall. I looked around to see if anyone saw me go in. No one did.

A saleswoman came up to me and asked, "Can I help you?"

"No, you can't!" I said.

"Okay, well, I'm Patty and if you see anything you like or need assistance, just let me know. Today we are having a forty-percent-off sale. And you can save another ten percent if you open a charge card with us today."

"Uh-huh," I said. I paid her no mind and continued to look around. I saw black skirts on the rack. I grabbed one. It was a size 26; that wasn't going to fit me. I put that back and then I saw a size 16 and a size 14. The saleswoman, Patty, noticed I had things in my hand. She said, "Let me get you a dressing room." I followed her to one.

"It's a nice day outside," she said as she opened the door. I agreed and went into the dressing room. "We have these great cute capri pants you might like. If you want, I can get you a pair."

"Okay," I said. I tried both skirts on. The 14 fit, thank God! I knew I was a size 14. I began to undress when she passed the pants over the door to me. The skirts fit perfect, but I liked to die when the 14 pants didn't fit. I had to ask for a 16 in the pants. I was about to cry when I thought I heard my phone ring. I looked at the phone, which had caller ID. It was my cousin Janelle. "Hey, girl, are you ready yet?"

"No, I just came from getting my hair braided and I am picking up a few last-minute things."

"You're going to be late. Where are you at?"

"No, I won't. I'll be fine," I said.

"What's wrong with you? Why you sound like that?"

"Nuttin', I'm just in the fat people store trying on clothes. I don't want to be fat."

"You just had a baby. You're not fat. You're nice looking. I would love to be married and have a little cute baby."

"And I would love to be your size."

"You are so crazy. Girl, I am so broke. I don't get paid until I get back and then when I get back, I have to pay my mom and my uncle Teddy back. I hardly have enough money to go. How much money are you taking?"

"Like five hundred. If you need to borrow some money I can take some out of the bank."

"No, that's cool. You don't have to do that. I should be okay. Well, hurry up and finish shopping. And good luck with Anthony. You're going to need it!"

"I know that's right. See you tomorrow. I'll try to call you tonight."

I walked out of the dressing room and a fat, fat, fat white girl with red hair said, "Don't you just love this store?"

No, I do not, I thought. I just gave her an evil look like, *we are not the same size, so don't ask me any questions.* I took everything I wanted to buy to the register. I had tried on about nine things and was only buying two. Everything else I laid on the counter. The girl said, "Do you want this stuff?" I told her no and she called another salesgirl over to hang everything back up.

Once in my car, I inspected my neck and chin. It did look like I might be getting a second chin. I don't know why it's been so hard for me to lose weight. I have been working out nonstop. Push-ups, sit-ups, running, jogging, walking, even swimming. Okay, well, I didn't really swim, but I did leg exercises while I was in the bathtub. For the last four days I have been exercising, so why did I only lose two pounds? All that work I have been doing, I should have lost at least twenty pounds! Goddamn. I should have stopped eating the soft, chewy chocolate chip cookies at McDonald's months ago. But I couldn't. They were so good they were calling my name and I answered them. It's all good though, 'cause I am just going to have a good time, nothing else.

My husband doesn't even know I am going on my trip. If I would have asked him, he wouldn't have understood and said no. He said women shouldn't take girlfriend trips after they are married. I don't agree with him. I haven't been on a vacation since about 1999. I am so overdue. I packed my clothes a week ago and put them in my trunk. My plan is to tell Anthony that I am going to the store this evening and instead go to the airport. I'm going to teach him a lesson, because Anthony won't change a fucking diaper and I'm sick of it. He expects me to take care of the baby, fix his food, clean the house, and be ready to service his needs when he gets home. He does the bare minimum with our son. He might pick him up and say, "What's up, big guy?" then put him right back down. Anthony just irks me. At night he will even wake me up out of my sleep and say, "Baby, I'm thirsty, can you get me something to drink?" I just ignore him. I blame his mother because she made him into the big baby that he is.

I said I am going to get another job so I can get out of the house. I used to do catering at the Sheraton at the airport before I had the baby. I did a lot of weddings, anniversary parties, and conventions. I also went to school for a couple of semesters at Weidner University and was a computer science major. It's been so many years I forgot everything I learned. Lately, I have just been helping my mom at her hair salon. She pays me to prep and wash her clients for her. I hate it. That's why I'm looking for a job. I have been looking for a while without any luck. I put the baby in day care because I thought I would have found something by now. I told my mom I wasn't helping anymore when I get back. So that's my life right now, working with my mom, Anthony, and the baby.

Initially, me and Anthony, our relationship was good, like all relationships are in the beginning, but then things changed. I don't know if it was the baby or what. We had him a year after we were married. All I can say is things have really changed for the worse. His mother, Ms. Renee, adds fuel to the flame by spoiling her son's ass. The first few months we were married she used to come over, wash his clothes, and call him over to her house for dinner every night. Even after I told her I had cooked. She is a bitch. I cuss her out all the time and my mother almost beat her ass at my wedding. She means well, I guess. I know she is lonely because her husband, Anthony's dad, died when Anthony was five. And she has been trying to compensate for his father's death with attention and gifts ever since.

Anthony is a mechanic at Foreign Car Imports, a dealership not too far from our home in southwest Philly. His uncle left him our house, so we don't have a mortgage. We don't have a lot of bills. However, Anthony wastes all of his money on his car. He has a 1985 brown Cadillac. It was a crashed-up bomb when he bought it. He has painted it and put rims on it, a stereo in it, and a bunch of expensive shit I know we can't afford. The car even has a leather interior. He had the audacity to say that the baby car seat couldn't go in it because it might destroy the interior. He bought me a green 1996 Ford Taurus from the auction. And I have to beg him to put brakes on my car. My husband thinks crazy. Sometimes I think he loves the car more than he loves me. And I hate when we are riding in his car and some guy likes it and says, "That's what up" or "What year is it?" and they start talking car talk at a traffic light. That makes me so sick. That gives him more incentive to keep spending on his piece-of-shit car. When Anthony is not playing with his car, he is playing with his Playstation 2. Yes, a grown man on a game. But his ass looks at me sideways when I buy anything for myself. He'll say, "Is that a new shirt? When you get that?" When I go to the mall, I have to hide my bags and shoe boxes because he tries to count my money.

I am so fed up with Anthony. He is very childish. That's why I'm going away for a couple of days so he can see how it feels to do everything, while I do nothing for a change. No baby waking up, no man bothering me. I am going to have so much fun. By the time I get back, he *will* appreciate me.

Chapter Four

Tanya

I waited around in the airport for Natalie. I was glad that I had picked up a *Source* magazine to read. I had to refresh my memory of what certain rappers look like, 'cause everybody dresses the same and I don't want to be rude or dis somebody that is somebody. *I am going to come the fuck up,* I thought. Memorial Day weekend in Miami. Please, that's the weekend when all the niggas come out. Rappers, celebrities, professional athletes. And I'm going home with *somebody*. Wife, no wife, I don't care. Once they see me, it's going to be a wrap. They going to be like, "I want a divorce." I brought every outfit to turn niggas out all weekend. I got bikini tops, panty booty shorts, my fuck-me-hard hooker sandals and ass-cheek-showing skirts. Wherever I go I always have no problem meeting men or getting attention.

When I was younger, everybody used to tell me I was so pretty and my hair was so long. They would say, "Oh my, you are so gorgeous, little girl. You're going to get everything you want." Grown men used to tell me, "When you grow up you going to be a little heartbreaker. You won't ever have to work. Somebody will always take care of you." They said I looked like a china doll. I have worn the same hairstyle since my grandmother let me come out of ponytails. The only difference is I cut my front bangs. They hang over my eyes a little like Aaliyah's, but my hair is still past my shoulders. Girls always come up to me and ask me what kind of a perm I get. I tell them I don't get perms. I just get it pressed out with a flat iron. Or I always get asked, "What kind of hair is that?" And I'll tell them it's mine, it's not a weave. My eyes are a little sleepy and slant. My skin is a bronzed brown like I have a natural tan. I'm an average height, about five eight with heels, about five five without.

Niggas always throw me out, take me places, and do shit for me. But I never met anybody like Barry. I never take any guy I deal with seriously. They are trying to get some ass and I'm trying to get some money. It's like this: you deal with me, we going out and you buying me shit. I'm not letting no nigga fuck me and I'm not getting anything out of it. I don't trick, but it is what is. If you ain't got no money, then you can't see me. Please. I like nice shit and so do my kids. If the money is right, then we can talk. Yes, and if he's your man. Yeah, you. If he got a couple dollars and he spending, then I'll fuck with him too!

I never had a job, and men do take care of me, but I'm tired of drug dealer dudes. I'm trying to meet somebody with some legal paper. Like a ballplayer, rapper, or something. Maybe even a producer like Pharell Williams of the Neptunes. Then I'm really going to come the fuck up. My mission for the weekend is to get money, party, meet a baller, and get paid.

Time was going by slowly. I was still waiting for Natalie to meet me at the ticket gate. She is not usually a late person. Damn, I hope Anthony don't find out. She better hurry, I thought, as I looked down at my square-face Gucci silver watch, another gift from Walei. I don't know why Natalie is married to that clown. You know how you look at somebody and say they deserve better or you can see their value but they can't? That's Natalie, she is a cute girl. I mean, she could stand to lose like thirty pounds, but she is pretty and nice, and her husband, Anthony, is a straight-up mama's-boy asshole. He needs a man to kick his ass.

I met Natalie back in the day in middle school. Back then I was a smart girl and I went to a good school. However, my mom was going through something. That something was just about any drug you can imagine. She always had me missing school and switching schools. I finally dropped out in the tenth grade. Me and Natalie became close around the same time I started dealing with Barry. I confided in her and she kept my secrets. She didn't look down at me, because she knew my mom was out there. I never had to worry about my business getting in the streets. Her mom, Sharon, is so cool too. The first time my mom went to rehab she took me in. I stayed over at their house for a month.

Natalie was so different from me, but yet we got along well. She did her schoolwork and got good grades. Back then Natalie was so decent because she had so much gold. She had gold triangle earrings, gold rope chains, and donut swirls. She also had red riding boots and a red leather trench jacket that everybody wanted. She used to keep her hair fly because her mom did hair. Natalie also had a mother and a father. I didn't even know my father. I remember going into her bedroom where she had her own pink canopy bed and her own stereo and television. She was so fly back then, right up there with Salt & Pepa. She was the only child. I was the only child too, but it didn't make any difference. My mom ain't buy me shit. All my mom did for me was put everything before me. Drugs before me. Men before me.

I remember the first time she left me with my grandmom. We lived on Thirteenth and Allegheny in north Philly, right around the corner from Temple Hospital. I was watching the Smurfs as usual, it was a Saturday morning. I remember Anita Baker's "You Bring me Joy" was playing, my mom's favorite song. I was eating Frosted Flakes cereal. She told me to get up and put clothes on. I tried to finish eating my cereal, but she gripped me by my nightgown, said hurry up and get dressed. She told me I was going over to my grand-mom's house. She didn't even wait for me to get fully dressed before she pulled me out of the house. We caught the bus to my grandmother's house. She lived on Lehigh Avenue. I was excited to see Grandmom because she would always let me go to the store to get cigarettes for her and buy whatever I wanted with her change.

That afternoon stay turned into two years. My mom was back and forth, gone for weeks and months at a time. Saundra would go to rehab, get clean for a few months, then relapse and be back out on the streets again.

My mom was real pretty, and I looked just like her. Men would always come around my grandmother's house looking for her. Men that if my mom wasn't getting high she would-n't think twice about. Every man she had would take care of her. Whenever she would get mad at my grandmother for not giving her money she would take me away. She would leave me with strangers sometimes. Other times we would stay with different men at motels. When she got tired of me she would send me back to my grandmother. My mom would al-ways say, "I'll be back tomorrow."

But tomorrow never came. I cried so much because Mom-Mom cried. Then I got tough and said why should I cry over someone who didn't want me? My grandmother said she was washing her hands of her and got an insurance policy out on her because one day she would have to bury her. A couple of people said they saw her down the bottom in west Philly. That always would amaze me. How could she be in the same city as her family and not call? I can't under-stand. Well, fuck her, she's not shit. If it wasn't for Mom-Mom and Natalie's mom, Ms. Sharon, I'd be an orphan. When I was younger, sometimes I wished for a mom and a dad. But after a while, life with my mom-mom became normal.

She took care of me. We were all each other had. My grandfather died before I was born. My mother was her only child and I was my mother's only child.

Natalie better hurry the fuck up! I will get on this plane without her ass, I thought as I looked at my watch again. She is probably going to get her ass beat for sneaking to Miami. She's my friend, but we are not that close anymore. I can talk to her about things sometimes, but we don't usually hang out. This is the first time we were going out in years. I usually hang out with this girl Monica, but she couldn't come. Her money wasn't right.

A few more minutes have gone by and Natalie is still not here. She has to hurry up before the plane starts to board. I know her husband is going to hate and prevent her from going. If he does, oh well, that's on her. I got my ticket. I looked in my bag and popped a Xanax. I needed it to relax me because I don't like planes.

Chapter Five

Natalie

After I left the mall, I went and picked Anthony Jr. up from day care. I had a little talk with him. He was smiling at me. His four little teeth were sticking out of his pink gums. My baby's smile is so awesome he could brighten up any room. "Mommy going to get some *me* time for a couple of days, okay?" He was only nine months, but he smiled at me like he knew what I was talking about. I felt a little guilty. I had never left my baby, ever. I didn't want to, but I had to teach Anthony a lesson. I pulled up in front of my door. I was so nervous. It was time to execute my plan. My plane was not taking off without me. I dug around in my bag for my keys and opened the door. *Play it cool, stay calm, your plan is going to work,* I said to myself.

Anthony was lying on his other home, the sofa, watching television. He had on his blue boxer shorts and white T-shirt. He needed a serious shower and haircut. His patch of premature gray was sticking up. Anthony used to be so handsome to me. They say women let themselves go when they get married. The opposite thing happened to me. It's like one day Anthony woke up and said, "Oh, we married now. I don't have to get dressed anymore." He had a belly and meat on his legs. He used to be my teddy bear. Now he has gained like thirty pounds and he is no longer so fresh and so clean. He would always look nice and get dressed. When we were dating, his boots were always new and he kept a haircut. Right now I could smell his underarms from where I was standing. I hated when he came home from work and plopped his ass on the sofa without taking a shower first. He left his clothes everywhere and expected me to pick everything up, like his mother, but I refused.

"Anthony, we're home. I picked up the baby early because I have to go to the market. Do you think you can watch him for a little bit?" I said as I kicked his funky mechanic's uniform out of my way.

"Can't you take him with you?" he whined.

"Anthony, I have to get so many things and he is going to distract me. I want to get in and out."

"Come over here, big guy," he said to baby Anthony as he extended his hands and took the baby.

"Your braids look so, so, so nice. Don't Mommy look pretty?" Anthony said as he looked up at me and was talking to the baby. I was surprised; he doesn't usually comment on anything.

"Thanks, babe," I said. I was still trying to figure out my next move.

"How much that cost?" he asked.

"Not that much. So can you watch him?"

"I don't feel like it. I had a hard day at work."

If Anthony did not take the baby, my plan was about to fail. My heart was pounding. Who would watch the baby? Could I leave him on our steps, ring the bell, and when Anthony came to the door, run? That wouldn't work, but I had to think of something and fast. The clock was ticking. I couldn't miss my flight. I had to try one more time. I asked Anthony again, "Baby, please watch him. I'm tired too. I have to go to the market. You want something to eat, don't you?"

"Okay, okay, I'll watch him, but you got to give me some before you go," Anthony said.

"Baby, I got to go!" I said.

"Come on, babe," Anthony pleaded. Anthony was getting under my skin.

"I have to go," I said as I looked into the kitchen at the clock on the wall. It was two forty-five. I was about to be late. Anthony put the baby in his playpen and pushed me into the kitchen. He began kissing me all over my neck and back. He unzipped my pants, put me on my knees, and slid himself into me. I just kept thinking about the time, and that I was not in the mood, and he needed a shower. He was breathing heavily and panting. Anthony was not coming fast enough for me, so I took control. I got on top and rode him. I faked a few moans and scratched his back. The sex was getting good, but I had to concentrate on getting out of here. I hurried up and gave Anthony the best five minutes of his life. He was damn near ready to go to sleep when I was done.

When I went back into the living room, baby Anthony was sitting there playing with his toys in his playpen. I ran upstairs, took a quick shower, and changed my clothes. When I came back down, both Anthonys were asleep. I grabbed my pocketbook and headed for the door.

"Hurry back, okay? I got somewhere to go. I have to pick this part up for my car," Anthony said groggily.

Yeah, all right, I thought. *Wherever you have to go, you'll be taking baby Anthony with you.*

I got in my car and screeched off. You would have thought I just robbed a bank. I was nervous and sweating and kept checking my rearview mirror to see if Anthony was after me. Somehow, some way I thought he would find out. I couldn't believe he didn't have a clue. I had slipped up a few times earlier in the week. I talked about my trip and he never caught on. Tanya even left a message on our answering machine asking me if I was ready for the weekend. Anthony asked me about it, but I changed the subject. I can't believe I'm getting away with this. I'm really getting away from him and the baby.

I drove myself to the airport and parked in the extended

parking. I caught the shuttle over to the terminal. I pulled out my suitcase, put my sunglasses on, and ran to the check-in counter. I checked in, went through security, and ran through the terminal. I was sweating and out of breath when I noticed Tanya sitting reading a magazine. I went up to her and tapped her on her shoulder.

She stood up and said, "I can't believe it. You made it. I didn't have any faith in you." We slapped hands. "I thought for some reason Anthony was going to find out."

"Why?" I asked.

" 'Cause he always up in your business."

"I did think he was going to figure it out. I am so scared. Anthony is going to kill me when he finds out."

"I know he is."

"At least I'll have a smile on my face at my funeral." I laughed.

They announced our row and we went to board. I grabbed my luggage and Tanya and I ran to the gate. We handed our boarding tickets to the agent. We boarded the plane and were greeted by the stewardess. I quickly put my luggage overhead and sat next to the window. I put on my seat belt, squeezed my eyes, and held on to Tanya's hand. She smacked my arm and pulled away. When the plane began to move I held tightly on to the armrest. The plane was turning on the runway; it started going faster and faster. I thought about screaming and saying let me off, I got to go home. But once I felt the plane take off, I knew it was too late. I looked at the clouds and tried not to think about what I had just done.

Our flight connected in Charlotte and we sat there and waited for three hours. It was only supposed to be an hour layover. But the plane was delayed in Pittsburgh due to rain. Me and Tanya got something to eat, bought magazines, and talked. I tried to call home, but the answering machine kept coming on. I couldn't leave a message.

The plane finally came and we arrived in Miami after ten o'clock. We took a cab to our hotel and the place was a fucking mess. When we had booked it with the travel agent, she said, "Beachfront property." It appeared nice from the outside; the beach was across the street. But when we stepped into the hotel, it was the state pen. There were concrete walls painted light blue, these bright bedspreads, the floor was gold. We requested double beds and were given a full-size bed and the other a twin bed.

"I'm not staying here," I said as I looked around.

"Neither am I, let's get out of here," Tanya said.

We went back to the front desk, demanded our money, and tried to make reservations somewhere else. Luckily we found another room just down the street. It was ninety dollars more a night, but we didn't care as long as it was clean. Tanya had inspected the room and she said it was cool.

We paid for the room, got our keys, and walked toward the elevator. I pushed the button. The elevator opened and we dragged our luggage on with us. Two men boarded the elevator with us. One had a big bush with a pick in it and the other had braids going back that were better than mine. They were laughing and joking. "What's up, ladies? Where y'all from?" the guy with the braids asked.

"Philly. Where y'all from?"

"Brooklyn." We got out of the elevator; we were all on the same floor. They asked us if we needed help. We said yes and they carried our luggage to our room's door for us.

"Y'all got some smoke?" Tanya asked the guy with the bush as I opened the door.

"Yeah. Why? You want some?"

"Yeah. Let me put my luggage in my room. I'll be right out," Tanya said.

"By the way, this is Todd and I'm Calvin," the guy with the bush said.

"She's Natalie and I'm Tanya," she said. We put our luggage in the closet of the room and went back into the hallway with the guys. I gave Tanya her room key and Tanya and Calvin went to the balcony-like fire escape. The other guy, Todd, stayed behind.

It is so crazy how people that smoke cigarettes or get high

got their own universal language. Like, sure, you can smoke with me.

"You don't smoke?" he asked me.

"No, and I don't want that mess getting in my clothes and my system," I said as I leaned against the wall.

"What, do you work for the police?" He laughed.

"No, I have a new baby."

"I don't smoke either. It's just funny the way you said that. How old is your baby?"

"Nine months."

"How long y'all staying?"

"Until Monday."

"We got drinks, food, and everything in between if you want something."

"Thank you, I'll think about it," I said and opened the door and went into the room and began to unpack. I hung up my clothes and put all of my toiletries in the bathroom. This room was bigger. There were two beds and a sofa bed.

Tanya came back into the room and said, "Those broke niggas better get out my face. Please. They wish I would waste my time with them. He asked did I want something to eat or drink and I said maybe we can go out later, right? Then he said, 'No, I got drinks in my room.' I looked at his ass like he was crazy."

"They seem nice, but they weren't my type either. The guy Todd asked me too!" I said. "Well, let's walk around and see what's going on," I suggested.

Tanya looked down at my hand and said, "What are you going to do about your wedding ring? You need to take it off."

"I'm not taking it off. I didn't come down here to meet anybody. I just want to have a good time and for Anthony to appreciate me a little more."

"Whatever. You need to leave him. You need to meet a baller down here and kick his ass to the curb."

"A baller isn't going to solve everything," I said as I shook my head.

I don't know what is wrong with Tanya, but she is so

dumb. I don't know what happened to her. She didn't used to think so stupid. Everything that comes out of her mouth is baller, get money, get paid. We unpacked a little more and then went outside. It wasn't really crowded yet. Tanya said that everything would start jumping tomorrow. We didn't do much. We walked around, got something to eat, and chilled. Tanya met this little short dude who invited us to this mansion party. He was old, had teeth missing, and thinning hair with spaced-out braids, trying to smoke on a cigar. He was claiming to be this important guy. He looked too old to be partying. I don't know why men think they can keep going out at forty and still be able to pick up somebody.

Friday morning we woke up and walked down the South Beach strip again. Everybody must have arrived this morning and late last night. Never in my life have I seen so many good-looking guys. And every girl was dressed as if they were in a music video. All I saw was short, tight skirts and high-heeled sandals. I felt overdressed in my knee-length jean skirt. It was so warm outside. It felt good getting attention. Guys were grabbing our hands and flirting.

"I told you everybody was going to get here," Tanya said excitedly. As soon as she said that, this drunk, short, ugly guy with dreads grabbed my arm, tried to spin me around, and said, "Ay, yo, Ma. You look good. I like your donkey."

"What?" I said, annoyed, as I stared at him.

"You got a fat ass," he said. I guess he was referring to my butt. Was I supposed to say thank you? Then he said, "I like big butts and I cannot lie." At this point, I wasn't even offended. I was laughing at his stumbling drunk ass. The guy was falling every which way trying to maintain his balance. "So what's up? Can I holla at you?" he asked.

"I'm married," I said as I flashed my ring and kept walking.

Then his friend caught up with us. He was a little chubby. "Sorry, my man don't have any sense. How ya nice ladies doing?" he said politely.

"Okay," Tanya said.

"I'm Monte and this my boy Tony. You got to excuse him. We from the Durdy. Where y'all from?"

"Philly. Where's the Durdy?"

"St. Louis. Y'all got to really excuse my partner, he's drunk," Monte said.

"How he going to be drunk already and it's only noon?" Tanya laughed.

"He never stopped drinking since last night." We all started laughing. "Y'all didn't party last night?"

"No, we had hotel drama, switching rooms and shit. Then before that, our connecting flight in Charlotte was late. We got here last night and chilled," Tanya said. Then she asked them if they were driving and told them how we had to pick Janelle up from the airport.

"Y'all want us to take you?"

"Yeah. Could you please?" she said, batting her eyes, then turned and asked me, "What time her flight get in?"

"Like one or two-thirty."

"Like one, that's cool. We'll meet y'all like quarter to. Is that cool?" the guy Monte said.

"We about to go get something to eat. Y'all want to go?" Tanya asked as she flirted with Monte and touched his hands.

"Naw, I got to get him back to his room, but I'll treat y'all," he said, as he wrote his number on a crisp fifty-dollar bill. He placed the money in Tanya's hand. We just both looked at each other and said thank you.

"Make sure you call me. We can pick your girl up from the airport," he said.

"You call me too!" the drunk guy said.

We walked away and agreed that Monte was trying to show us he had money. He validated our thoughts seconds later when he yelled from halfway down the street, "There's more where that came from." We didn't care about Monte or his friend, but we were about to have lunch on him and a ride to the airport to get Janelle.

WHAT'S REAL   39

I hadn't been out in such a long time it felt a little strange. When I get home, I'm going to get out more. I'm young, I need to do stuff and have fun. I have been with Anthony forever, and he is my baby, but if I wasn't married. I certainly would have met me a husband down here.

Tanya and I went and had lunch at Fridays with the fifty dollars Monte gave us. The restaurant was crowded. We sat down and waited for our name to be called. I had time to think and then I began to feel guilty about all the fun I was having. I called home again. The phone just rang and rang and then I finally hung up.

"Stop calling home, Nat. Make the best of the situation. You're on vacation. Act like it," Tanya said as she attempted to take my cell phone from me. She then tried to convince me to have a good time. No matter what she said, I was starting to think I might have made a mistake by coming. I was feeling guilty for having fun. I missed my baby and my man. I was wrong. I shouldn't have left them, not like this. I needed to check and make sure they were okay.

"I feel bad, Tanya."

"I don't know why, girl. Please! You need a break, girl. He don't do shit. Let him take care of the baby."

"You're right," I said as I put my cell back in my pocketbook and contemplated my choices.

"I be right back. I got to go to the bathroom," Tanya said. As soon as she walked away, I called Anthony again. This time he answered.

"Hello, babe," I stuttered.

"Where are you, Natalie? Are you okay? I have been calling and looking for you. I called your mother. I was about to call the cops, but your dad told me not to. What's going on? Me and the baby went to the market searching for you."

"Yes, Anthony, I am okay. Um, Anthony, I am in Miami. . . on vacation—"

"Miami where?" he yelled before I finished.

"Miami, Florida. Anthony, I needed a break."

"Natalie, you got to be fucking kidding me. I got stuff to do and who is going to watch baby Anthony?"

"He's your son too, Anthony. You are going to watch him. Take him to day care or your mother," I said.

"I don't believe you, Natalie! Who are you with?" he yelled even louder.

"Janelle and Tanya."

"Your cousin and that slut Tanya," Anthony said angrily.

"Tanya is not a slut," I said defensively. "I'll be home on Tuesday. Okay?" I was trying to calm him down.

"Natalie, we won't be here when you get back," he snapped.

"Where will you be then?" I asked.

"Don't worry about it." Anthony hung up the telephone on me. Now I really felt bad for leaving my baby and husband. I hope this weekend is going to be worth it. I put my phone away before Tanya got back.

I will have to talk to Janelle about everything when she gets here. She always has good advice. Tanya can't give me any advice. She can't even advise herself. My cousin Janelle and I are close. We have the same grandfather. My father is Janelle's mother's half brother. My grandpop was married to Janelle's grandmom and cheated on the side with my grandmom and had my dad. Our parents didn't meet until they were teenagers. My grandmother and Janelle's grandmother kept them apart. But when they got older they met and made sure their kids knew each other.

My mother owns a hair salon in the basement of her house. I always tell her she needs to take a refresher course because she's in a time warp with her hairstyles. But she doesn't listen. She has an older clientele, so I guess it doesn't matter. I still let her do my perm, from time to time. She tries to get mad at me when I go to another stylist. My mom and me are like best friends. I can tell her anything. We have the best relationship. My mom always talked to me about my body, love, and life. Because of my mom, I didn't lose my virginity until I was with Anthony and I ran right home and told her.

Chapter Six

Janelle

I was curling my hair. I had just had it dyed wine red a few days ago. At first I thought it was too much, but when I went to work the next day, I got so many compliments. I have a few weave tracks that blend right in. The color goes great with my cocoa-brown skin and dark brown eyes.

"Mom, have you seen my suitcase?" I screamed from the bathroom. I don't know why I waited until the last minute to pack. I wanted to take everything, but I couldn't.

"It's in the closet. Ted said be ready, he is on his way," my mom yelled from the kitchen.

I searched in the closet and found my blue suitcase. I rubbed the dust off it. I opened my suitcase and dumped all Jamal's Hot Wheels cars and coloring books onto the floor. I threw all my clothes in. Then I ran into the bathroom, grabbed my toothbrush, and went into the living room to get my other bag. I checked off all my stuff on the list I made to remind myself of things to pack. If I didn't write my list I would forget just about everything. I ran back into the room to grab my contacts and solution. I definitely needed them. I wasn't blind, but at night I couldn't see far away. My mother handed me a bagel for the road. She was dressed in a black pantsuit and had her hair in a short layered Cleopatra bob. She looked really nice. "Mom, thanks for the bagel, you look nice. Do you have an interview today?"

"Yes, downtown at a school. Cross your fingers for me."

"I will. Well, good luck," I said as I left out the door. *I hope she gets a job so she can move the hell out,* I thought.

As I opened the door my uncle was coming up the apartment steps. My uncle was light skin, is about five ten, with a little protruding belly. He was wearing brown slacks and brown loafers and a cream rayon shirt. He kept a toothpick hanging out of his mouth and a pair of sunglasses on. I gave him my first suitcase. Then I went and grabbed my other bag.

"How long are you going for?"

"Until Tuesday."

"Why do you have so many bags?"

"I haven't decided exactly what I am wearing, so I got to bring everything."

"Niecey, you're going to have my back hurting."

The ride in my uncle's Cadillac was smooth. You couldn't feel any potholes or bumps, and it smelled like strawberries. He kept it washed and waxed. My uncle was listening to sports radio. He was a big baseball fan. I hated listening to that station. We pulled up to the terminal and my uncle got my luggage out of his trunk.

"Do you have everything?" he asked.

"Yeah, I got everything. I can always use some more money."

"How much we up to now?" he asked as he went into his wallet.

"I don't know."

"Janelle, you lucky you're my favorite niece. Here, I want my money as soon as you get back," he said as he placed the money in my hand.

"I got you. Thank you, Unc," I said as I gave him a hug and walked to the curbside check-in. I checked in my luggage and headed for the terminal. My flight was on time and

I didn't have to wait. I called Natalie to let her know I was on my way and the flight would be on time.

"What's up, girl? You down here?" Natalie asked.

"No, not yet, I'm about to get on my flight. Are y'all still going to meet me at the airport?"

"Yeah, you got to get down here. It is so nice and the weather is beautiful. Hold on, Tanya wants to talk to you."

"What's up?" Tanya asked.

"Nothing, on my way."

"Well, you better get you ass down here now. It is the fuck off the hook, let me tell you. I seen players from the Heat and Fat Joe already," Tanya said, all excited.

"Are you serious?"

"Yes, girl, it is like that. Niggas is writing their number on fifty-dollar bills. Here go Natalie."

"Hello. Oh, by the way, we switched hotels," Natalie said.

"When y'all do that?"

"Long story. I'll tell you later. We're staying at the Penguin on Tenth and Ocean Avenue. We are in room 417 right across the street from the beach. You know, Tanya got like eight numbers already. I even got a few numbers. I threw them away though. Some guy invited us to a mansion party tonight."

She was trying to tell me everything all in one breath. I wrote the name of the hotel and the room number down.

"Save some friends for me and come meet me at baggage claim for American Airlines at one p.m. That's when my flight comes in, don't forget."

"I won't. See you later. We'll get these guys we met to bring us to the airport."

Once I arrived in Miami I was like a little kid in a candy store. This was my first time passing Virginia Beach. My mom didn't have any money to take us anywhere. I never could afford to take myself anywhere before now. The only time I ever saw Miami was when I was a kid watching the television show *Miami Vice*. I couldn't wait to lay eyes on the pretty people, palm trees, and fast cars.

The Miami airport was so-so. I was actually not impressed yet. I got my baggage and needed help outside. An older Latin gentleman came up to me and said, "*Ayuda?*"

Of course I didn't have any idea what he meant. But he seemed nice and placed my luggage on his cart. I assumed he wanted to help me. I told him I needed to go outside to pickup and he said, "*No hablo inglés.*"

I nodded and said, "*Gracias.*" That's all I could remember from Spanish class. We went outside to arrivals. I didn't see Tanya and Nat yet, so I tipped the man and had a seat. I sat outside in the heat. Fifteen minutes had gone by and I was still waiting. Damn, Miami is hot and everybody was getting picked up but me. I called Natalie's cell phone. I got her voice mail. Where was she? She was supposed to be here. I left a message on her phone.

I then went back inside and walked over to the information desk. I asked one of the ladies sitting there in the dark blue uniforms how far I was from South Beach. She told me at least twenty-five minutes; with traffic, maybe thirty to forty minutes. I asked the woman if I could catch a cab and how much it would cost. She handed me a sheet with the prices. I didn't have much money to begin with, so I decided not to waste any money on a cab and just waited for them.

I looked down at my watch again and it was 2:00 p.m. I wanted to get a snack, but I couldn't because I didn't want to miss them. So I pulled out the half-eaten bagel from this morning. Then I called Tanya. Her phone said something about this subscriber is out of the service area and could not accept calls.

I really didn't care too much for Tanya. We got along sometimes. She was my cousin Natalie's friend. They were total opposites. Natalie was married, a good girl, and somewhat quiet. Tanya, on the other hand, would fuck anything walking as long as they gave her some money. Tanya's mom was on drugs. She lived with her grandmom, had two kids, and never finished school. Natalie always had a job. How they maintain a friendship, I don't know. I guess opposites attract. They met back in middle school. My aunt took Tanya in when her mom was in rehab. I can tell that Tanya is jealous of me. She always looking me up and down and staring. She think she is the shit and can't handle competition. I guess I'm going to have to put up with her ass, at least for the weekend.

I looked down at my watch again, it was almost two-thirty. They really must have forgotten me. I decided just to catch a cab. I went into my pocketbook and got the name and address of the hotel where we were staying. I got in a cab and gave him the address to the Penguin. He loaded my luggage into his trunk. He was playing this crazy music I never heard before. It wasn't Latin or reggae. It sounded like both fused together; I don't know. I wasn't feeling it, but he seemed to enjoy it because he sang along. I was relieved to be in the cab, but I was upset once I realized my taxi driver was pretending to be lost. I saw a sign to South Beach pointing in the other direction. I didn't have enough money to play games with him. I tapped the driver on his shoulder and said, "South Beach is that way."

The driver said, "Sorry, I don't know what I was thinking." He got off at the next exit and turned around. Once we were in the right direction, I took in all the sights. I rolled down the window and a warm breeze hit my face. We went over this long bridge. I could see yachts, the ocean waves, and oceanfront houses. It was beautiful. At the end of the bridge, we began running into traffic. I saw so many cars and people. Hummers, Benzes, and even a Bentley. We sat on one block for about ten minutes. My bill was thirty-one dollars. I asked the cab driver how much farther I was from my hotel. He said about four blocks, so I decided to walk the rest of the way. I paid him and began to walk.

I had two pieces of luggage, I was not dressed, and did not feel cute at all. But guys were still beeping their horns up and down the street. By the time I reached the hotel I was sweaty, my hair was looking a mess, my spiral curls were gone, and I needed something to drink. I called Natalie's cell again. I heard her answer, but she didn't say anything.

"Hello, hello, Natalie," I said.

Then Natalie finally said, "Oh, my bad. I thought you might have been Anthony. You know, he's mad. I told him I was down here. He's not going to kick my ass! Don't say that! What's up with that?"

"Huh? What?" I said as I tried to comprehend what and who Natalie was talking to.

"Stop talking to people. Listen, Nat, I'm here at the hotel."

"Okay, here we come."

"What's our room number again?"

"It's 417. We left you a key at the desk."

"Okay, well, I'm going to the room."

The hotel was light yellow. It had an art deco feel. I went to the front desk, gave them my name, and they gave me a key for my room. I got in the elevator and went to the fourth floor. When I opened the room's door, I noticed stuff was all over the place. There was no closet or drawer space left. Where was I supposed to put my clothes? I thought. There were two double beds and a pull-out sofabed. I heard music blasting from outside. I opened the drapes and saw the beach sitting right across the street. I looked over the balcony and saw hundreds of cars for miles and miles, their lights glaring. That got me excited. I had to hurry up and get dressed. I got out of the musky clothes, wrapped my hair up, put my scarf on, and jumped in the shower. After I finished showering I heard Natalie and Tanya walk in. "What's up, Nellie Nell?" Tanya said.

"Don't what's up me," I said as I came out of the bathroom with my towel on. "Y'all bitches was supposed to meet me at the airport."

"I know we were, but we was looking for the guys from St. Louis that said they was going to take us," Tanya said.

"We was looking for them. You know we wouldn't have left you stranded like that, cousin. Plus, Tanya said you would find your way." Natalie laughed.

"No, I didn't," Tanya said.

"Yes, you did."

"Well, the good thing is, you made it," Natalie said as she tried to hug me. I nudged her off me. They were officially getting on my nerves.

"I don't want to hear I made it. Y'all left me to fend for myself. That shit ain't cool."

"Janelle, I meant to tell you, we had to pay extra for this room, so you owe us sixty dollars."

"Sixty dollars apiece?"

"No, thirty apiece. You can give me mine when we get home."

"I need mine now," Tanya said.

I didn't even have sixty dollars to spare. I went into my bag and counted out thirty dollars. I told Natalie I'd give her thirty dollars when I got change. My money was dwindling fast.

Chapter Seven

Janelle

We all wanted to go out to a club. I was ready. They had walked around, saw, and met people, but I hadn't and I could not wait to get some numbers. Natalie looked so cute. She did her makeup real pretty. I don't mess with makeup because it irritates my skin, but it looked good on her. I only wear lip gloss and a touch of eye shadow every now and then. She wore black satinlike capri pants and a pastel lavender low-cut shirt that flattered her pear shape. I had on a powder-blue dress and blue crisscross sandals that came up to my calf.

Tanya came out of the bathroom looking like a whore, but she kind of looked cute. She had on tight white low-rise jeans, with her black thong hanging out, and a black bikini tank top. I studied myself in the mirror. I looked cute but not cute enough. I wasn't happy with what I had on.

"Y'all ready to go?" Natalie asked.

"I'm ready," Tanya said as she put on her mascara and brushed her eyebrows into shape. They both turned to me to see if I was ready.

"Um, y'all give me a minute," I said. They both said they were going to meet me in front of the hotel. As soon as they walked out of the room, I slipped off my dress and sandals. I dug around in my suitcase and tried to find something else to wear. I pulled out white shorts, a red skirt, a black dress, but finally decided to put on a denim miniskirt. I located my red stiletto sandals and a rose-red corset shirt that matched my wine-colored hair. Now I was ready to go out. I met Tanya and Natalie outside and Natalie said I looked nice. I thanked her. Then Tanya asked, "Why you change your clothes?"

I didn't owe her an explanation, so I just told her, "Because I felt like it."

We walked down Collins Avenue toward the strip of clubs. Everyone was out; the vibe in the air was really festive. Cars were honking their horns at us and traffic was jam-packed. All the clubs were lit with different-colored neon lights.

We first went to a place called Wet Willie's. It was free to get in and the drinks were reasonable. I wasn't really trying to spend any of my money on drinks. Somebody was going to buy us drinks. We had a few watermelon shots, then left. We walked up and down the street for about an hour, then decided we were ready to go to a club. The problem was which club to go into. The prices varied. Seduction wanted fifty dollars and Club Level was free until midnight. We knew all the broke people would be in the free club.

"I'm not paying fifty dollars to get into a club," Natalie said.

"That's not shit," Tanya said.

"Not shit to you. You know what I can do with fifty dollars?"

"Why are you bitching?" Tanya asked.

I interrupted them and said, "I agree. Why should we pay all this money to get into this club? We should try to see if we can get in for free."

Tanya said, "Hold up." She walked up to the bouncer, batted her eyes at him, and smiled. She even stretched a little so he could see her thong. We knew he was about to let us in free, because he was all smiling and looking. She walked back over to us and said, "He is not doing nothing. He said everybody that wants to get into this club is paying fifty no matter what. Girls fifty and guys one hundred."

"Okay, so what we going to do?" Natalie asked.

"I say we go in. What do you say, Janelle?" Tanya said.

"It's whatever y'all want to do. If y'all want to go in, then I'm with that. I just want to have fun."

"I want to go in, so I say we go in," Tanya said again.

"I think it's going to be corny. Let's go to that other one, Club Level, and see how that is. It might be crowded because it's free," Natalie said.

"It might not have the right people in that crowd," Tanya exclaimed.

"We can see how it is. If it's not jumping, then we can come back here," I said.

Everybody agreed, and I was happy. I didn't really have fifty dollars to spend and I didn't want Tanya to know it. We walked two blocks down to Club Level. The bass was extra loud because the club was totally empty. We got our complimentary drink and headed back up the street to Club Seduction.

Seduction's line was now wrapping around the corner. It was packed inside and it was all white. The chairs and the bar were white and all the servers wore white. There were white roses and white tables. As soon as we walked in, Tanya met a guy that worked for Def Jam. He was really nice looking, light brown, about five ten, with short twisties on his head. He got us into the VIP room. Him and his friend were cool and ordered us food and drinks.

Me and Natalie wanted to dance, so we left the VIP room. We went out onto the dance floor and right away I got asked to dance. We danced to "Get Low" by Little Jon and the East Side Boys. I danced with the same guy for six songs straight. I was exhausted. I was having a good time though. I felt relaxed and liberated. I had to pee very bad and wanted to make sure my hair was still in place. I walked into the bathroom and even that was made of glass and white. It was small and dimly lit. I came out of the bathroom drying my hands and saw Tanya grinding with the guy that got us into VIP.

"Um, Natalie, look at your girlfriend, she feeling it," I said as I patted Natalie.

"That's what I was just saying." Natalie giggled.

"You better get her," I said.

"She is okay. She knows what she's doing. She parties all the time."

"If you say so." We both continued watching Tanya from the sidelines of the dance floor. She was making a complete fool of herself. She was dancing all around the party, winding her body as if she were a dance hall queen in a reggae video. She was letting the guy rub on her breast and his friend came up and started dancing with her from behind. I couldn't watch it anymore. A crowd was forming to look at her gyrating hips. I didn't want anybody to know she was with me.

Me and Natalie walked to the bar and ordered two apple martinis. I went to pay for our drinks and the bartender said they were already covered. She pointed to an appealing guy in a Lakers jersey who was standing at the bar. He raised his glass. I lip-synched a thank-you, and me and Natalie drank the next half hour on him. He kept sending us drinks and more drinks. I put a white napkin in front of us to let him know to stop sending drinks. Out of nowhere, Tanya walked up and said, "Where y'all been at? He said he is going to fix me real good." We both looked at each other and started to laugh because we were borderline drunk ourselves.

"What? Who said that?" Natalie asked.

"The guy who gave me a drink," Tanya stuttered. "He said he going to fix me real good," she repeated and then she did a twirl and fell to the floor. I was tipsy no more.

"What is going on with you?" Natalie asked as we tried to lift Tanya from the floor.

"What else did you have?" Natalie kept asking her. As

badly as I didn't want to leave, it was time to go. Tanya was sweating profusely and could barely walk. We had to hold her up to get her out of the club. She was holding on to us, stumbling. But she managed to flash her breast to a bunch of guys as we walked down the street. We thought the fresh air would help, but it didn't. She was singing and trying to dance to "Naughty Girl" by Beyonce. We walked Tanya to the hotel. She collapsed on the bed and was still singing.

"Shut up, Tanya! What did you have?" Natalie asked her again.

"Nothing." Then she smirked. "I didn't have anything but an E-pill."

"What, you mean Ecstasy?" Natalie shouted. "I told you to leave that shit alone. The last time you were high for two days and so dehydrated you almost had to get rushed to the hospital."

"They make me feel good all over," she said as she rubbed her legs.

"No wonder she was all touchy-feely in the club. She was feeling it," Natalie said. Natalie told her if she didn't sit up and stop squirming she was going to call 911.

Tanya then threw up and said, "Don't call 911. Please. I'll be okay; just get me water and a ginger ale."

Chapter Eight

Tanya

I was dressed to fucking kill. These bitches had no clue. I looked the best, I thought as I applied my black eyeliner. I'm that bitch. Fix your shirt, I told Natalie. Her outfit was cute. She was cute, but she would look better if she lost some weight. Her stomach was hanging out a little on the side; it was almost a spare tire. I wore white pants and a black bikini top with black high-heeled sandals. I looked so good Janelle went and changed her clothes to keep up. The minute we walked onto the strip, all eyes were on me. A few guys called me over to their car, but I was not walking up to any guy's car. If they wanted me, they would either have to see me inside the club or leave their car running and come to me. Niggas was begging to take pictures with me. I didn't stop and take any, because I don't want my picture to be posted all over the Internet or on their friends' walls in prison.

When we entered the club the music was loud and the bass was booming. I met this dude James who worked for Def Jam. He was all right–looking, but he was like a cornball. He had twisties on his head and he wasn't my type. Him and his friend got us all into VIP. He was nice. He bought me, Nat, and Janelle drinks. His conversation was kind of typical like. You so pretty. Where yo' man at? Can I spend the night with you? He was all trying to fall in love, talking my ear off in the club. I wasn't feeling him or his conversation, so I left him in VIP and headed to the dance floor. I went and was dancing by myself. Then this big tall dude came up to me and started dancing with me. He was holding a bottle of Cristal.

"Where's my glass?" I asked.

"Right here, Ma," he said as he went and got me a glass and started pouring. The champagne bubbled over my glass a little. I sipped it down and said thank you. Once I finished that glass, he poured me another and another. By the sixth glass I stopped drinking because my head was spinning. Then he gave me a yellow butterfly- stamped Ecstasy pill. I remember he walked me to the bathroom and told me he would be waiting outside for me. When I got in the stall I could hardly pull down my pants. When I finally managed to get them down, I almost tilted over toward the door. I had no control of myself. There was no toilet paper and it was very dark. My body was feeling warm and I was tingling all over. I felt like I needed to be touched.

Sadly, that's the last thing I remember happening. The rest is a blank. I shouldn't have taken that pill he gave me. I don't really drink, I smoke. So, when I do have a drink I get real fucked up. I looked through my cell phone this morning. I got all these numbers and don't remember what anybody I met looks like. I checked my messages and that guy with the bottle of Cristal was on there. He said, "Hey, Ma, this is Rah from New Jeruse. I'm the one that gave you the glass of Cris, and the E. Call me when you wake up, so I can eat that cat out all night again." I threw the phone down and screamed.

Chapter Nine

Natalie

I always wear black pants because they're what look good on me. They hide everything. My braids looked pretty and I put on blue eye shadow, a little foundation, brown lip liner, and a frost purplish gloss. The color flattered my skin and went with my lavender V-neck shirt and open-toe sandals. I had to deal with Janelle trying to talk about Tanya. And Tanya asking why Janelle got that on. She's not cute the entire night.

There were so many people out. I was having an okay time, but I was still thinking about Anthony. I tried to call him a few times, but he just kept hanging up on me. *He probably will just be mad for a couple of days, not a big deal,* I thought. I needed this trip. I would have gone crazy if I didn't get away. As mad as Anthony is, he will get over it. At least I hope. I decided just to have a good time.

Miami was lit up and lively at night. I was having a little more fun at Club Seduction. It was all white inside and was majestic like a queen's palace. I didn't want to touch anything. I met this spoken-word poet named Miles from Boston. He worked at a hip-hop magazine as a graphic designer. We had a real deep conversation and he was attractive. He gave me his number and invited me to this party in his room. We danced for a couple of songs. He was trying to feel all up on me. I would move his hands off my back; then he would place them on my hips. When we started dancing we were in the middle of the dance floor. Now we were at the end because every time he would move in closer, I would step back.

"What, you scared of me?" he asked.

"No, I just don't know you and I am married," I said as I showed him my wedding ring.

"And where your husband at now?" he asked.

"It doesn't matter. I'm faithful."

"No girl's faithful down here. You can try to be, but someone is going to break you down," he said.

"I don't think so," I said and walked away.

I ran into Janelle back at the bar. A guy she met kept sending over drinks. I hadn't ever drank so much in my life! I didn't know I could hold liquor. Surprisingly, I didn't throw up or act goofy. It was Tanya who was acting crazy, dancing all over guys. I had to nurse her from stupidity all night. She was mixing drugs with liquor and was sick as a dog. All I wanted to do was go to bed.

Chapter Ten

Janelle

I stretched and awoke. Natalie was already up watching television on the sofa. Tanya was stretched out on the other double bed on her cell phone, with her clothes and shoes on. I got up, looked in my bag, pulled out my jeans, and put them on.

"What time you get up?" I asked Natalie.

"Eight o'clock."

"Why so early?"

"You know I get up early with the baby every morning."

"What time did we get in?"

"I think like four?"

"What time is it now?"

"Eleven?"

"Oh, I'm thirsty. I need something to drink. I'm going to walk to the soda machine. You want something?"

"I want a Sprite," she said as she gave me change out of her pocket.

"You want anything, Tanya?" I asked.

"Yeah, get me a Pepsi. Y'all got any Tylenol? My head is spinning. Hand me my purse, Nat."

"I got it. I'll be right back," I said.

I walked down the hall to the soda machine and got our

three sodas. Then I pushed the ice button on the ice machine. I noticed a set of guys getting off the elevator. One of them looked familiar. I turned my head because I didn't want to stare. The guy I thought I recognized approached me. I now realized who he was. I didn't want to get too excited. I kept saying in my mind that he is just a regular guy, just a regular guy. That's how I was trying to act, like I didn't notice the biggest rapper in the South was standing right across from me and was looking good. He was tall, about six three, with a medium dark brown complexion. He had ice wrapped all over his neck and wrists and a do-rag on his head and a Yankees hat on top of that. A blue Yankees baseball jersey and untied Timbs. His only flaw was the gold-capped teeth in his mouth.

I turned and tried to still act like I didn't notice him. Then he said, "What's up, shawty?"

I turned around to see if he was really talking to me. I said, "Shawty? Where you from talking like that?"

He looked surprised and said, "What, you don't got a TV? You don't know who I am?"

"No. Who are you?" I said as I continued to play dumb.

"Spinal Rap's biggest artist, Mannis."

"Oh. Okay, well, I never heard of you. I don't listen to rap," I said as I tried not to look at his gigantic platinum chain. It was long and rested in the middle of his chest with a big spinning M in diamonds. It was the size of a grapefruit.

"Well, maybe you should start. What room are you in?" he asked.

"Why?"

" 'Cause I'm coming to get you and show you what Mannis is all about."

"Oh, really? Well, I'm in 417."

"Yup, really. I'll be there at eleven to pick you up and play some of my music for you and let you know about Mannis and how we get down round here," he said as he looked down at his multicolored diamond-face watch with a royal-blue band.

"All right, see you then," I said as I got in the elevator. As soon as the door closed, I jumped up and down. The elevator opened on the fourth floor and I ran down the hall. The door was open. I walked into the room, put the sodas and ice on the dresser, and said, "Guess who I met and wants to take me out?"

"Who?" Tanya asked.

"Who got the hottest song right now, 'What the fuck You Ain't Like Me'?"

"I know you not talking about Mannis?" Tanya asked.

"Yup."

"You are lying. How you do that?" Natalie asked.

"You know I got skills. I don't know what to wear," I said as I dumped my clothes out of my suitcase.

"I wouldn't wear anything. Mannis could get it," Tanya said as she looked me up and down.

"No. Don't you know he is used to freak bitches? I'm going to be different. I'm going to wear something conservative."

"Conservative? Please," Tanya said.

"Somewhat conservative. I'm going to be real respectable and by Christmas y'all going to see me in a Spinal Rap video," I said as I started doing the booty bounce around the room. I flashed smiles and winks at the girls through the mirror. I could tell by the look on Tanya's face the hating was about to begin.

"How you know he is even going to show up?" the hater Tanya asked.

"Because I know," I said confidently.

There was a knock on the door and Natalie answered it.

"Huh? I think you got the wrong room," I heard Natalie say. I walked over to the door to see who she was talking to. It was this young guy with these dark shades on.

"Who you looking for?" I asked.

"How much for a sloppy one?" he asked. Then I told him he had the wrong room.

"Yo, dude, you got the wrong room," Tanya said as she came to the door like she was ready to fight.

"Nisha ain't here?" he asked.

"No," I said as I began to shut the door.

Then the boy said, "Well, what's up with the big girl anyway?"

"We told you, you had the wrong room," I said as I shut the door and called down to the front desk to report him.

"I wonder who he was looking for," Natalie said.

"I seen these girls last night down the hall. Dudes was going in and out of the room," Tanya said.

"Um, they getting it in," I said.

"There is nothing wrong with getting paid, but damn, be selective and don't fuck everybody," Tanya said.

"I don't care what the situation is. My body ain't for sale," I said.

"I know that's right," Natalie added.

"Well then, you're giving it away for free," Tanya said as she sipped her Pepsi.

Mannis came to our room on time. I was shocked he even showed up! I invited him into our room and introduced him to Tanya and Natalie. They said their hellos and Natalie, like a dummy, was like I love all your music. Can I have a picture? He said sure and I took the picture. I know Tanya wanted a picture too, but didn't want to ask.

Once we reached the lobby, people started running up and asking him for autographs. He signed a few as I stood on the side. Then a group of girls walked up and asked to take a picture. I took the picture for them. One girl wanted Mannis to sign her shirt. He did one better and signed her breast. We then made our way to the white Hummer limo that was waiting outside. I tried to act unimpressed, but inside my heart was pounding and I was screaming. He asked if I wanted something to drink. I asked him what he had. He said Hennessey, Moet, Hypnotiq, and some Cristal. I tried to act classy and said I'll take some Cristal. I don't even like champagne, it tastes like beer to me. I took a sip of the champagne, then asked where we were going.

"We're going to the biggest party in Miami."

"And where's that?" I asked.

"The Spinal Rap yacht party."

"Yacht party?"

"Yeah, you scared of water or something?"

"Not at all," I said.

We pulled up to the dock moments later. I never been on a yacht, but I acted like I had. There were plenty of limos lined up. We boarded the yacht and I saw a few well-known faces in the crowd. I knew them from watching television. There were people from the NBA, the NFL, and the music industry. I tried to pretend I belonged. I was in heaven. Mannis introduced me to everybody, including other rappers on his label. Again, I was screaming on the inside. I couldn't take it anymore. I told him I had to go to the bathroom. In the bathroom I called Natalie. She picked up on the first ring.

"Nat. I'm not going to tell you. I'm on a yacht in the middle of the ocean with a bunch of millionaires and celebrities."

"What?" she yelled.

"Yes, girl, I just saw Trina, Missy, and Timbaland."

"Oh my God, really? I need to be there!"

"Then Trina asked me where I got my sandals from and we started talking. This party is so banging I can't take it. Well, I got to go," I said. I had exaggerated a little bit about Trina. I only saw her in the bathroom and we didn't talk. I just wanted Tanya to know what she was missing out on.

"Ooh, that is not fair. I should be there!" she said.

"Where y'all at?"

"I don't know, some place on the water."

"Well, call us when y'all hit land."

"Okay."

I went back out to the party and Mannis was up on me the rest of the night. He was trying to hug and kiss on me. He was trying to let everybody know I was with him. That was cool. We danced all night. I mingled around the party, met a lot of industry people, and got a few business cards.

After the party was over, our limo was waiting for us. Our night was going so good. Mannis invited everybody back to an after party at his hotel suite. He was staying at the Marker Hotel. The room lights were dim, it was a large suite, everybody was coupled up and sitting back drinking and smoking. The room had a little haze over it.

He yelled, "I'm real. I'm a boss nigga, don't step to a nigga before I pull the trigga!" as he bounced around, moving his shoulders from side to side. Then he started freestyling. Everybody was all up on him like he was a king, pouring his drinks and holding his cup as he rapped, hyping him up.

This one friend was a true sucker; he kept trying to complete every sentence Mannis rapped like he was his echo. We went into Mannis's room, and he said it was hot so he took his shirt off. He had a wife beater on under his shirt. The room was big. He had posters and CDs scattered all over the floor and dressers. He put one of his CDs on and started rapping in the mirror. He looked like he was practicing for his next video. It seemed a little weird, but I guess that's what rappers do. He played more of his music. He gave me some CDs and I put them in my bag. I could give them to my brothers. We started kissing, touching, and feeling. He wasn't all thugged out, he was caressing me softly. Then I thought I heard someone come into the room. I asked him what that was as I tried to sit up. He nudged me back down and said it was nothing. Things started getting hot again. I didn't have a problem with that, but when his friend rubbed my leg, I had a problem with that.

"Get off my leg," I screamed.

"My man can't join in?" Mannis asked as he tried to kiss me some more.

"Hell no, I'm not with that," I said as I pulled away from him.

"That's my man, we get down together," he said as he looked at me.

I got out of the bed. "Well, I don't get down like that."

"If you want to be down with Mannis you will."

"Then I won't be down with you. I'm not that type of person."

"Whatever, ho. All hoes are tricks and tricks suck dick or we put them out," his man said.

"What?" I said as I looked at Mannis's friend. He was a straight-up flunky.

"You heard me, bitch."

"Nigga, you wish you could get this."

"Bitch, we get better hoes than your ass."

"Whatever," I said as I grabbed my pocketbook and headed for the door.

As I walked out, Mannis threw a pillow at me and said, "Bye, bitch."

I was fuming but didn't let it show. I kept my composure without making a scene as I walked out of the suite. I couldn't believe what went down. If it was Tanya, she might have been down with that three-way shit, but I wasn't. I would have fucked Mannis, but not his friend too. Nigga, please. I got into the hallway and pressed the Down button to the elevator. I fluffed my hair, pulled out my gloss, and touched up my lips in the mirror of the elevator.

As I got off the elevator I saw a group of guys talking. I walked past one of them. "Excuse me, miss, what's your name? Can I take you out tonight?" one guy sang like Jay-Z.

I didn't bother looking up. I had had about enough of men for one night. I walked out of the hotel, down the street, and then realized I did not know where the hell I was. I called Natalie and Tanya. Neither picked up. I went back into Mannis's hotel. There was nobody at the front desk. It had a sign that the front desk would open at 7:00 a.m. It was close to two. I went back outside and stood. I didn't know which way to walk.

"Do you know where you are going?" a sexy deep voice

asked. I turned around and saw a cashew-brown, attractive, muscular man.

"No, not really. I know my hotel is on Ocean Drive." I laughed.

"Ocean Drive, that is a ways from here. You can walk it, but it's a good walk. I would give you a ride, but you don't know me, and I know you wouldn't ride with me."

"You're right I wouldn't go with you. Can you just point me in the right direction?" I asked.

"Well, how about I walk you to your hotel?"

"Thank you, but I'm good. Just tell me what direction to walk in." I didn't want to talk to anyone. I was mad as shit and just wanted to get back to the room. The guy asked me if I was sure. I told him I was. One block later, my feet started burning in my heels and I did not feel like walking because I had danced all night. I was walking slow and I noticed the guy running up behind me.

He approached me again and said, "Listen, I'm not a stalker or anything, but I don't want you walking by yourself. Let me at least call you a cab. I don't want anything to happen to you."

"I don't need a cab," I said as I was about to cross the street. Then I said, "Okay, how many blocks do I have?"

"About twenty. How about this, you don't want to walk with me, you are too scared to get in my car, so how about we take a cab together?"

I thought about it for a moment and told him I would take a cab with him. If he only knew how my feet were burning and I couldn't walk anymore if I wanted to.

He called a cab. He closed his cell and said, "The cab will be here in a few minutes. Since we are going to share a cab, you got to tell me your name."

"Janelle, and yours?"

"Damon."

"Where are you from?"

"Orlando, Florida, but I live here."

"Really? I would love to live here. I live in Philadelphia."

Damon was very courteous and mannerly. It took the cab about a half hour to come. Within that half hour, we shared so much about one another. We had many things in common. We both were the oldest, loved Alicia Keys and the show on HBO *The Wire*. Damon's older sister's middle name was Janelle.

The cab finally arrived and we were still talking. Damon told me he'd gone to Syracuse, graduated, and had lived in Miami for three years. He did a lot of traveling with his job and loved steaks. I shared with him that I never went to college and had worked in retail since high school. Once we reached my hotel we wanted to finish talking. I felt comfortable with him, so we went to get something to eat. I was starving. I hadn't eaten because I was trying to be cute with Mannis. We ate at a bar and grill called Charlie's. We just talked and got to know each other the rest of the night. Damon talked about being from Orlando and all of his brothers and sisters; he was one of four. Out of nowhere Damon asked, "Have you ever been fishing?"

"No," I answered.

"My dad used to take us fishing all the time. You would like it. I love fishing," Damon said as he smiled.

"I'm sure you do, but I like eating fish, not catching it. Damon, you are real country."

"I'm not country. Every once in a while it comes out. That's because I went to school in the North and I'm starting to talk like y'all up there."

"Look at you, you just said y'all."

"You say y'all."

"No, I don't."

"Yes, you do. I think I heard you say it."

The food was good and our conversation was better. Damon had this kind demeanor to him. We were getting ready to leave and a young man walked up to the table, shook Damon's hand, and said, "How's it going, man, ready for the season?" Damon said he was ready. The man told Damon to take it easy and left.

"What is he talking about?" I quizzed.

"I play for the Dolphins."

"Dolphin what?" I asked.

"The Miami Dolphins, the football team."

"Really?" I said, shocked. I had no idea. Here I was sitting here talking to him and he never even mentioned it. "Do you know him?"

"Yeah, I eat here all the time. Remember when I said I do a lot of traveling with my job? I didn't want to tell you, I hate putting my business out there," he said as he opened the door for me to exit.

Damon said he had played football since he was six years old. His dad was his coach and had coached him until he got to high school. We walked back to my hotel. Damon told me more stories about his life and growing up in Orlando. We took a long walk along Ocean Drive. The beach was to the right of us and the sun was beginning to rise. So we walked onto the beach to get a better view. There were people all along the beach waiting for the sun to rise. It was so beautiful to see. The ocean water was an aquamarine green. In the distance it was blue. The sun emerged from the ocean water. The rays' colors ranged from bright orange to a pink. It looked like you could swim out and touch it. After a few minutes it was up in the sky.

We exchanged numbers and Damon gave me a warm, long hug. He asked me if I wanted to come back with him to his room. I told him no but maybe we could get together later. He said he would call me when he got up. I started walking toward my room, when my phone rang.

"I just wanted to say good-bye, Janelle," Damon said. My heart was fluttering out of my chest.

"See you later, Damon," I said seductively as I held the phone tightly. His scent was still on my clothes from our hug. I inhaled it. I wanted him so bad. I wanted to wrap my arms around him and stay with him. But where would that lead? Us having sex, having a good time for one night, and him never calling me anymore. I know how athletes can be.

I got somebody to fuck. Sean. I need more than that. When I walked into the room, Tanya and Natalie were sitting on the bed, waiting for me to tell them everything about my date with Mannis.

"Did y'all go out?" I asked.

"Yeah, we had a good time. Now tell us about your date," Natalie said.

"How was he? Was it good?" Tanya asked.

"Nothing happen, y'all." I laughed as I took my sandals off.

"Whatever. Why you coming in the next morning then?" Tanya questioned.

I broke down what had happened in the limo, then at the party, and then how he tried to play me with his three-way shit.

"Oh, I don't like him no more," Natalie said.

"Me neither, he's a dirty dude. I would have fucked them, but he would have had to pay me. Um, so if everything went bad why are you sitting here smiling?" Tanya asked.

"Because I met a Miami Dolphin. We just came from breakfast and a romantic walk on the beach."

"You did?"

"Yup."

"How do you know he really plays for the Dolphins?" Tanya asked.

"While I was with him a guy asked him was he ready for the season, and he shook his hand," I said confidently.

With a big smirk on her face Tanya said, "Some of these guys down here are suspect. A lot of fronting, saying they got this and that. I met a fake producer today. I asked him who he produces and he couldn't name anybody I ever heard of."

"Well, he's real. I was with him since two and when I wake up we are going out again."

"If you say so. I'm going to bed," Tanya said.

"Turn the lights off," Natalie said.

Chapter Eleven

Tanya

Janelle stepped off with Mannis, who should have been my come up. Now it's just me and Natalie. Me and Nat got dressed. I put on a tube top short flair black dress. She wore a black skirt and a pink-printed shirt. After we were dressed we walked to the elevator and saw the girls that were tricking down the hall. They were busted chicks. They were real friendly and one said in a country drawl, "Ladies, where the party at tonight?"

"I don't know. We're trying to find somewhere to go," I said.

"Where y'all going?" Natalie asked.

"We probably go to Crobar, or maybe Club Zno." The little chunky one said.

All three of them were a mess. The first one had a played-out tongue piercing, an eyebrow earring, and a tattoo of a cherry on her neck. She was wearing a baby doll dress and big clunky-heel square sandals. The second girl was short and fat. Natalie was thick, but this bitch was fat; they should have left her ass home. A drunk nigga wouldn't fuck that. She had frizzy curly hair and it was twisted in the front. She didn't even bother to shave under her arms. She had her hair packed under her arms with white deodorant balls hanging.

The last girl was tall and had chipped polish on her crusty sausage toes that were hanging over her sandals.

We all got on the elevator together. We all introduced ourselves. She said that's Meka, I'm Tiffany, and that's Nisha. "Hi, I'm Natalie and this is Tanya," Natalie said.

"So y'all want to hang out with us?" Natalie asked.

These girls reeked *cheap* and Natalie going to ask them to go out with us. My heart dropped. No, she didn't invite these busted chicks with us. I pulled her to the side and asked her why she did that. She said she thought it would be fun, the more the merrier.

"I heard all the ballers with money is going to be at Opium Garden," the tall one said.

"Really?" I said sarcastically. I was steady, thinking, *who would want you?* Talking about some baller, please. They was all in my dick telling me how fly my sandals were. I was so embarrassed to be seen with them. We walked down Ocean Drive and no one, not one person, tried to talk to us. We reached Club Opium and stood in line, and when we got to the door, we could not get in.

The bouncer looked over at Boomkisha and friends and said they had reached capacity. "Sorry, we're not letting anyone else in."

Me and Natalie walked across the street and the girls followed. We stood across the street and watched as they let these regular chicks in and groups of guys. I pulled Natalie to the side and said, "We got to drop these dirty bitches, they the reason we couldn't get in."

"All right, what are we going to tell them?"

"They're your friends, tell them something," I said.

"I don't know what to say," Natalie said.

"Tell them we about to go back to the room."

Natalie convincingly said, "Hey, y'all, we're going back to the room. So we're going to see y'all later." They were like, bye. And we walked away.

We went to this other club called Crobar. On the way there, Janelle called.

"How is it?" Natalie asked Janelle. She turned to me and said it was good.

"Here, she want to talk to you," Natalie said as she passed me the phone.

I grabbed it and said, "What's up?" Janelle started naming all the people she saw. I said okay and to call us when she hit land.

"All right then, bye," she said.

"Why is she calling us from the party? I'm not there, so I don't care. I know she just trying to rub it in our face that she with Mannis," I said.

"No, if she could have taken us with her, she would have," Natalie said.

"Natalie, your cousin's all about herself. She left you. She is not my family, so she didn't leave me."

"Janelle is not like that, Tanya."

I wasn't going to argue with her. As soon as we went to the bar and started drinking piña coladas, I seen the girls from the hotel. I told Nat and we tried to turn the other way, but they had spotted us. The big girl walked over and said, "See, y'all didn't decide to go in after all, huh?"

"Naw, we changed our minds," I said.

We started dancing and I felt a hand rub up against my butt. I turned around, but the dance floor was so crowded I couldn't tell who it was. I started dancing again. I tapped Natalie and said, "Yo, somebody keep feeling my butt."

"Some pervert," she said.

The next time the person grabbed my butt, I was going to grab their arm. So we danced some more and then the hand tried it again. I grabbed the arm and it belonged to this chick dancing beside me. She started smiling. I looked at Natalie, she looked at me, and we couldn't control our laughter. After she saw I wasn't flattered, she came over and apologized drunkenly. "Sorry, boo, I thought you was with it."

I asked Natalie if she was ready to go. She said yeah.

"Come on, girl, let's go," Natalie said as we exited the club.

We went back to our room. Janelle wasn't there. She probably was somewhere giving it up for free.

Chapter Twelve

Janelle

I woke up and saw that Tanya and Nat were gone. I yawned and opened my eyes. I wondered if Damon would call me today like he promised. I wanted to make sure he really played for the Dolphins. Tanya made me think that he could be a fake, so I called my uncle, who is a diehard football fan.

"Uncle Teddy, listen, have you ever heard of a guy named Damon Scott that plays for the Dolphins?"

"No, but I have heard that name before. Why?"

"I met this guy last night and he said he plays for the Miami Dolphins. I just want to see if he is telling the truth."

"Really? Let me log onto my computer." I heard him typing away and then he asked, "What is his name? I'm on the team's Web site."

"Damon Scott."

"Okay, what does he look like?"

"About five ten, brown skin."

"Is he from Orlando, Florida, and went to Syracuse?"

"Yeah, that's what he said."

"He's been with the Dolphins for three years as a second-string cornerback free agent."

"What does second string mean?"

"That means he is a backup player."

"So he sits on the bench?"

"Not necessarily, second strings still play. What, you didn't believe him?"

"No, I just heard about guys posing as athletes trying to get girls, that's all."

"Y'all young girls are so rough on these guys. They got to lie about who they are."

"No, we're not."

"Good luck, niecey. Be good and I'll see you and my money when you get back."

"I got your money. Bye, Unc," I said. I got up and attempted to get dressed. I couldn't make up my mind what I was going to wear. I tried on a few outfits. I laid my clothes across the bed. I decided to put on my white shorts and my white and gold sandals. I had a gold and white shirt. I put on my gold bangle bracelets and gold hoop earrings. I threw my hair up into a ponytail and I took a shower. Tanya and Natalie came in with breakfast when I got out of the shower.

"What's up for the day? Are we going to the beach?" Natalie asked.

"I'm not messing my hair up at the beach," I said.

"This is supposed to be my vacation. I got to get some sun and sand," Natalie said.

"Natalie, you have braids, we don't. I want to walk the strip and see who we meet. Then we'll try to set up shit for tonight," Tanya said.

"I'm with that," I said as I lotioned my legs down with baby lotion.

We walked down Washington Avenue and did some light shopping. We went into a small boutique. The salesgirl welcomed us into the store and said, "All of our pieces are one of a kind."

"And so are their prices," I said as I glanced at a pair of plain black shorts for $110.

Natalie held up a dress and asked the salesgirl what the biggest size was that they carried. The salesgirl giggled a little and said, "The biggest size we have is a ten." Natalie looked at her like, what?

"Why is that?" she asked.

"We just don't carry plus sizes. They don't sell."

"Let's get out of here," I said. I didn't like the girl's attitude. I was nudging Natalie toward the door when she said, "Hold up. I like this shirt. Do you like it?"

"It's okay. What are you going to wear it with?"

"I don't know," she said.

I didn't know how to tell her that her shirt looked like a grandmom's. I picked up another shirt. "I like this one better," I said.

"So you don't like this one? Tell the truth."

"Not really. It's okay, but I like this one." She valued my opinion more than her own. So she bought the shirt I suggested. We walked out of the store and went into a shoe store. There were so many pairs of sandals, boots, and shoes in different colors. Natalie picked up thigh-high, pointy-toe sandal boots and said, "Get these, Janelle."

"You get them, Natalie, wear them for Anthony," I said as I joked with her. I wanted these peach-colored sandals that were $115. If I bought them, I would be practically broke. So I pulled Nat to the side and asked if I could borrow a hundred dollars from her. She said sure, went into her pocket, and gave me the money. Tanya didn't have any money problems. She bought three pairs of sandals and said she was going to meet us outside. I paid for my sandals and we met up with Tanya outside. She was licking a strawberry ice cream cone walking down the street trying to get attention.

By the time we came back from shopping, we were all hungry. It was just about three o'clock. We ate at a restaurant on Ocean Drive. I had a chicken Caesar salad and Tanya had a turkey club. Natalie ate a big order of buffalo wings as an appetizer, a cheeseburger and fries as her meal, and she slurped down three Pepsis. You would have thought Natalie hadn't eaten in three years. She probably was trying to eat away her fears. We were sitting outside and just taking in all the people riding past on motorcycles and scooters. It was sunny, breezy, the beach was right across the street and was the backdrop for everything

"We should rent some scooters, it looks like fun," Natalie said.

"It does look like fun, but we can ride scooters back in Philly. We need to be trying to link up with some niggas so they can tell us what party is going to be doing it," Tanya responded.

"I'm with Tanya," I said as I looked over at Natalie. "I really want to have a good party night before we go home. That's what I came down here to do." Natalie shrugged her shoulders and said forget about it. We continue to walk down the street. We ran into a Spanish speaking woman selling cigars. Natalie bought one.

"You're a cigar aficionado now," I said.

"No, what is that?" she asked.

"It just means you like cigars," I said as I shook my head.

We debated about what club we wanted to go to. People were giving us free passes and discount admission to various clubs. We weighed the pros and cons of each club we heard about. We all decided that we were going to go to this place called Opium Garden. That was supposed to be the hottest club and really exclusive. Last night all these rappers and athletes were there and Tanya and Natalie couldn't get in. I mentioned to them that I was going to go out with them, but if Damon called, I was out. I wasn't passing up an opportunity of being with him. I only met him last night, technically this morning, but I liked him already.

Right after we finalized what we were going to wear, and what time to leave, Damon called. He asked if I could be ready in a half hour. I let him know I'd be ready in an hour. I hung up with Damon and broke the news to Natalie and Tanya.

"Ah, y'all, I'm going to go out with that guy Damon. He called."

"Damn. What, you trying to be, in love?" Tanya asked.

"No, I'm just enjoying myself."

"She's right, Nellie. We are in Miami. You should not be with one guy the whole weekend. You just said earlier you were trying to party and have fun," Natalie said.

"I know, Ms. Snuck Out of The House ain't talking."

"Yes, I am," Natalie said, like she wanted to get in my face.

"Natalie, if you could go home right now, you would," I said.

"If I was you, Janelle, I would have got his number and been out. I would have told him holler at me when I get back home. You going to fuck around, and fuck him, and he ain't going to call you no more."

"Whatever, y'all can still have fun without me. I don't make the party," I said.

"You right you don't make the party, but you playing yourself, boo, loving that nigga you just met," Tanya said.

"Nell, you're right, we can have fun without you, but it just won't be the same. This is the second night in a row you are dissing us. This was supposed to be our vacation together."

I was tired of arguing with them. They were just jealous. Natalie was already married and had a husband at home waiting for her. And Tanya doesn't need any more men. But me, I don't have nobody waiting for me but Sean, and he doesn't count. There was no discussion. I am going out and having a good time.

Chapter Thirteen

Tanya

Bitches are acting real foul and shady in Miami. I don't even fuck with Janelle like that, so I don't know why I'm mad. Here it is, I thought we were going to have the bomb time and this shit is just okay. So right now I'm not feeling Miami or their niggas. You know what I'm saying? Ain't nobody got no dough and my pussy ain't for free. We were all supposed to be going out together, but Janelle left us for the second time. Natalie said she don't feel like going out. So, I'm going to call the dude from St. Louis, Monte. He is sweet and I know I can get a couple dollars. I can tell because of the way he was throwing money at me.

I called Monte. The phone rang like four times.

"Yo."

"This is the girl Tanya. You trying to see about something or what?"

"Yeah."

"How much money you working with?"

"How much you want?"

"It depends on what you want?"

"I want the works." *Yeah, whatever*, I thought. I told him I cost three hundred and if he wanted the works, he better get somebody else. I was not licking or sucking him. He was too fat and I don't like fat guys.

As soon as I entered his hotel room, he immediately pinned me against the door. He said, "You smell good" and began rubbing my breast under my shirt. He then knelt down and opened my legs wide. Then his head went farther down and his beard began tickling my clit. Monte took off his shirt and released his grizzly-bear chest. His body was a little chubby and then he unzipped his pants. As he undressed, I asked him if he had a condom. He said he didn't have one. I told him to go find one. He was pressed, so he went and got one.

When he went to get a condom I looked around the room. He had bottles of beer under the bed and his wallet on the dresser. I opened his wallet and saw pictures of a fat little girl that looked like him. He had plenty of credit cards and money. I took three hundred and put the rest back. I put the money in my bag and lay back down. He came back into the room and began kissing and licking on me fast. I told him to slow down and that I wasn't going anywhere. He put his dick into me, and it was smaller than my lipstick. I could barely feel it. He said, "Damn, girl, you got some good shit." Only about three minutes had passed and he was done. He came too fast. I know he was paying me, but he owed me some more money for putting me through this shit. He wasn't even a good fuck. I don't know the last time he had some, but he came entirely too quick. He was breathing hard like he just finished a marathon or something. *Please*, I thought. I slipped out of the bed and dressed myself. He started snoring and I woke him up and asked for my money.

"Monte, I'm about to leave."

"Why you leaving already? Stay awhile."

"No, I got to go," I said with an attitude.

"I'll give you your money, but you should think you're worth more than three hundred. For what you got down there, you could probably get a whatever. If you stayed the night and give me some more you could get a gee," he said as he pointed to my butt.

I got mine, I thought, as I shrugged off his comment. I couldn't care less about what he was talking about.

"No, I'm cool," I said. I couldn't imagine staying the night with him. He gave me my money and then drove me back to my hotel. So far, I had made only six hundred dollars. That was cool, but I wanted to make more. I soaked in the tub when I got back to the room. I wanted to tighten my pussy just in case I met somebody tonight. Natalie was being the depressed lady over Anthony, and Janelle was still somewhere with that guy Damon. How the fuck that bitch going to come down with us and get lost like she has all fucking weekend? That bitch make me sick. That's why I don't really deal with her like that.

I couldn't look at Natalie, she looked sickening. I didn't feel like being in the room with her. She is a negative fucking pain in the ass. She is complaining about everything. Giving me a fucking headache saying how Anthony said he going to leave when she gets back and she don't know what she going to do. I wasn't going to listen to her sob story.

I changed into a camel-colored tan dress. I didn't wear any underwear intentionally and went back out. I hated going out by myself. Natalie was a wrap and those smuts down the hall weren't an option. I had no other choice. I told myself that I was only here one more day and I had to "come up" before I left. I had to meet some type of baller and get paid.

I walked down the street from our hotel to this Sports Bar. There had to be some men in there. I walked in and all heads turned. I tried to act like I didn't notice all of the attention. I sat at the bar and ordered a Grey Goose and cranberry juice. Nobody approached me at first. Then this real good-looking tall man came over and sat next to me. I knew exactly who he was. I recognized him from seeing him on BET. His name was Kamani Johnson and he was one of the comedians on *Comic View*. He had to be getting money. I turned around and uncrossed my legs for him. I wanted him to see I didn't have any underwear on.

"You have some pretty lips," he said.

I didn't bullshit him. I got straight to the point and said, "Thank you, and for a thousand you can taste them."

"A thousand? Um. That's not bad," he said as he rubbed the few hairs on his chin. He smiled and said, "I can handle that."

He bought me a few more drinks and then we went to his hotel room. It was four times the size of our hotel room. The suite was huge with a bar and a living room. He told me as soon as I walked in to get naked. He went into the bathroom and I went into his pocket. He only had one platinum card. I took that and slipped it in my bag. He then threw me on the bed.

"You got to work for your money," he said as he ripped my dress off me. He was already hard, so I grabbed all of his erect nine and a quarter inches and put it in my mouth. I licked it slowly up and down. I tried as hard as I could to put it all the way down my throat. I wanted to deep-throat that shit better than the best porn chick. After I finished, he got on top of me and banged my back out. Goddamn, he was so powerful. He pulled my hair and spanked my ass. I fucked the shit out of him back. He hit the back of my walls. Every time he hit it I screamed.

"Stop screaming," he said.

"I can't," I said.

"Touch your toes," he demanded. He went from smooth to rough and strong. *Bitch, you going to be calling me, sending me tickets to your shows, telling me to come and see your ass,* I thought. For about two hours straight, we went at it. He had never had sex like that in his life. I could bank on that. I know I was the best he ever had. Every time he stroked I felt it in my back. After we were done, he asked me for my number and put it in his Blackberry phone. I put my ripped dress back on, asked him for my money, and if he could walk me to my hotel because my dress was ripped. He said he didn't have any money and the door was that way. I still wanted this to lead to something, so I said, "Kamani, I need my money."

"I heard what you said. Maybe you didn't hear what I said. I don't have it." I could not believe I had just been burnt for my money.

"You got it on a credit card, Mac card, something," I said.

"Did you hear what I said? Get out before I call security."

"So what you think, you're just going to burn me?" I asked.

"Pretty much," he said as he tried to show me the door.

"I don't think so," I said as I got up in his face.

He said, "What you going to do, call the cops?" He was right, I couldn't call the cops. But I could run up his fucking card. I'm glad I took that shit. All I could do was leave. I was going to max his credit card up for trying to play me.

Chapter Fourteen

Natalie

Janelle and Tanya were out. I was in the room by myself watching television. Janelle was making me so mad. She was leaving me and Tanya. She was having a great time going to all these parties meeting celebrities. I finally broke down. I called home and I heard my baby crying. Anthony was yelling at me, saying, "My wife does not go out of town for the weekend! I'm done with you, Natalie. I'm washing my hands of you."

"Listen, Anthony, just listen," I cried.

"Listen to what? You think it's a game or some type of joke, don't you? When I said I want to marry you, I meant every word. I saved up to buy your engagement ring. I wanted to propose to you on your birthday in November, but I was broke, so I bought you a necklace. But as soon as I got enough money, I bought you the biggest ring I could afford and gave it to you on Christmas. I never did that for any other woman. I didn't even pay my bills to get you that ring. Then I married you right away. I didn't say let's be engaged for a year. I married you against my mother's wishes. But you don't appreciate me."

"I know, Anthony, I just needed to get away, I'm sorry, I'm so sorry," I sobbed.

"Natalie, those bitches don't have a man. Tanya is a slut. You told me that yourself. And Janelle don't have a man or a baby. You have a family, but you left it for a stupid trip. You left me for the weekend with your cousin and your girl-friend."

"Anthony, I said I'm sorry."

"Sorry is not good enough. I know you down there part-ing your legs for niggas."

"No, I am not. I'm not sleeping with anyone. Why would you say something like that?"

"Yes, you are, I'm not stupid. That's what women do when they go on girlfriend trips. If you want to save our mar-riage you better get your ass home."

And once again, he hung up on me. I couldn't stay in Miami anymore. Janelle was with that football guy and I don't know where Tanya was. All I knew was I had to get home. I was sitting on the bed and then I started crying harder and harder. I couldn't help it. I had to go home. I grabbed the yellow pages out of the night desk, called Delta, and asked them if I could catch an earlier flight. Delta told me the earliest flight was leaving Monday, tomorrow. It would be fifty dollars to switch tickets and an additional two hundred for the ticket. That was the day before I was sched-uled to leave anyway. American Airlines said they didn't have any available flights. Then I called Air Tran, nothing, United, nothing. Then I thought about taking the bus. I called Greyhound. They did have a bus leaving at 5:00 p.m., but it wouldn't get back to Philadelphia for almost a day and a half. It had all these stops.

I cried again and paced around the room. I felt trapped. I needed my baby, my husband, and they needed me. I had let them down. I sat back on the bed and tried to think of ways to get home. Then I thought of renting a car and called Enterprise. It was five hundred dollars and some change for a one-way trip. I couldn't really afford it, but I wanted to go home.

I went downstairs to the lobby and asked if the front desk

agent could check on mapquest.com for me. The site said it would take me about twenty-seven hours to drive home. I was not going to drive that long by myself. I couldn't fly until Monday, the bus was too slow, so I guessed I was stuck. Anthony was just going to have to yell at me some more. I did all I could do. I tried, I really tried.

I went back to the room, turned out the lights, and went to sleep. I couldn't sleep because there was too much noise going on outside. I just thought about my life and how I had really fucked up. I heard a knock on the door. I went to answer it. I turned the lights on and saw Todd had knocked on the door. "I know you not asleep. Where are your girls?"

"Out somewhere."

"And you in the room by yourself?"

"Yup."

"That's not right. You want to go get something to eat?"

"No, I think I'm going to stay in. I'm tired from last night."

"You sure you okay? Well, if you don't want to get a drink, at least get something to eat."

"No, I don't feel like it. I just want to go home."

"Home? You are in Miami. Come on, let's go and get pizza. You shouldn't be sitting up in a room crying and lonely. The fresh air will be good for you. Okay?"

"Okay, I'll go."

We walked to this small pizzeria, got our pizza to go, and walked back to Todd's room.

"My husband is mad at me for coming down to Miami. I shouldn't be down here. I don't belong," I confessed as we walked down the street.

"This is not really my scene either. I have a girlfriend back in New York. It seems like if you don't have a Benz or a platinum chain on, a female can't even holler at you."

I laughed at his comment. "All these girls have stilettos on with everything hanging out. I don't dress like them. I went into the store and the biggest size they had was a ten. If you bigger than a ten, then you don't get no love down here."

"Well, every store I go into, there is an Antoine or Salvatore saying how can I help you, with their hand on their hip. I can't take it. Then if they are not gay, they don't understand me. No offense but everybody speaks Spanish. I went into Denny's and I felt like I was in a different country because everybody was speaking Spanish. I was the only person speaking English."

I started laughing. It was the truth. I had noticed that too!

We talked a little more and I was enjoying our conversation until Todd said, "Do you think your husband will mind if I give you a kiss?"

"What?" I said. He had caught me totally off guard.

"I'm telling you. Take you clothes off and I'll massage you, and kiss you all over your body, and that will make you forget all your worries."

"No, I'm okay. Actually, thanks for the pizza, but I got to go." I had just cried and spilled my guts to Todd and his mind was still on trying to fuck me. Unbelievable! He had seemed like he was sincerely concerned. I can't wait to get home to my baby.

At least I know my husband and my baby love me regardless of what size I am.

Chapter Fifteen

Janelle

I showered, dressed, and met Damon in the lobby. He showed up with small-rimmed eyeglasses on. They didn't make him look nerdy. He looked really good. His muscles weren't popping out of his shirt, but they were noticeable. I never liked a big muscular guy with muscle shirts on, but his were nice. He had on a long black T-shirt and blue jean shorts with a pair of white Air Force Ones. His eyeglasses matched his platinum chain. He had a trimmed mustache and light facial hair. His ears were studded with large square diamonds. He didn't have all that jewelry on last night. We walked toward his car. It was a new shiny silver BMW 745i. He opened my door for me and I got into the seat and melted. The leather was so soft. "So where are we going?" I asked.

"I don't know. I just wanted to see you. We can do whatever."

"Whatever? Um, I don't know about that."

"Well, if you not with whatever, how about we get something to eat?"

"No, I just ate. We can get drinks," I said.

"All right, then I can show you around Miami."

"What, you trying to get me home?"

"No, I'm just trying to spend time with you," he said as he looked at me. "You are so cute."

"Thank you," I said as I blushed.

We went to get drinks at a bar in Coconut Grove. I ordered a mai tai drink. It was served in a coconut with an umbrella and pineapples and a cherry adorned it. I was really enjoying his company. After our drinks we walked and talked more about our families, growing up, and our passions in life. Damon's father was in the navy and his mother was a teacher. His sister's name was Yolonda and his younger brother, Corey, went to Bethune-Cookman College, his baby sister, Kisha, was still in high school. Damon began interrogating me about relationships, past and present.

"Who are you seeing at home?"

"I'm not seeing anybody. How about you?"

"My girl left me."

"Why did she leave you?"

"Another woman."

"Are you serious?" I said.

"It's true."

"I don't believe that," I told him as I tried to keep from laughing.

"Do you believe this?" Damon said as he pulled me close to him and kissed me right in the middle of the street. People were walking past and couples were holding hands, children were getting their faces painted. It was a short, simple kiss. His lips were succulent. We walked past a movie theater and he asked if I wanted to see a movie. I told him there was nothing out I wanted to see.

I couldn't believe Damon wanted to chill with just me. His boys kept calling him all day telling him about different parties and things going on. "She must be a dime. You not coming out. She got to be gorgeous," I overheard his friend say over the phone.

"She is beautiful to me," he said as he glanced at me.

"I'm going to stop answering this phone now. I'm cool. I met who I wanted to meet," he said as he grabbed my hand.

We rode back down to Southbeach near my hotel. There were all these girls, pretty girls, half naked, and down for whatever was walking around, and Damon didn't want them. It didn't matter to me that I was missing the parties. All the cars, guys, and rappers were walking and driving by. It was so much chaos going on, but we were together taking everything nice and slow, like we had been together for years. We parked and were walking down the street holding hands while everyone else was trying to have a one-night stand and a quick thrill.

We went back to his house, which was about thirty minutes away from my hotel. It was in north Miami. He had a house with a two-car garage. The outside and neighborhood was very nice. The inside was very simple and basic, not what I expected. It was plain and lacked pizzazz. It looked lived-in though. His table had place mats and dishes set up, but it looked like it was never used. He told me to look around as he went upstairs into his bedroom. He had cream marble floors and a crystal chandelier. There were glass tables, a multicolored sectional, and a plasma-screen television.

He yelled from upstairs, "If you want, there is juice and wine in the refrigerator."

I walked over to his kitchen and opened his stainless steel refrigerator. He had bottles of water, an Italian Garden to-go bag, a few bananas and oranges, Gatorade and plenty of high-protein maintenance shakes. I pulled out the white wine and cranberry juice he was talking about and poured myself a glass. I noticed his green and white marble countertops were shiny and spotless. There wasn't one dish in the sink and his copper-colored pots looked like they had never been touched. I brought him a glass of juice up to the bedroom, as an excuse to see what his room looked like. He had two extra bedrooms. I peeked outside. There was a large gated backyard big enough for a pool.

"I'm renting this. I didn't buy a house down here yet because I'm not ready. When I'm ready I will. I got one at home in Orlando though."

"It's nice and neat in here."

"I have a housekeeper, Rita, comes in once a week. She buys my food and straightens up."

"Must be nice," I said as I continued to look around.

The bedroom curtains and comforter were a masculine tan and cream color. His bed was tall and grand with coliseum poles at the end of it. I would need a stepladder to get into it. It looked comfy and had about twelve pillows on it. I glanced into his huge bathroom. There were two walk-in closets and a big Jacuzzi tub. There was a double sink and a standing shower next to it. I went back downstairs to the living room and flipped through his CD collection. He had a mixture of R&B and rap.

"What are you doing with a Justin Timberlake CD?"

"That's not mine. I swear to God. My sister Kisha brought that when she came to visit."

"Whatever. You can admit it."

Damon put on an Alicia Keys CD and poured us glasses of white wine. We stood on his patio. The view was so pretty, the city lights and horizon in the distance. I wished I could stay here forever right in his arms. This was the first time in my life I wanted time to stand still, at least for another week.

Chapter Sixteen

Janelle

I stayed with Damon last night. Being with him is total bliss. I don't care if we've only known each other a little while. I still haven't given him any yet, but we have come very close. He was probably used to girls who give it up fast. I wanted to be different from them. He didn't even really try anyway. I guess it will happen eventually. I am going back out with him today. He dropped me off at the hotel and I went to get dressed. Natalie wasn't in the room and Tanya was asleep all balled up under the covers. I saw her head come up from under the covers. She looked at me and asked, "You going back out?"

"Yeah, I'll see y'all tomorrow before we leave. Where Natalie at?"

"I think she went to the beach."

"Tell her I said to call me."

Damon was waiting outside. His windows were rolled down and he had his sunglasses on.

Tomorrow I'll be back to the everyday hustle and bustle, cleaning, arguing, and cussing my brothers and mother out. Today I was going to have fun. Damon said he had to show up at this party his friend was throwing. If he didn't go his partners would be calling him soft and talking about him. I didn't really want to go to a party with him. If I wanted to party I would have stayed with Nat and Tanya.

We went to the party his friend was throwing at the Loew's Hotel. It was a mixed crowd, Spanish, white, black, and every other nationality. The music varied from room to room. One room had hip-hop, the other was techno, another reggae, and another soca. Damon held my hand and led me through the party. The strobe lights were fuchsia, yellow and white flashing all around the party. At first I felt a little nervous because I thought I might run into Mannis, but then I realized he wouldn't care if he saw me. He probably wouldn't have even remembered me. Everybody kept coming over to Damon, speaking and shaking his hand. I was just standing there feeling out of place. One guy was walking around with twins. One on each arm like he was the man.

"You want a drink?" Damon asked.

"No, not right now, I have to go to the bathroom. Hold this for me," I said.

I went to the bathroom to check my hair to see how it looked. When I came out of the bathroom, I saw Damon talking to this white girl. She was very thin with brown hair and blond highlights. I walked back over to where Damon was standing. I stood to the side of him.

Damon turned around and said, "Janelle, I want you to meet Kelly." She was wearing a low-cut, draped, revealing dress, and her hair was resting on her shoulders. She had a white multicolored monogrammed Louis Vuitton bag. I said hello awkwardly. I still didn't know who Kelly was to Damon, so I stood quietly. If she was his girlfriend, I didn't want to play him, and if she was just a friend, I wouldn't want to get upset. Besides, we'd only known each other a day or two. I was still trying to figure out who Kelly was when a guy built similar to Damon came over to her and kissed her on her neck. He was a little taller and huskier than Damon with dark skin and a small blow-out haircut.

"This is my partner Carl from Chicago, he plays with me on the team," Damon said. Carl smiled at me and shook my hand. They were talking about the upcoming season. I made small talk with Kelly. She seemed to be cool. I stepped away from Damon and attempted to buy a drink. "Hi, can I get an apple martini?" I asked the bartender.

"One minute." The bartender walked away, opened a few Corona beers and put limes in, then poured three glasses of white zinfandel. She came back, wiped up a spill, turned around, cashed out a check, waited on another man. I said excuse me four times. She looked over at me and said, "One minute."

I get it, she doesn't wait on females. She was only catering to the men. Damon's friend Carl walked over and said, "Hey, Jen."

"Hey, Carl," she said as she smiled. Carl was sipping champagne and Red Bull.

"Get her whatever she's drinking. Here go my card, keep my tab running," he said as he handed the bartender his green American Express credit card. Twenty minutes after trying to get a drink I finally had one. Not only did she take my order, she got extra friendly. "Hey, what you drinking?"

"An apple martini."

"Coming right up," she said as she began to pour the apple pucker mix into a mixing glass. I located Damon and went and stood next to him. We danced a little until this drunk guy accidentally spilled his drink on my dress. Damon grabbed some napkins from the bar and I began to blot the stain. It was smearing so I asked Damon to hold my bag while I went into the bathroom. I walked to the rest room and put a little water on the stain. It was coming out. Now it just had to dry. When I came out Damon introduced me to his friend Stephen. He was a light skin guy with a bright smile. He kept laughing. I guess he thought I didn't get the joke. I just smiled like I didn't know what he was talking about. "I see you got my partner holding your pocketbook already," he said.

"Man, be quiet, some drunk spilled something on her dress. Go find your wife," Damon said.

"I left her home," he said as he laughed.

"Well, you better leave me alone before I call her."

"Nah, don't do that," Stephen said as he shook Damon's hand.

Me and Damon danced all night and drank cocktails. We left the party and walked toward the door. "Did you have fun?" Damon asked as we left the club and got in the car.

"Yeah, I'm enjoying myself," I said as I sat in the car.

"Can't believe you about to leave me," he said as he pulled my face toward him and he kissed me.

"Just enjoy me. While I'm here," I said between kisses. We kissed a little more, then pulled off. I was feeling the drinks I had and Damon, because I climbed over the console and began rubbing all over him while he was driving. I unzipped his pants and placed his dick in my mouth. I stroked it up and down. It became firm and harder every time I licked. I could see lights whizzing past my head as I bobbed up and down.

"Baby, I can't drive like this, stop!" he said unconvincingly. His phone rang and he located it and tried to talk. "Hello, um, man, um I'm . . . going to . . . call . . . call you back." He threw the phone in the backseat. He was still driving with one hand. The car was swerving a little. He grabbed my hair and pushed my head up and down. His dick was so erect that I didn't have to hold it anymore. It was standing straight up by itself.

He took his hand off my head and put it up my skirt. He slid my panties over and played with my clit, stroking it back and forth and slowly patting it. He then pulled my shirt up and raised my bra, releasing my breasts. My breasts were now hanging out as Damon cupped them, rubbed them together, and played with my nipples. He said he couldn't take it anymore and pulled over on the side of the highway.

He got out of the car. I exited on his side. He kissed me wildly, then pushed me into the backseat of the car. There wasn't a lot of room, so I placed one leg all the way back and held it with my arm. My other, I spread back. His pants and boxers rested at his ankles. He licked his finger and smoothly traced the opening of my vagina. He primed it for his entrance. He then placed all of himself inside me. It didn't slide right in, because I was a little tight, but after a few slight strokes, it was in. It was so tender and not rough, it was passionate. His motions were slow and intense. He was creating an extreme sexual energy inside me. My heart was racing. I had always wanted to have sex outside in a car, but never had. The warm breeze was whipping past us as cars sped by. He kept going at it, giving me all he had. I was pumping back at him. It felt so amazing and so wild. After we finished I jumped back in the front seat, fixed my hair, and pulled my skirt down. He kept looking over at me the rest of the ride home. As soon as we got back in the house, he picked me up and placed me on his bed. He tossed all the pillows off and we went at again and again. It was like he couldn't get enough of me.

Chapter Seventeen

Natalie

It was my last day in Miami, so I decided again I was going to enjoy myself. I can't get home and Anthony is going to be mad. I just have to live with that. I am in a nice hot place near the beach. I needed to enjoy it. I went to the beach by myself. Tanya didn't want to go. She was still sleep. I met a couple and played Frisbee in the water with them. It was fun to dive in and out of the water. Once I was out of the water my legs felt like they weighed a hundred pounds. I got a henna tattoo on the beach with Anthony Jr.'s and Anthony's names on it. I relaxed in the sun and went back into the room, took a nap, then caught the bus to the Bayside Marketplace. It was like a minimall next door to the Miami Arena. On the way home I didn't want to catch the bus, so I took a cab. I stopped at a pharmacy and bought a magazine. I picked up a sandwich from Subway and went back to the room. I began to pack and was about to get ready for bed when Tanya called.

"What are you doing?" Tanya asked.

"Nothing, about to go to bed."

"You should go out with me."

"I'm going to stay in again."

"Natalie, you can't stay in again. Look, I met these guys from Baltimore. They cool and they're paying for everything. Get dressed, I'm coming to get you."

I hurried and got dressed. I had plenty of outfits to choose from. I didn't wear anything I brought. This was my last night in Miami and I was going to make the best of it. I met Tanya in the lobby of the hotel.

The guys Tanya met were cool. They took us to a party. They had their own table at the club and all these bottles of champagne and Hennessey on the table. Tanya's friends kept asking us if we were okay and if we wanted anything else. I danced with Tanya's friend Lamar. He was spinning me all around. I asked the deejay to play a Ludacris song. I got really drunk and was dancing with Tanya on top of a table. It was fun at first. Tanya was dropping it like it was hot. I was moving back and forth to the music.

I climbed down and got another drink. Then my heart started racing and I felt really hot, like I was going to pass out. I tapped Tanya on the leg and told her I needed to go to the hospital or something.

"Natalie, that is the drink, sit down, it will wear off."

"Tanya, I really feel sick."

Tanya got off the table and walked me over to the bar and got me a cold bottled water.

"Drink this," she said as she handed me the bottle.

I opened it and drank and felt a little better. Tanya got back on the table and continued to dance. I sat at the table and put my head down. My head was spinning and I felt like at any minute I was going to spit up.

I decided to wait outside the club and get some fresh air. I sat on the ground. The sun was coming up and it was cool and breezy. I knew it was time to go home. I started seeing people taking their morning jogs and restaurants opening for business, spraying hoses against the concrete. Did I need to run away from reality that bad, I asked myself, that I had to come hundreds of miles and get so intoxicated that I could hardly walk? To make me forget about my problems? Tanya came out with her friend, and I told her I was ready to go. She said she wanted to go to breakfast.

"Tanya, I am so tired, I feel so nauseous."

"I'm going to breakfast. We can drop you off at the hotel."

Her friends came out of the club. The one I was dancing with pulled a towel out of his pocket and wiped sweat from his forehead.

"You okay, lil' mama?"

"I'm fine," I said.

"You don't look so good. Y'all need to take her home."

"We about to," Tanya's friend said. Then he told them he would meet them at the restaurant in the hotel after they dropped me off.

Before I got out of the car I asked Tanya if she was cool. She said yeah, she felt comfortable with them and that she would bring me some breakfast back.

When I got back to the room, I was crying and crying. Partly because I was drunk and I couldn't wait to wake up and pack my clothes and go home.

Chapter Eighteen

Tanya

I woke up and Janelle was getting her stuff, trying to hurry and get dressed and leave again with her friend. That was not cool. She is not my friend, but she is Natalie's cousin and left her like this since Saturday. That football guy ain't going to do nothing but leave her ass anyway. She is putting in too much time too soon. She didn't even bring him to our room, because she knew if he had seen me, then he would have wanted me. She is real intimidated by me, I can tell.

After Janelle left, I checked my voice messages. That guy, Monte, was on there saying that he had a really good time and wanted to get with me again. *No, thank you,* I thought. I guess he didn't realize his money was gone yet. Oh well, today is the last day before it's time to go home. I didn't meet anybody that I really liked or clicked with. Until I met this guy named Keith by the pool at our hotel. He said, "Hey, sexy. I'm taking you home with me," and grabbed me.

"Where's home?" I said.

"You going to Baltimore with me."

"Oh, really? I don't think so," I said as I eyed his rose-gold chain with a cross and bracelet. Flooded with diamonds. He had his hat pulled all the way down and a little goatee. "So here, put your number in my phone."

I took his cell and dialed my number and entered my name and saved it.

"So what's your plans for the night?"

"So far nothing. Why? What's up with you?"

"Me and my boys got a table at—" His cell phone ring was a loud song. How corny, I thought.

Keith then said, "You can party with us all night."

"Where y'all going?"

"We got a table at Krave. You got some friends for my boys?"

"Yeah, I do."

"Well, call them and tell them to get ready so we can go out and show y'all a good time."

I called Natalie and she was still in the room being depressed. I convinced her this was our last night and we needed to go out and have some fun. We all went and got her. They took us to a party and bought us all these drinks. I got on top of the table and danced like Tina Turner and a belly dancer combined. Keith and his friends cheered me on and put dollars in my waist. Natalie was so drunk she got on the table and danced too! I was trying to make sure Natalie had a good time and she did.

After the club we went back to Keith's hotel. I told him I was fucking, he said he didn't want to fuck. He begged me to eat my pussy. I let him. He came from eating me out. He said some bullshit like he was into pleasing his woman, whatever. "Tanya, I'm going to be in Philly by the weekend to see you."

Chapter Nineteen

Janelle

I couldn't help but reflect on last night. Just the thought of how he made me feel, brought my body into an automatic frenzy. The last two days have been a dream come true. Damon is so sweet. We have had the best time doing everything from salsa dancing to walking on the beach. He is so funny and playful. He is real kissy-feely and I love it! We've stayed together almost every moment since I met him. We already talked about me coming back down before the summer was over. I just wish I could stay a little longer. My weekend went by too fast. He said he'll come to see me. Hopefully I'll be able to take off from work. I was in the bathroom doing my hair. Damon walked up behind me, put his hands around my waist, kissed my ear, and said, "One more time before you leave me."

"Dame, I'm going to miss my flight."

"I don't care about you missing your flight. Damn, girl, you leaving me. I can't take it."

"I'm coming back, I promise."

"I'm coming with you," he said.

"You can't come with me."

"I'm only joking. For real though, I'm going to miss you."

If I said all the attention that Damon had showed me didn't go to my head, I would be lying.

My flight was leaving at noon. Damon said he would take me to the airport. He kept saying I don't want you to go, and I didn't want to leave him or Miami. Everything was going so great. I went back to the hotel to pack my stuff. Natalie was already packed and Tanya was getting packed. I told them Damon was going to drive us to the airport.

"That's good. I didn't feel like catching a cab," Tanya said.

"I just want to get home," Natalie said as tears ran down her face. She looked like she had been crying all night.

"You okay, Nat?" I asked.

"I'm cool. I got a hangover and I'm tired."

We checked out of the hotel and headed for the airport. In the car, Damon kept kissing me and telling me how much he was going to miss me. Tanya smirked at me through the rearview mirror.

"I'm going to miss you too! I'll call you as soon as I get home," I said.

Once we were at the airport Damon walked me as far as he could to the security checkpoint. I took my bags from him that he was carrying. I gave him a hug and he said, "I wish you didn't have to leave me," as he gave me one last long hug.

"Damon, I have to go."

"How about if you stay for a couple more days?"

"I can't stay, Damon. I wish I could stay, but I can't. You're so silly. I can't stay. Where am I going to stay?"

"With me," he said.

"What about my job? I don't even have any more money. Plus, I have to pay some bills back home."

"How much are your bills? I'll pay your salary for the week," Damon said as he smiled. He pulled out a wad of money. Then he said, "I'll give you two weeks' salary." He put the money in my hand.

"You don't have to pay me to stay," I said as I gave him the money back.

I thought about it for a moment. I thought about my job. I couldn't call out. There was no way. I hadn't even paid my bills before I left, and what about my mom and brothers? I still owed my uncle money.

"Damon, I'll be back. I promise," I said as I gave him a kiss on his lips.

"You can't leave me now. We are getting along so good and we need more time to get to know each other. What's keeping you from staying and saying yes? Don't you want to stay with me?"

"I want to stay but . . ."

"But what?"

"I got bills to pay and a job to go back to."

Natalie and Tanya were waiting for me. I said good-bye once more to Damon, and he started walking away. We all began walking toward the terminal. I mentioned to them that Damon wanted me to stay and I wanted to stay, but I was scared. I stopped and stood still and thought about staying. I knew it could only get better between Damon and me and I loved the weather and the beach. I couldn't decide what to do; then finally I went with my impulse and said, "I think I'm going to stay for a few more days, y'all. Have a good flight."

I screamed, "Damon, wait!" He turned around and started walking toward me.

I walked with my luggage and said, "I'm staying."

"What, the dick is that good?" Tanya mumbled under her breath as she marched down the corridor to the security checkpoint. She yelled to Natalie to come on.

Natalie ignored her and said, "You're doing what? You better get on this plane and go home. You can't stay with him. You barely know him. He could be crazy."

"I'm staying. I'll be okay. I'll call you. If he was crazy he would have got me already."

"That's true." Natalie looked at Damon and then back at me. She changed her tune and said, "Well, be careful. I'll call you as soon as I get home, and good luck." She gave me a hug.

Damon grabbed my luggage and kissed me. I knew I had made the right decision. The only bad thing or problem I had was calling my mother. I asked Damon for a moment alone while I called. He said sure and went downstairs. I closed the bedroom door and called her.

As soon as she answered, I blurted out, "Mom, I met a friend and I'm not coming home today. I'm staying for another week."

"What? What friend are you talking about, Janelle?" she asked.

"A guy I met over the weekend. He plays for the NFL." I whispered as I didn't want Damon to hear me.

"Are you that dumb, Janelle? Don't you know those kind of men get women all the time? What about your job?"

"Mom, I'm going to call my job. It's okay," I said, trying to reassure her.

"Janelle, you be careful in Miami."

"Mom, I'll be okay. I'm going to Western Union you the bill money. And pay Uncle Teddy back."

"Where did you get money from, Janelle?" she quizzed.

"Mom, I didn't spend any of the money I had. Guys have been treating us all weekend."

"Janelle, what's this guy's name and address?"

I gave my mother everything she needed on Damon. That was easy. I called my Uncle Teddy and got his machine. I left him a message and told him I was staying in Miami and to pick up his money from my mom. I hung up the phone and began to call my job when Damon peeked in the room.

"Is it okay to come in yet?" he asked playfully.

"I'm trying to call my job now." He said okay and shut the bedroom door. Now it was time to call my job. I was due back tomorrow, and that's not going to happen. I began to think of a clever lie. Everybody knew I went out of town. I sat on the bed and thought a little more. Different scenarios came to mind, from having an accident to pneumonia. I called in and got Shana. I asked her the number to the district manager's office. I figured I'd go over Joan's head. She could find out I was staying another week from corporate. Shana gave me the number and then said, "Hey, girl, we need you so bad. This store is going crazy without you."

"I'm not coming back until next week."

"Are you okay?" she asked.

"Yeah. I'm fine. I met somebody."

"What? You go!" She laughed loudly.

"Shh, don't say nothing. I'll see you next week."

"I'm not going to tell anyone. Have fun."

I had called everybody I owed to settle all my business, except for Sean. If I call him he is going to be asking questions. I'll deal with him when I get back.

The first night I slept at Damon's house he was wonderful. It was just the best moment in my life. First, we got into the hot tub and gave each other massages. He had vanilla candles lit everywhere. We engaged in an intense kissing session. We just held each other, cuddled, and drank champagne. We fell asleep in each other's arms. I was awakened by gentle kisses to my butt, back, and legs. His kisses started at my foot and traveled up my leg. Damon was making a warm rush come over my body. Everything was playing out like a storybook. It was going too good. What if what my mom said was true? I don't know what came over me, but I looked Damon in the eyes and said, "Damon, please don't hurt me."

"Where did that come from?" he asked, puzzled.

"It's just that everything is moving so fast and I'm here and everybody is saying I'm insane for staying."

"I promise I won't hurt you. Now lie back down," Damon said as he playfully pushed me back on the bed. And we made love again. Damon put my body in every position possible. Kamasutra enthusiasts would have been proud. I didn't know I was so flexible.

Right after our long session the phone rang loudly. Damon told me to answer it.

"Can I speak to Damon?" a male voice asked.

"One minute," I said as I tapped him on the shoulder.

"Who is this, Alicia?" the man asked.

"No," I said as I gave Damon the phone. Damon talked

for a few minutes. He hung up and said, "Alicia is my old girlfriend. That was my brother. He didn't know we broke up."

"How long have you been broke up?"

"A month."

"A month." I was starting to feel like I was Damon's rebound chick. I got up and went to the bathroom.

"Come here, Janelle."

"What?" I said as I turned around.

"Sit down. I want to talk to you." I sat on the bed next to him. He grabbed my hand and said, "Listen, Janelle, I know it seems like we are moving fast and we haven't got a chance to talk about everything."

"We haven't known each other long enough to tell each other everything," I said with an attitude.

"You're right, Janelle. We can start right now. Since we being honest, tell me where you were coming from that night I met you. You were coming out of the elevator of the hotel."

I was speechless. I didn't know what to say. I didn't want to tell Damon I was with Mannis.

"I was at a party with this guy I met."

"Why didn't he drive you home?"

"Because the next thing you know he invited me to this room. He tried to make a move on me and I left."

"I was wondering what you were doing that night."

"You should have asked me. So what is the story on Alicia? Okay, did she really leave you for a woman?"

"Yeah, I'm not lying. I met her at a strip club, Rolex. I took her personal. I got her to stop dancing, I was taking care of her and her son. I didn't know she was a dyke. I knew she got high, but I didn't know she messed with girls. I started getting suspicious about her being a lesbian when her one friend, Shanita, kept calling, getting smart with me and hanging around all the time. Come to find out, that was her girlfriend. The girl was spending the night here when I was at away games. I confronted her and told her that I wasn't with the gay shit and she had to make a decision. She told me she like dick and pussy and she couldn't live without either. I kicked her out right then and there. I was hurt and I called Carl. And he went and told everybody I fell in love with a trick."

"And you still his friend?"

"Yeah, that's just Carl. He just is playful. I mean now, if it go down I know he got my back. He was the only one who showed me the ropes when I first got down here. He showed me everything."

I was trying to act like I wasn't fazed. Like he didn't just drop a bomb on me. But I was. I couldn't believe what he had just said. It was a hard pill to swallow.

"So that's my story, Janelle. Who are you seeing back at home?"

"Nobody really."

"Janelle, I'm not going to hurt you. I don't want to be hurt either. Okay, baby? I promise you I won't hurt you."

He held me tightly and I felt safe and warm.

We woke up around 11:00 a.m. I went into the bathroom and heard someone downstairs. I ran into the room and told Damon. He told me it was probably Rita.

I walked downstairs and spoke to her. She said hi. I asked if she wanted any pancakes, and she said no. We ate breakfast on the patio. I read the *Miami Herald* a little, then began to clear the table.

"No, no, sit down, señorita," Rita said as she stopped me from cleaning up.

"I'll help you."

"No, no," she said as she walked away, throwing her hands up, and started speaking fast in Spanish.

"Damon, what's wrong with her?" I asked.

"She wants you to sit down and let her do her job. When she is here, just let her do her thing."

"Okay," I said. I wasn't used to anyone cleaning up after me.

Chapter Twenty

Natalie

I was so happy to be going home. My cousin Janelle *has* lost her damn mind. Okay, Damon was cute, but she don't know him. He could be a crazy football star or not. He seemed nice, but he could have skeletons in his closet. They've only known each other a couple of days. Plus, what is she going to tell Aunt Linda? Oh well, I got to go home and fix my situation. Forget her. I got problems of my own. I was still worried about Anthony.

When we boarded the plane, I threw my carry-on luggage overhead and took my seat. I rested a little easier because I was on my way home, finally.

We were watching the informational video they show every flight. The one they play that shows you what to do in case of an emergency. They had asked everyone to turn off their electronic devices. I turned off my cell phone and sat back and closed my eyes. This girl the next row over was still on her cell talking loudly. I guess she didn't hear the announcement. I shot her a glance like, didn't you hear them? She didn't care and she continued to ramble on to somebody about how she didn't know where their fucking sandals was and she didn't give a damn because she was on her way home. The informational video was still playing and I felt the plane begin to move. All of a sudden the video went off and all of the lights went out on the plane. I couldn't believe the power had gone out, and the plane jerked a little more.

I looked over at Tanya and she said, "What the fuck was that?"

I told her I didn't know. I unhooked my seat belt and stood up to see what was going on just as the pilot announced that the plane had a power problem that was standard before takeoff and the problem was in the process of being solved.

A man's voice from the back of the plane said, "Don't let that shit happen while we are in the air." A few people laughed. I didn't find it funny. Was I supposed to feel secure traveling on a plane whose power went off right before takeoff?

Then the plane began making a banging noise in the back and all the lights came back on. I asked the stewardess what the banging noise was. She said it was normal and that it was just the gears changing. Wasn't I on a plane, I thought, and not in a stick-shift car? I didn't want to feel or hear the gears shifting.

A few minutes later, we took off. Everything seemed okay. I tried to fall asleep, but I couldn't. I kept thinking that the plane's power was going to go off again in the middle of the air.

"Man, this plane better make it back home," Tanya said, then, "I'm tired as shit. If we crash I won't know. I'm going the fuck to sleep. My head is hurting." She pulled a jacket out of her bag and threw it over her face. She then asked the stewardess for something to drink. She pulled out two pills.

"What's that, Tanya?"

"Something that will keep me calm before I beat a bitch up on this plane."

"Another Ecstasy pill?"

"No, a Zannie?"

"A Xanax."

"Yup, you want one?"

"No!"

"Well, wake me up in Philly."

I tried to read a magazine and just kept praying that I made it home safely to my family. I couldn't wait to see my baby. As soon as I see Anthony I'm going to hug him and tell him how much I miss him.

The plane was descending and I could see twinkling lights from the buildings and homes below. I was home. My stomach began to turn and I became so anxious. The plane hit the runway and I tried to be the first to get off. But there were people in front of me being slow grabbing their bags.

As soon as I managed to get off the plane, I ran to baggage claim. I left Tanya. She would have to find her own way home. I was out. Once I reached baggage claim, the luggage hadn't even come out yet. I took a seat next to the conveyor belt. Tanya walked up to me and reminded me to throw all the numbers I had in the trash. I told her I'd thrown all the numbers away. If Anthony had found them, I would have been dead. I asked Tanya if she wanted me to drop her off. She said that her friend Walei was coming to get her. I was happy. I didn't feel like taking her home anyway. She said I should hurry home. The yellow light started blinking and the conveyor belt began to move. I had black luggage. I leaped and grabbed almost every bag that passed me. Everybody had black luggage. At last I saw my bags. I grabbed them and said, "Okay, I got my luggage. I'm out."

"All right, good luck. I'll call you later," Tanya said.

My car was at airport parking. I caught the shuttle. The shuttle driver grabbed my luggage and put it in my trunk. I gave him a tip and closed the trunk. I started my car and began to say a silent prayer on the way home. I usually only ask God for really important stuff like to keep my parents, baby, and husband healthy. However, today I was praying to God to help me out with something a little trivial. "God, please don't let Anthony be mad at me anymore. Please let him get over it." I hope my prayer works.

I walked into my house. All the lights were out. I turned the light on and noticed a letter propped up on one of the sofa pillows on the floor. I read it and it said:

> Natalie,
> I hope your little trip was worth losing your family. I don't want you anymore. God knows what and who you were doing in Miami. You can pick up baby Anthony from your mother's house.
>
> Anthony

I threw down his letter. Anthony was bluffing, but he was still mad. He wanted me to be regretful about what I had done. I was sorry, but maybe if he would have helped me I wouldn't have gone. I went upstairs, took my clothes out of my suitcase, and put them into my hamper. On my dresser, there was another note from Anthony.

> Natalie, here is my ring.
> Anthony

I opened my closet door to see all Anthony's belongings gone. He had packed his clothes and shoes. I walked into the bathroom to see that all his colognes and razors were gone. In our middle room that he used as a gym, all his weights and workout equipment were gone.

I called Anthony's mom's house to talk to him. Her voice mail came on. "Praise the Lord. This is Sister Renee. I am not home, but I'll call you as soon as I get in. God bless you and have a nice day." Listening to that message, you would think she was a saint and not the mean devil she really is. I hung up and didn't leave a message. I didn't know what to think or do. Anthony was going a little too far. Leaving his wedding ring on the dresser and taking all his clothes was dramatic for Anthony. Real dramatic. What did he want me to say, I'm so sorry, I'll never do it again? I then tried dialing Anthony's cell. He didn't answer. I jumped into my car and drove to my mother's house. I used my key to get in the door. My mother was sitting on the sofa playing with the baby. I watched them for a moment. My mom's skin is creamy brown with light freckles and she has reddish-brown hair. She keeps it short and natural. She is usually so busy doing other people's hair she doesn't have time for her own. I tried to suck in my tears, but I couldn't. I busted out and said, "Mommy, Anthony left me because I went on my vacation." I startled my mom. She jumped up, gave me a hug, and patted my back. Baby Anthony was still smiling.

"Natalie, what did you expect him to do? You left him. You took wedding vows. To love and obey, and you can't just get mad and leave for the weekend."

"Mom, he gave me his ring back," I said as I showed her his ring.

"Well, Nat, you know I tell you how I see it, and you are wrong."

"I'm wrong? I never get to do anything! I'm a good wife. He never helped me with the baby and I'm wrong?" I said as I grabbed baby Anthony and took a seat on the cream leather sofa.

"Baby, you are wrong. You don't know how your baby's been eating or if he was missing you. You're crying now, but when Anthony dropped the baby off he was crying to us."

My dad walked in the door, just coming in from work. My dad is a police officer, a sergeant. He had his blue pressed shirt on and blue-striped uniform pants that fit kind of snug on him. He is average height and husky. My mom said I get my weight and complexion from his side of the family, but that's to be decided, because my mom is not that slim herself.

He gave me a hug and said, "Stop crying, I talked to Anthony, and he is really upset. But it will all work out, baby girl." He took off his hat, rubbed his bald head, and then said, "You can't take vacations without your husband and not let him know."

"I know, Dad, but—" I stopped midsentence. There was no use. Nobody was seeing my side. They had talked to Anthony before I got a chance to talk them. I just grabbed my son and went to lie down in my old bedroom. My mom still had my sheets and everything fixed up like when I left. I had a pink canopy bed with stuffed teddy bears and posters. I got into bed and tried to go to sleep. Anthony did not want to go to sleep, so I took him back to my mom. I went back into my room, closed the door, took off my shoes, put the quilt over my head, and began to cry. Right now I didn't want to talk to anyone but Anthony.

The next morning my mother brought the baby in and said that he was ready for his bottle and that her client was downstairs. I got up and fixed him a bottle. I made myself scrambled eggs, hot sausage, and toast and I called Anthony.

"Hello, Anthony, I want to talk to you," I said as I paced around my mother's living room waiting for his response.

"There is nothing to talk about, Natalie. What kind of mother leaves her baby and man for some stupid bitches? You are not anything, Natalie," Anthony said as he hung up the phone on me once again.

I called back and his mother, "Holy Ms. Renee," cussed me out. She called me a slut, tramp, promiscuous prostitute, and bitch and said her son was getting a blood test on that baby. She told me her son deserved so much better than me. Ms. Renee and her son were getting me so frustrated. *Anthony is so fucking stupid,* I thought. *I hate him. He needs to grow the fuck up.*

I walked downstairs into the basement and smelled the aroma of oil sheen, spritz, and burning hair. My mother already had one woman under the dryer. The other she was putting a perm in her hair and one was waiting. Everything was set up like a salon. My mother had three stations with a mirror and hair dryers.

"Mom, do you need my help today?"

"No, but I might Saturday."

"Okay, I'm about to leave."

"Lock the door and call me later."

"Is that your grandbaby?" the lady under the dryer asked my mom.

"Yeah."

"Oh, he is getting so big. How you doing, Natalie?" the lady under the dryer said.

"I'm fine. I didn't know that was you, Ms. Pat," I said.

"Well, see you later."

I got the baby dressed and went right to Anthony's mother's house and knocked on the door. Ms. Renee came to the door in a gray oversized sweatsuit, white slippers, pink and purple rollers in her dyed black hair, and 1950-cat eye style eyeglasses on. Her glasses sat on the tip of her nose, looking down at me.

"Is Anthony here?" I asked.

Ms. Renee looked me and the baby over a couple of times and said, "It's warm outside. Why you got all the clothes on that baby?"

"Because he has a summer cold," I answered her with an annoyed tone. She told me that if I was taking care of him like a mother is supposed to he wouldn't be sick.

"I do take care of him. Very well," I said.

"Well, I know you wasn't taking care of him this weekend, because my son had to. Anthony's not here and don't come here for him no more. He doesn't want to speak to you."

"Whatever, tell Anthony I was here."

Ms. Renee closed the door and I got back into my car. I tried Anthony's cell phone, but had no luck.

Chapter Twenty-one

Tanya

As soon as I got back in the city, I called Walei to make sure he was outside waiting for me. Natalie had run off the plane and left me. I met back up with her at baggage claim. I told her I had a ride and I would see her later. I claimed my luggage and walked outside. I saw Walei standing, with red roses in hand, smiling. He was all happy, looking like a frog. I grabbed the flowers out of his hands and he took my bags.

"How was your trip?" he asked as he tried to hug me.

"Please, Walei, I'm tired," I said as I exchanged my luggage with him for the flowers.

"These are nice, but you know I like pink roses," I said as I looked down at the flowers.

"I know, but I couldn't find any pink roses. I missed you, Tanya."

"Um, Walei, I said I'm tired. I have to meet up with Monica and go see my kids."

"Okay, I'll go get the car."

I waited at the curb as Walei went and got the car. He put my luggage in the backseat and opened the sunroof.

"What cologne do you have on?"

"Aspen aftershave."

"It's too strong. You smell like a grandpop. Don't wear it again."

"I won't. So how was your trip, Tanya?"

"It was okay. I didn't do as much shopping as I wanted to."

"I can try to take you to the mall this weekend." He said exactly what I expected.

"Why do I have to wait till the weekend?" I asked as I crossed my arms, annoyed.

"I have to send money to my sister, she is in London at school. I told you this."

"Can't she wait?" I asked. I don't give a fuck about her. She will make it. I thought.

"Tanya, I will call and ask her if she can wait. Are you going to Monica's house?"

"Yeah, and then I'm going home from there. Can you drop my luggage off at my house?"

Monica was a chick from around the way that I hang with every now and then. She is like thirty and still into dumb shit. She is okay at times, but really I don't trust that bitch. She is good for going out, playing niggas, and getting money, but I would never trust that bitch with my man or a secret. She would tell the world. She's really not that pretty, but dudes be liking her 'cause she got a nice shape. She lives in a small bi-level apartment in southwest Philly. She do hair sometimes. She used to do my wrap when we was younger.

We got to Monica's apartment building and he asked if I wanted to go to dinner. I told him no and that I would see him later.

I knocked on Monica's door. Nobody answered, so I checked to see if it was open. It was; I walked in and yelled, "Monica!"

I heard her say, "In here." I walked in the back to her bedroom. I opened the door and saw her lying on her stomach with the pillow tucked under her chin. She was watching *Maury* on television. Her hair was pulled back into a pony-tail. She had on low-waist jeans that revealed her gigantic tattoo that read *Lil' Ron* with this big swordlike figure on her back. *I don't know why she got his name on her back. He still messes with his kid's mom. And every girl in the city,* I thought.

"Hey, girl, what you doing here?" she said as she turned around and sat up at the edge of the bed on her maroon plaid comforter.

"Just got back."

"I know you came up?" she asked.

"Not really. It was okay. Fucking Natalie's cousin was down there thinking she was the fuck cute. That bitch came up! She met a fucking dude that play for the damn NFL," I said as I sat down.

"Damn, she ain't even all that cute."

"I know, I said the same thing."

"She don't look better than you. Pass me my cigarettes," she said. I stood up, grabbed Monica's cigarettes off the dresser, and handed them to her and continued to rant about Janelle.

"Plus, she got a fucking weave. I got my own hair. She is average and I'm cute. Everybody say how good I look. I know all that bitch got on me is that she ain't got no kids. She still down there. She's staying for another week. But she left me and Natalie the whole entire weekend. Then Natalie was acting like a miserable little bitch. She going to get her ass beat when she get home."

"For what?"

"Her dumb ass went away without telling her husband. I got to call her to see if she made out all right. You got any weed?" I asked as I stood up again and checked my face out in her mirror on her dresser.

"No, Lil' Ron just left, he went to go get me some. Why you think I smoking some cigarettes? Did you meet any-body?"

"A few people, but not really. I met this guy from Baltimore, he was cool, and this other comedian dude that tried to play me. So I took his credit card." I pulled out Kamani's credit card. "That's why I came over here. To tell you that I had some work."

Monica asked how long I had it. I told her a couple of days. She sat on the bed and said she had to call this guy Mike-Mike to see if he could make a license to go with the card. My cut would be 60 percent of whatever we got. Monica got dressed and we got in her 1992 aqua-colored Honda Accord to ride to the gas station.

"Yo, you don't have no air in this car?" I asked Monica, annoyed.

"No, I need some Freon. I'm going to get it tomorrow. Just roll down the window," she said.

"You got me in this fucking sauna! My hair is going to get all frizzy and fucked up," I yelled at her as I glanced over at my hair in the side-view mirror.

We drove to the gas station to see if the credit card was still active. You didn't need ID at the pump and if it didn't work, we could pull off, if it was reported stolen. The card was still working. We filled Monica's car up.

We met up with Mike-Mike. He already had a new laminated license with Kamani's name on it and his picture. I didn't know his right address, so he just made up an Atlanta address for him. He got in the car and started rolling a blunt. We smoked the blunt and then I sprayed perfume on my clothes so I wouldn't smell like that shit. We walked into the Best Buy in Springfield, right outside Philly. We couldn't go to any electronic store in the city, because they would be hip to the game. Plus, they would ask too many questions because they got burnt before. Mike-Mike walked up to the register and within a few minutes, he walked over to us and said they gave him five thousand dollars' worth of instant credit. We walked outside and decided on what we were going to get. Should we get a couple of televisions or one big-screen or flat TV? With the five thousand, we got a big-screen television, ten car stereo systems, and three Play-stations. I went and got the kids some DVDs. The cashiers just rang everything up for him. We had like a thousand left. I told them to spend the rest at another Best Buy, the one on the boulevard. There was a computer store down the street from there. We went right over to Computer World. They gave him four thousand dollars' worth of instant credit.

"This nigga got good credit." Mike-Mike laughed.

We got three computers and a laptop. We had shit all over the place. Monica's dumb ass was talking about going to buy a fur coat.

"No, not in June, asshole, we would look suspicious." We gave Mike-Mike all of the stuff and he went to sell it. On the street, even though we had over eight thousand dollars' worth of stuff, we could only get about half. That was the rule. Half off the original price. Mike-Mike had regular customers who bought from him. So he wouldn't burn us.

After it was all said and done, I had twenty-five hundred, a new computer, and a few DVDs and Playstation 2 games. We went back to Monica's house. Her daughters, Sabrina and Alexis, were home. They were too damn grown and looked like her sisters instead of her daughters. They only were eleven and twelve. They get smart and be trying not to go to school. The younger one had already been left down twice, but ask her about how to do a dance and she could do that. Sabrina's ponytail was like thirty-six inches, too long for a little girl. The youngest one was built, a little tiny waist and a big ass like her mom. Monica leaves them in the house all the time. Their asses going to be pregnant real soon if she keeps letting them be grown. Little boys already be knocking on the door for them. Wait a few more years. She'll be a grandmother before she is thirty-two.

"What you bring me?" Alexis asked Monica.

"Nothing. Get this fucking living room clean," she said.

"Lil' Ron called, Mom," Sabrina said.

"When? Where did you tell him I was?" she asked anxiously.

"I didn't tell him nothing," Sabrina answered.

"Get me the cordless so I can call him."

Lil' Ron showed up at the door moments later. They called him Lil' Ron because he was short. I didn't like him. He was like a dwarf to me and he wasn't that cute, with bad skin. I said, "What's up?"

"Nothing. Same shit. Let me talk to you, Monica," he said as he began walking toward the kitchen. She walked him in there and they talked for a little bit and then he left.

After Lil' Ron left, Monica took me home. I had to carry all my boxes and bags into the house.

"Mommy, we missed you! What did you bring us back?" Deja asked as she ran to the door to greet me. I had managed at the last minute at the airport to buy all three of them shirts and a key chain. My grandmother gave me this stare like *you know you wrong*. I ignored her. Deja gave me a hug and Davon just looked at his shirt. I pulled out my bag and I handed Davon the games and DVDs.

"Thanks, Mom, this is the game I wanted," Davon said.

"Tanya, you got my money?" my grandmother asked as she eyed me down.

"Yeah, Mom-Mom. I got your money."

"About time," she said as I placed the money in her hand.

"That fellow brought your luggage. Where did you stop before seeing your children that you haven't seen in days?"

"I had to make a few runs. What's in here to eat?" I asked as I walked toward the kitchen.

"Ain't shit here to eat. You didn't leave these kids here with any money, but I bet your ass been eating like a queen," my grandmother said as she followed me to the kitchen.

"I didn't have any money," I said.

"I hope they broke the mold when they made you, girl."

"What's that supposed to mean?" I asked as I pulled some leftover chicken out of the refrigerator.

My grandmother told the kids to go upstairs and then said, "For someone so much into their looks you need to take better care of your kids. Then you need to stop smoking that mess."

"Grandmom, I don't smoke at all."

"Yeah, right, what you think, I don't know? You smell like that mess every time you walk in the door. You try to spray perfume over it, but I still smell it. You are setting a bad example for your children. Your mother is an addict. It is in your genes to be an addict. Don't you see that you need to stop?"

"Mom-Mom, I'm in control. I got this. I take care of my kids."

"You need to buy these kids clothes. It's a hundred degrees outside and Davon running around with sweatpants on. You are a part-time mom, when you find the time and it is convenient for you. I shouldn't have to spend my last on these kids. I raised my child. I should be out and seeing the world. I did this already."

"Mom-Mom, leave me alone. Davon got clothes. That's what he chose to put on." My grandmother had better get out my face. I was unfazed by her comments. I sat down at the table, ate my chicken, and continued not to listen to her.

All that traveling and riding around with Monica, I was exhausted. I went to my room and closed the door.

My bed was a gold-frame daybed. Department store bags, a jewelry box, perfume, deodorant, makeup were everywhere. I didn't have enough room for all my clothes, so they were piled all over the place. My shoe boxes and pocketbooks were aligned next to my closet. I listened to all my messages on my answering machine. I had a separate line from my grandmom. I'd had my own line since I was like fifteen when my mom-mom first told Barry he couldn't call after nine. I unpacked and took off my clothes. I dumped all of the numbers out of my bag. I had to throw away a lot of them. I'm not calling Kamani for obvious reasons.

I called this guy I met named Aaron. His phone was disconnected. I called Keith. He didn't answer, so I took a nap. Almost as soon as I fell asleep, my phone rang.

"Hello," I said, annoyed as hell.

"Hello, can I speak to Keith?" a woman asked.

"Don't no Keith live here," I said

"Do you know a Keith?"

"What? Who is this?"

"All I want to know is if you know Keith. You might have met him in Miami, he is from Baltimore," the woman said as she tried to put a little bass in her tone.

"Look, I don't know what the fuck you talking about, bitch, and I'm asleep. Don't call my house." I hung the phone up.

The woman called right back and said, "Listen, I'm not trying to come at you. I just want to know if you know him. I'm his fiancée. He was in Miami this weekend for his bachelor party. I want to see if he was cheating on me. We are about to get married next week, and he said he didn't meet nobody. But I found your number. We got three kids together and I just wanted to know if he is telling me the truth." Her little sympathy story did not mean a damn thing to me. I was tired and she was interrupting my sleep.

"Yo, I don't care who you are. I don't give a fuck if you getting married or not. You playing yourself by calling my phone. You want to know who I am? Ask your fucking man, bitch. If you call my phone again, you are going to have a problem."

Keith talked all that shit to me and he's about to get married. I picked up my cell phone and erased his number. I am so tired of bitches calling me about their niggas. They need to get their niggas in check. All niggas do is lie and lie some more.

"Mom, can you buy me some construction paper for my project?"

"Davon, close my door, I'm asleep."

"Mom, my project is due."

"Boy, you heard what I said, I'm asleep. Shut my door." I tried to go back to sleep, but it was useless.

I went into the kids' room; they weren't in there, so they must be outside. They had a bunk bed. Davon slept on the bottom that was a full-size bed and Deja slept on the top that was a twin. I decorated her bed with Dora the Explorer sheets and pillows. Davon didn't like cartoon sheets. He already thought he was grown at times. I went downstairs. My mom-mom was on the phone and I asked her where Davon and Deja was. She said she sent them to the store. I stood in the doorway and saw them coming down the street.

"Mom I need to do my project." I looked down at my watch it was almost seven.

"Davon, I don't know where I'm going to find construction paper. You should have told me before about your project."

"I did tell you."

"No you didn't. I don't feel like going to the market or walking to the Rite Aid. You're just going to hand the project in late."

Chapter Twenty-two

Janelle

It had been three weeks and I was still in Miami. Every time I was ready to leave, Damon asked me to stay again. My first week down here I kept calling my job saying I was sick. The second week I said my mother was sick. Then he said, why don't you just live here? I didn't think twice. I called my job and quit. I don't want to ever go back home. I love it here. I drive his BMW and he drives his Yukon truck. The first time I got in that thing by myself I almost crashed. I slightly put my foot on the pedal and the car took off. I think if Dame kicked me out today or tomorrow I would beg for change, or become a cigar girl and do dishes, just to live by the beach. Sean has been calling and leaving messages. I don't have the heart to talk to him. I just ignore his calls. When Damon asks who's calling my phone, I just tell him it is Natalie whining or my mom. And my uncle, I haven't been able to catch him. I have been leaving him messages. I know he is going to have something to say. I called my mother to tell her the news. She had a fit.

"Mom, I'm not coming home. I'm going to stay."

"Stay where?" she asked.

"In Miami. I'm going to live here."

"What do you mean? What in the hell is wrong with you, Janelle?" she yelled at me.

"Nothing is wrong with me," I said, annoyed.

"What about your job?"

"I quit, Mom."

"You are not supposed to quit your job for a man. I know he is in the NFL, but next week when he meets somebody else what are you going to do?"

"I'll deal with that when it happens. I'm grown and can do whatever I want to do."

"If you're so grown you wouldn't have to tell me you're grown. And what about Sean? He has been calling here almost every day. What do you want me to tell him?"

"I don't know, tell him the truth. Mom, don't worry. I'm going to get a job. I have been working since I was fifteen. You think I'm not going to get a job? There are plenty of places down here." I was getting tired of explaining. I felt like I didn't have shit to explain to my mom. She was in my apartment.

My mother was silent for a moment, then said, "Well, I guess I could have your room."

"For now, Mom, but listen, I don't want them boys destroying everything."

"Janelle, I think you should think again about moving."

"Mom, I already made up my mind. I'll call you later."

I tried to reassure myself that I was doing the right thing. I went and got some orange juice out of the refrigerator.

I'm not explaining anything to anybody. I'm the fuck grown. I'm twenty-three without any responsibility. No kids, no man, my only bill was my apartment. So, I was free. I mean if we don't make it, so what the fuck? I get to live in Miami without working, chilling by the beach for a couple of months. Philly will still be there. So will jobs in the mall. I have manager experience, so I can work anywhere.

I was warm in Damon's arms. The sun was bright and filling the room through the drapes. He gave me a kiss and asked me what time it was. I looked over my shoulder to the nightstand and told him it was eight-thirty. Damon got up out of the bed, went into the bathroom, and turned on the shower.

"Dame, why you jump up? Where you going?" I asked as I yawned.

Damon came back in the room with a towel wrapped around his waist and said, "Preseason is about to began. I have to practice. Go to the gym, work out." He flexed his muscles.

"Huh, already?"

"Yeah, how you think I am going to get money for us?"

"I know, but doesn't football start in the winter?"

Damon laughed at me and shook his head. "No, Janelle, training camp begins around the third week of July each season. The first game is in August against the Jaguars."

"So, Damon, I'm going to have to stay here by myself?"

"Kelly is going to come and take you to the mall. I know you need some things. She is cool. You remember her, right? I'll leave you some money on the dresser, okay?"

"Yeah."

"Well, she will be over around noon." Dame dressed, gave me a kiss, and walked out the door.

Kelly showed up exactly at twelve. I went and opened the door and she said, "Hey, girl, what's up?" She sashayed past me and into the house. She had a pastel Chanel pink pocketbook that matched her dress and sandals. Her scarf was tied around her hair like a headband. Her stringy brown hair had light blond streaks in it. Pink lavender and purple-pink-tinted sunglasses with a big double G on them concealed her eyes. They were probably Gucci, I thought.

"So where you want to go first?"

"I don't know. I need everything. There is a nice shoe store I like on Ocean Drive."

"Please, that's where the tourists shop. I'll take you to Bal Harbor Mall. They have all the stores like Saks and Hermes."

"Well, let me get dressed," I said as I walked into the bedroom. I glanced at the dresser and noticed Dame had left me eight hundred dollars in cash and his Visa card to go shopping. He gave me more money to shop with than I would make in two weeks working.

Her car was a shiny mint-green Mercedes Benz CLK convertible. It was freshly waxed and the sun was shining against it. It was so clean it appeared like it was glowing.

Bal Harbor had all the stores and we went in every one. The mall didn't have a roof. You could see the bright sun. It was very different. Shopping with Kelly was no limit. I was in awe. Kelly spent four hundred on seven jeans, twenty-seven hundred on a tangerine dress and heels to match. We went to the next store and I was pondering over a pair of sandals that were three hundred.

"Buy them, girl, shit, I spend all of Carl's money. He can't make it fast enough for me," she insisted.

I didn't buy the shoes, but I did see sandals I liked. They were $565. I never spent more than two hundred on sandals, but they were Prada. They matched a dress I had seen in Neiman Marcus. I decided to charge it. The lady at the cash register did not give me any problem. She didn't ask for any identification like I would have done at the store I used to work at. She just said, "Thank you, Mrs. Scott."

She turned to Kelly and said, "How's it going, Kelly? I see you're back again." Almost every store we went in, the clerks knew Kelly on a first-name basis and gave her the red carpet treatment. They must be working on commission.

Kelly tried on a few outfits and said, "I am getting so fat. I used to run every morning. Now I do Pilates."

"What are you, like a five? That's not big," I said.

"Yeah, but I used to be a three. You're in good shape. Do you work out?" she asked.

"Please, skinny, but I eat practically whatever I want. I wear a size eight and I don't work out at all."

"Really, you don't look that big. No offense, you look really thin. I got my breasts done last year," she said.

My breasts are a little smaller than I would like, but I

can't do anything about that. I don't believe in breast implants and push-up bras. Take it or leave it, I thought. I bought sandals, two dresses, lingerie and perfume.

After shopping for what seemed like forever, we went to have lunch at the Blue Door Café down the road from the mall. Kelly's cell phone rang. She answered and said, "Hey, Lisa. . . . No, I'm not home. I'm with Damon's girlfriend, Chanelle."

I looked over at her, corrected her, and said, "It's Janelle." I couldn't believe we had spent the whole afternoon together shopping and she didn't even know my name.

"I meant Janelle. So what's up? Come join us," she said as she toyed with her hair. She hung up her phone and said that Lisa and Amber were on their way. Kelly gave me the quick word about Lisa and Amber. Lisa was Cuban and married to Stephen, a defensive tackle on the team. Amber was a white girl who had been engaged to James, a tight end, for four years. Kelly said James was not going to marry her, but they had kids so she wasn't going anywhere. Once the girls arrived, I could tell they were looking me up and down trying to figure me out and price my clothes.

"So, where are you from?" Amber asked.

Lisa didn't give me a chance to answer before she asked, "Oh, so how did you meet Damon?"

I answered their question even though I knew they were just trying to pry. These girls were pretty, in shape, stylish, but something was ugly about them. They were nauseating, eyeing me up and down. They were so fucking phony I couldn't take it. They would smile at me, then smile at each other in some secret smiling language only they could understand.

"Guess what? You know Bobby bought Dana a car for her birthday?" Amber said.

"That is so nice. What kind did he buy her?" Lisa and Kelly asked in unison.

"A micro Benz," she said, laughing.

"A micro Benz, not a Kompressor. What? You can't be serious."

"Yes, a Kompressor, can you believe it?"

"Was it brand-new?"

"No, it wasn't. It was a 2002 and he leased it. Now you know he just renegotiated his contract. He has money. He could have paid for it in cash," Lisa said.

"Why would he try to play her like that? With that little-ass car? That's not a good sign," Amber said.

"If Stephen tried some bullshit like that, I would have left him," Lisa said.

"Right. Didn't he promise her a six hundred? Oh, he is a cheap bastard. She is not getting a ring, so she might as well pack her shit." Amber laughed.

I sat and just looked over at Kelly.

"Well, that's what she gets. She thinks she is so hot because she was in a stupid rap video."

"Yeah, that's right, she was only in one video, and the song was not even that hot. She probably only got paid a couple thousand."

"I don't think she got anything," Kelly said.

"And the rapper was a nobody. His record only did good overseas. It's not like he's 50-Cent or Jay-Z," Amber chirped.

"Right. Whoever heard of that guy? What was his name?"

"Kep or something like that," Lisa said.

"Well, speaking of rings, I need an upgrade. I saw this six-carat pear ring. It was so nice. I hinted around to Stephen. I'll probably get it for my birthday," Lisa said.

I looked over at her three stone diamond ring. It was enormous and she wanted something bigger. I didn't fit in with this group. I was thinking, *What is wrong with a Kompressor Mercedes Benz?* I'd be happy with a car, any car that didn't break down.

The conversation went on and on. Kelly, Amber, and Lisa were so materialistic and egotistic it was sickening. Anyway, after forty-five minutes of mind-numbing conversation I had had it. Fortunately the dullness was broken up by the ringing of my cell phone. I looked down at it and it was Sean again. I didn't want to take the call. I hoped I didn't look nervous looking down at my phone. I looked up to see if anyone was paying me attention. They weren't. They were still talking. I thought about picking up the call, but then Sean would be asking all kinds of questions I didn't want to answer in front of them. I decided not to answer the call. I pushed Sean's call to voice mail. He called right back four more times. I kept sending his call to voice mail. I hoped he got the message. They all said they had to go. Amber had to pick up her children. Everyone began fighting over who would pay the bill. That was a first. My friends and I usually argue about what we are not going to pay on the bill. Amber eventually paid because they all agreed that Kelly had paid the last time and the time before that Lisa paid.

When I got back in the house I checked my messages. Sean was on there saying since I didn't know how to answer the phone could I at least give him his money back he loaned me? He was so petty. I made a mental note to send my mom the money to pay him back. I checked on my mom and called Natalie. Damon came home and asked to see what I had bought. I modeled all my new clothes for him.

"Let me see you in that," Damon said as he held up some lingerie that I had bought.

"Look at my boo's butt," he said as he slapped my butt.

"Baby, I need to go home and get some things together."

"Like what? You just went shopping."

"My birth certificate so I can get a job and just bring some of my personal belongings."

"I told you, you don't have to work."

"I got to work."

"No, you don't. Baby, can't your mom mail that stuff to you?"

"Babe, I have to go home. I'll only be gone for a couple of days. Plus, you will be at practice."

Chapter Twenty-three

Natalie

I have called Anthony repeatedly for almost a month. I sent him flowers, I offered to cook for him, to just talk. I have called him, left him messages, and begged for forgiveness. I have been going crazy. I need him. I miss him. I am plain old exhausted and frustrated with him and this whole situation. Me chasing Anthony, it is getting so old. Sometimes I feel like yes, I'm free! Let him go. He left me and I didn't do anything wrong. Then the next moment I feel like I was wrong, I shouldn't have gone to Miami without his consent. Anthony is a good man, he never cheated on me. He is a good-looking brother and I don't want to lose him. My biggest fear is that Anthony is really serious about leaving me. If he goes and marries somebody else and starts a new family, that would hurt me so bad. *This* hurts so bad. It really hurts. I miss him. Anthony is right in his thinking in some ways. There are a lot of desperate and not so desperate women in Philadelphia that will want my man. Every time Anthony and I would go out to dinner, he made it his business to point them out to me. The women would be huddled in groups, acting like they were having fun with their friends. They knew they came out to look for a man. Don't get me wrong, women can go out with their friends. But you know the fat-girl cliques, drunk-as-hell, no-man cliques of girls. They hang out at every restaurant. Those are the bitches that be eyeing your man until they see you behind him. Then they try to sip their drink and turn the other way like they weren't looking at him. Or when you go to the bathroom they will try to pass him their number. I don't want Anthony to meet a woman that just gave up all her self-respect and hope and is ready to put up with all his shit. A kind of woman that is willing to spoil and buy her man. I can't compete with someone like that. I'm still young and I'm not ready to give up my freedom just yet.

I couldn't take him ignoring me anymore, so I decided to go up to his job. I drove to his job, put the baby on my hip, and marched into the waiting area of the garage. Telephones were ringing and people were sitting in the waiting room watching the midday news. I saw a few mechanics walking past and I pulled one to the side and asked, "Is Anthony Grant here?" The guy said yes and went to the back and got him. I waited fretfully. I didn't know what Anthony was going to say. Anthony came out in his dirty uniform and wiped his soiled hands with a rag. He walked out of the building. I followed.

"What, Natalie? What are you coming up here for?"

"I just want to know. Is it over?" I asked as I looked him directly in his eyes.

"Yeah, it's over," he said as he shook his head. Then he said, "Why are you up here at my job, with the baby, making a scene?"

"So it's over just like that, Anthony?" I asked.

"Yeah, Natalie, I think so. You just hurt me too bad, I don't think I can trust you anymore."

"What do you mean you can't trust me? I made one bad decision."

"Look, I got to go back to work. I can't talk about this right now. I'll talk to you later."

I couldn't control my emotions. Anthony was right in

front of me. I was missing him and wanted him to come home. I started to cry and said, "I love you, Anthony."

"No, you don't," he said as he pushed me out of the way and went back toward the building.

"Anthony, please don't do this to me! Please, I love you! Think about our son," I pleaded.

"I have been thinking about our son. Well, my son. You should have thought about that when you went away," he said as he continued toward the building. Then he turned around and walked back over to me. I thought he might have wanted to talk or was having a change of mind. But he grabbed my hand and began to pull my engagement ring and wedding band off my hand.

"You don't deserve or appreciate this," he said in a mean voice. My finger was somewhat swollen and fat so the ring wouldn't budge. I tried to get my hand away from him. He finally got a good grip and pulled it off. I looked down at my hand. It was bleeding and sore. "You're dead to me, Natalie. I'll never take you back after you fucked and sucked somebody else."

He went back into the building. I didn't want to start a scene, so I walked back to the car. I put baby Anthony in his car seat and drove home. With Anthony out of my life, I had nothing to live for. My man was gone. I went to my parents' home and cried myself to sleep.

"Natalie, Natalie," my mom called out. "Are you okay?"

"Yes," I said. I had fallen asleep on the sofa, snot and tears all over me. The baby was still in his car seat, asleep.

"What's going on?" she asked.

"Nothing, just Anthony."

She walked over to me and gave me a hug and said everything was going to be okay.

I got myself together and asked my mother if she could perm my hair. I cut the end of my braids, put Vaseline around my edges and began taking them out. My mother had shared my story with a few of her clients.

"Mom, stop telling my business," I said. I didn't want everybody in my business. But it was good to get other women's opinions.

"Honey, your husband will get over it. Women need lives outside their husbands. If I didn't do little stuff like go get my hair done or go shopping, I would have to kill my husband. You need an outlet," my mom's regular client Ms. Donna said.

"Donna, you need an outlet but you don't go on vacation by yourself," my mom said.

"Ms. Donna, that's what I was trying to tell my mom."

The other lady under the dryer joined in on the conversation and said, "See, the problem is that these young girls are taking these guys on dates. My son got women asking him do he want to go on a vacation? Young girls spoiling these young guys too much. Buying them gifts and taking them out, we didn't do that in our day."

I started laughing and then I heard Anthony crying upstairs. I ran to go get him. Once I got upstairs he stopped. My dad was already taking Anthony out of his car seat.

"Are you doing your hair?" he asked.

"Yeah, Mommy's about to do it."

"Then he can stay upstairs with me. I don't want him hanging around down in that hair salon."

"Thank you, Daddy." I went back down to the salon and shampooed a few ladies for my mom and she paid me for helping her out and did my hair.

Chapter Twenty-four

Tanya

I didn't have anything to do and I was bored. My grand-mother had decided that since I didn't take the kids any-where yet, she would take them to Ocean City, Maryland. I gave her the money and drove them to the bus station in her car. Since I was driving, I went to check on Natalie to make sure she was taking Anthony's leaving her okay. Her hus-band was so stubborn and mean. If Barry was still alive, I'd get him to scare him nice or stick him up. Something to put some sense in his dumb-ass head.

Natalie's baby was crawling all around trying to go up the steps when I came in. She pulled him off the steps and placed him on her hip.

"What are you doing here?" she asked.

"I dropped my mom-mom and the kids off."

"It's a mess in here. I have to clean up," she said as she sat down on her tan love seat.

"What you have to eat?" I asked.

"There is some pizza."

"You didn't cook a big Sunday dinner? What? I can't be-lieve it."

"I haven't felt like cooking the last couple of weeks. The baby don't eat a lot of food yet, and Anthony's not here, so why should I cook?" Natalie's baby crawled over to me. I picked him up; he was cute and fat, like a sumo wrestler.

"What size are you buying him now?" I asked.

"Like eighteen months."

"When I get the kids some clothes I'm going to pick him up some things. So what's going on with Anthony?"

"He's still acting like a fool. I am so depressed. I don't know what to do."

"You need to ignore his ass. He is trying to break you and you are falling for it."

"You think so? Janelle said the same thing."

"Yeah, I'm telling you. He is missing you just like you are missing him. Men have feelings too! He's not only mad that you got over on him, he is mad because you did it and he had no idea. He is used to sweet, innocent Natalie that doesn't do anything. The Natalie that listens to him and has his food ready and waiting for him. You need to start going out and having fun. You are young! Fuck that nigga."

"You're right."

"So what's up with Janelle?"

"She is still in Miami."

"What? Damn. I should have met her friend. I need to be living in Florida." I stayed a little while trying to make Natalie feel better about her situation. Natalie was still a close friend of mine. No matter what, I know she had my back. I told her if she needed anything to call me and I left.

I got back in my grandmother's car and the gas light came on so I pulled over at the first gas station. As soon as I pulled up to the pump, a smoker came out of nowhere trying to pump my gas. He was like five ten with a scruffy beard and mustache. He was prepared to put air in my tires, wash my windows, and pump my gas for some loose change. This man was strung out on that shit. "Yo, sis, what pump you on?" he asked. I know he probably got a family, like my mother, wherever she is. Her smoking ass is probably some-where pumping gas, or since she got a pussy, she's probably getting fucked for a couple of dollars. Last time I seen my mom was when Deja was born. She said she would never touch that shit again. She told me how she would sleep in abandoned houses and how she rode down South with a dead body just to buy crack. She never wanted to go through that again. The next thing I know she was back out there again. She came around for a couple of weeks and then vanished again, like a ghost.

I asked her why she treated me the way she did. She said to me, like I was nothing, "I could have left you on the street. Or maybe I could have killed you or even aborted you at birth. Did you ever think of that? Get out of my face, I birthed you. That is enough. I don't owe you shit, Tanya." Then she said, "When you was a baby I thought of putting a pillow over your face to make you stop crying. I thought about falling down the steps when I was pregnant with you all the time. You know that? I hated you. You took away everything from me. I was only sixteen when I had you. Your dad went away to college and I never told Mom-Mom who he was because he would have denied me and you."

I told her she could have taken him to child support court or something. She said, "Back then we didn't do all that." Then she told me, "You should just be lucky that I had you. My mother wouldn't help me. No, she made me go and get my own apartment and work and live on my own. All my other friends, they had kids, but their mothers helped them. When I first left you I wasn't thinking about not coming back. I was only supposed to go away for the weekend. Then when I got out there, those streets felt good. It felt real good. Then I got with my girlfriends and we met guys and they introduced me to crack. I didn't know I would get hooked."

After that conversation I never looked at Saundra the same. I hate that bitch. They tell you in school don't do drugs, don't sell drugs, because you're going to die from them. They say if you take them and if you deal them, you're going to get killed. If that's true, how come every smoker around my way is still alive? When I was younger my mother would come and would stay for a few months to try to get clean, go to rehab, then go back to the streets and not call for months. I don't think she is dead. A couple of times my grandmother went to identify bodies that matched my mother's description, but they weren't her. I wished one was her so I could finally cash in the insurance policy my grandmother had on her. And I could stop thinking about her and my mom-mom could stop worrying so much and we could go on with our lives.

Chapter Twenty-five

Janelle

I went home to get some of my stuff. To my surprise, every-thing looked the same.

"Mom, I can't believe it's not a mess in here!" I said as I walked into my apartment. I gave her a hug and we caught up on everything that had happened in the last few weeks. It felt good to be home.

I went past my old job to pick up my last check. The line was still to the back of the store. Hundreds of people still in line, looking frustrated. The store looked so unorganized. I saw Shana behind the register. She ran from behind the counter and gave me a hug.

"Your skin is glowing. You got a good tan," she screamed.

"Thank you."

"So, you just up and stayed in Miami?"

"Basically," I said. "Where is Joan?"

"She went to go get lunch."

"That figures. Do you know where my check is?"

"No, but you know they gave me your job."

"What?"

"Yes, and it has been on-the-job training. It's the blind leading the blind."

"I can't believe that," I said as my phone rang. It was Damon.

"I miss you, baby girl," he said.

"I miss you too, Dame. I'll be back tomorrow." He blew me a kiss over the phone and said bye. I hung my phone up and Shana said, "Goddamn, can I be you? Nobody ever calls me to say that they miss me in the middle of the day." She then told me she would get my check for me.

I looked at my check. It was seven hundred dollars after taxes. Now I spend that on a pair of sandals. I was relieved that I didn't work there any longer, 'cause I hated that job. I don't know why I stuck around so long. Why do people continue to work jobs they hate? I know why—money.

I went to see Natalie. She was at her mom's house.

"How is everything going with Anthony?"

"The last time I talked to him, he snatched my ring off my hand. I have been so sad. I tried calling his house. Ms. Renee answered and told me that I was the child of the devil and not to call her house anymore."

"Don't pay him any attention. He'll come around. He will call you and want to come back home. He thinks he is paying you back for having fun. You didn't do anything wrong. Nothing! You are a young person, you deserve to have fun and enjoy yourself. Yes, I will admit, you were wrong for going on vacation without telling him. But that still does not give him any right to disrespect you or divorce you."

"So you know I'm staying in Miami for good."

"What? Are you serious?"

"I'm just up here to get my clothes and stuff."

"What about your job?"

"I quit. I have been going shopping all the time and just relaxing. Miami is just so beautiful."

"That sounds so nice."

"So how about Sean keep calling my phone?" I said.

"What you say to him? I know he asked where you been."

"I haven't answered his calls."

"Wait till he catch up with you," she said.

"I know. Well, I got to meet my mom. Then I'm going to the airport. I'll call you tomorrow. Try not to worry about everything."

"I'll try not to, but it's hard," she said. I gave Nat a hug and left.

I took my mother out to eat at Outback Steak House. We hadn't been out just us two in a while and my mother loved their bread. She told me how she liked her new job, how Uncle Teddy was dating one of her coworkers, and that the boys had had contact with their dad.

"How is that going?"

"It's okay. I had left him a message saying your sons are right down the street, call them. They are boys, they need a man. I guess his conscience got the best of him, because he called."

Then my mother told me that she revealed to Sean that I was coming home.

"Mom, why did you tell him?"

"I got tired of him calling."

"So you just tell him all my business?"

"I didn't tell him anything."

"When was the last time you talked to him?"

"He called today when you were downtown."

"So what did you tell him?"

"Nothing."

I gave my mom a look.

We ate our meal and drove back to the apartment. My mom was going to drive me back to the airport. I just wanted to get out of there before Sean showed up. I did not want to see him at all. He is going to be mad as shit at me. He probably wants to hurt me. I haven't returned or answered his calls. I don't think he is actually missing me. I think he is more upset that he doesn't know what I'm doing. I don't know; he will just have to get the picture. I sent him his money. What else does he want?

I had grabbed my suitcase and we were halfway out the door when I saw Sean in the hallway. My mother looked at me and said, "I'm going to leave ya'll alone for a minute."

I was left by myself in the hallway. Either Sean had perfect timing or my mother set me up.

As soon as she shut the door, Sean pushed me up against the wall and said, "Janelle, where the hell have you been?"

"I moved," I said as I pushed him away.

"Okay, you moved. Does that stop you from calling me? I mean damn, you don't know how to return a nigga's phone call?" he asked with a real serious look.

"I have been busy. I'm sorry I didn't call. I just didn't know how to tell you I moved," I said.

"Yo, you ain't even checked on me. That hurt me. I'm doing good though. Me and this guy John from Camden are going to be promoting hot Tuesdays at this bar in Olde City."

"That's nice. I'm so sorry."

"All is forgiven I just wanted to make sure you were okay. Your mom wouldn't give up any info. Can I get a hug? I miss you, Janelle." He extended his arms out to me.

I gave him a quick hug.

"That's nice. Your body looks all good and tight," he said as he touched my waist.

"Thanks."

"Damn, so who you living with down in Miami? What, you met somebody? Dude got to be major. The nigga must got paper. You quit your job and everything."

"How you know I quit?"

"You ain't come home since your trip. I told your ass you were a groupie."

"I'm not no damn groupie."

"Then I went to your job and that girl that worked there told me you don't work there no more. So what the dude do?"

"I'm not telling you."

"What, you got an NBA player?"

"That's not important."

"You at least got somebody that gets a little time, that don't warm the bench?"

"He is not in the NBA."

He started naming players in the NBA. I began laughing at him. He was so simple.

"Sean, don't worry about him, but he don't play for the NBA."

"Oh, you got a big-ass NFL dude. Oh, okay. Well, how much money he make?"

"Sean, you are so crazy."

"I ain't mad at you. Miami is treating you right. I'm not mad at him either. Or them down there," he said as he looked me over once more. "When you going home?"

"Right now. Why, you feel like driving me to the airport?"

"I'll take you."

I got the rest of my things. I hugged my brothers and my mother and gave them some money. The moment I got in Sean's car the phone rang.

"Hello, baby," I said as I answered my phone. It was Damon making sure I was on time for my flight. I turned to see Sean say to himself, "Baby," and then laugh. "I'm on my way to the airport. I'll call you when I get there." When I hung up I looked at Sean and asked him what was so funny.

"Nothing, just you haven't been with him that long and you calling him baby. You never called me baby."

"Please. We said we were only friends, right?"

"Yeah, that's true. But you know I love you, Janelle," he said as he looked in my eyes.

"Sean, you don't love me."

"I do love you. But I guess it doesn't matter now." he said as he looked away.

That was the first time he told me he loved me. It was too little too late. I was on my way back to Damon.

I was in the terminal waiting for them to call my flight

when my phone rang. It was Damon again. The first thing that came out of his mouth was, "Who took you to the airport?"

"My mom," I uttered, trying to think on my feet.

"I just spoke to your mom, Janelle. She called me to make sure I met you at the airport. She said that a friend from high school drove you. Are you lying to me, Janelle?"

"Dame, I didn't think you would understand."

"Damn, baby, you lying to me already. That is not good."

"Dame, it's nothing. It's not like that. He is just somebody I know from school, that's all." *Shit*, I said to myself. I was fucking up by lying to him.

"You used to deal with him?" he asked.

"No! He is just a friend."

"Don't lie to me, Janelle. If we don't have trust we ain't got shit."

"I'm not lying, Dame."

"Okay. Well, I'll meet you at the airport." I should have told him the truth. Especially about stupid-ass Sean. Sean is a trip trying to tell me he loves me. *I bet you do now.* A man always got love for you when he sees somebody else loves you.

Chapter Twenty-six

Tanya

It was the end of the school year. Deja got a good report card and I had to pick up Davon's. I went to his classroom. His teacher was a young black girl. She didn't even seem old enough to be teaching. She looked like she kept herself up and was into the latest fashions. She said hello, then pulled out Davon's report card. I glanced over at it and saw that he had straight Fs and Ds. There was a stamp on the bottom that said *will repeat grade again*. His teacher said that he wasn't a bad kid. But he didn't do his homework, projects, or study for tests. She said he was doing good in the beginning.

"So he's left back. There is nothing I can do?" I asked.

"He can go to summer school."

"How do I sign him up?"

The teacher, Ms. Davidson, went to her desk and handed me a form. She circled the dates and start time for me. Then she said, "Now, summer school is no longer free. It's two hundred and fifty dollars per class. Davon needs at least three classes."

"Okay, that's not a problem. Thank you," I said.

I went to walk out of her classroom when she said, "I don't want to get in your business, but maybe you should talk to Davon's father. He always talks about his father."

"His father is dead, Ms. Davidson."

"Really? I'm so sorry. Well, maybe that's one of the problems. Davon's friend Naim's father comes and picks him up every day from school."

"Thanks again," I said, as I walked out of the classroom. I walked home. Mom-Mom wasn't home yet. I saw Davon outside playing touch football with his friends.

"Davon, come into this house!" I yelled.

At first he acted like he didn't hear me and just kept playing. Then I screamed his name again. All his friends turned around and he started walking toward me.

"Get your ass in this house, boy." He came in the house smelling like a little puppy and with sweat stains everywhere. I pulled out his report card and showed it to him.

"What is this, Davon? You're going to summer school."

"No, I'm not going to summer school."

"Yes, you are, and I have to pay for it. 'Cause if you don't go you will be in fourth grade again. You are on punishment."

"I didn't do anything. I hate that lady."

"What lady," I asked.

"My teacher. She is stupid. Mom I told you she said if I don't do my project I'm going to get left down."

"Go in the house. You want me to buy you a new bike and you getting left back? I don't think so."

He ran past me and started crying.

"Why is he crying?" My mom-mom said as she walked in the house.

"Because he is on punishment."

"For what?"

"Because he is getting left back."

"How are you going to get mad at him when you don't even help him with his work? Davon, come out here."

"I said he was on punishment."

"Girl, please." Davon walked past me and ran back and played with his friends.

Chapter Twenty-seven

Natalie

I was picking Anthony up from his day care and the director came up to me and said, "How you doing today?"

"I'm fine," I said.

I went into Anthony's nursery and grabbed his bag and said good-bye to his teachers. I was halfway out the front door when the director approached me and gave me an envelope. I opened it and it was a bill for three hundred dollars. I gave the bill back to her and said, "My husband pays it."

"I know, I called him. He said you were paying for it," she said.

"Okay, um, can I write you a check?" I asked as I started fumbling in my pocketbook with Anthony on my hip.

"No, we don't accept checks. Just bring the money in tomorrow."

I thanked her and walked out to my car.

I put Anthony in his car seat. I rolled his window halfway down and mine all the way down as it was a beautiful June day. It smelled and felt like summer had arrived. As soon as I fastened my seat belt, I dialed Anthony's cell phone.

Anthony didn't pick up. He probably was looking at the caller ID and didn't want to speak to me. I waited about five minutes, then called back by *67, blocking my number. He picked up.

"Anthony!"

"What, Natalie?"

"I just picked Anthony up from the day care and they said you haven't been paying."

"I'm not paying for him to go to day care while you are home doing nothing."

"I'm not home doing nothing. You know I work with my mom."

"You want him to go to day care, you pay for him."

"I'm trying to find a job, Anthony. How am I going to find a job if he is with me?"

"I don't know and I don't care." He then hung up the phone on me. I couldn't believe Anthony was still so angry.

I was getting more hyped by the second. I called him back.

"Listen, Anthony, okay so you not going to pay for his day care, right? Can you at least give me some money?"

"For what?"

"So I can get him diapers, milk, and baby food."

"I'll pick some up and I'll drop them off later. I'm not putting any money in your hands." He hung up on me again.

I took Anthony Jr. to the park and tried to forget about Anthony. I called Janelle to see what she was up to.

"So how's everything going?"

"Girl, I love it here. Damon is the best. I'm so glad I moved here. What's the latest with Anthony?"

"Same thing, he still mad."

"Damn, he really mad. Nat, it's been a minute now."

"Yeah, I don't know, he stopped paying for Anthony's day care. I got four hundred dollars in the bank. Either I take three hundred and pay his day care and only have one hundred dollars to my name, or I don't send him to day care anymore."

"I owe you a hundred. I can send it today."

"I forgot about that money. Send it when you get a chance."

"I'll Western Union it to you."

"No, just put a check or a money order in the mail."

"Okay, kiss the baby for me. Bye."

"See you."

"Natalie, don't forget you got everything going for yourself. I don't even know why you bother with him. You know his ass was crazy when you married him. His mother is a nut too."

"I know, I know," I said as I agreed with Janelle.

"Nat, sometimes people need time apart to find themselves, cool their head. Then they can come back to the situation as a new person, or he really wants out."

"I wanted out too, but not like this. And he told me his mother was right all along about me, that I was a whore and wasn't shit," I said.

"See, Ms. Renee needs a good ass kicking. Maybe you could come down, Nat."

"Really?"

"Yeah, Damon said that I could invite someone to keep me company while he is away at his games."

"Oh, I need that. When I get my money together I will be down."

I was going to have to continue helping my mom out and work off the money I was about to borrow.

"Mommy, can I borrow some money?"

"What you need it for?"

"Anthony didn't pay the day care, so now I owe them three hundred dollars."

"Why don't you let Donna watch him? Then you can come help me."

"I'm going to help you. But I want to get a real job."

"Natalie, how much do you need?"

"I don't know. Whatever you can spare, Mom."

"I got five hundred for you and it's not a loan. I'm giving it to you for my grandson."

"Thanks, Mom. I love you,"

"You're welcome."

I read baby Anthony a bedtime story. He was so funny trying to grab the pages and put the book in his mouth. I was trying to make him right-handed, but he favored his left hand. After I put him to bed I took a long, hot bath. I needed to soak. I just sat in the tub thinking that my marriage was over. It was really over and I couldn't believe it! I was missing Anthony so much, I wanted us to be back together. I wished I could call him. I wanted to hold him and tell him let's try to make our marriage work. I wanted to tell him to stop listening to his mother. She is just miserable because she doesn't have a man. He is being so mean to me. I got out of the tub and dried off and threw on a nightshirt. I turned the air conditioner and television on and watched the rest of *Law & Order*. That was my show. I decided to call this guy I used to date named Darnell. I dated him before I got serious with Anthony. I almost didn't marry Anthony because of Darnell. Darnell was immature though, so I left him alone. The only thing that made me want to speak with him now is I knew it would make Anthony so mad, because he hated him. I dialed his number and he answered.

"Hey, Darnell," I said.

"What? I know this is not . . . no, can't be." He acted like he didn't know who I was.

"It's me, Natalie," I said.

"What are you doing calling me, Miss Married?"

"I'm separated now."

"Yeah, right. I doubt it."

"No, I am serious, we are separated."

"That man is not letting you go. He is crazy over you. Separated don't mean single. You still legally married."

"We're getting a divorce."

"Whatever," he said.

We talked a little more and I realized why I broke up with him. He still sounded immature and only made me want to talk to Anthony more. I called Tanya for advice and she said the answer to all my problems was to get another man. Once Anthony saw I wasn't chasing him anymore, he would start to wonder why and come running back to me. Then she said, "Have some hot shit parked outside your door and he will be mad like, 'who the fuck is in my house?'"

"You might be right, Tanya. But I don't feel like meeting anyone right now."

"Well, at least you got your mom and dad to help you out."

"Yeah, I guess I'm lucky."

"So why don't you lose some weight? That will make him run back."

"It is not that easy to lose weight. I have tried."

"Well, can't you go to one of those places?"

"Places like what?"

"A fat diet place."

"Tanya, shut up. I'm hanging up. Good-bye."

Chapter Twenty-eight

Janelle

I was looking for a new hair salon. I didn't know what the black or white areas were in Miami. I heard one of the black areas was in Liberty City somewhere. Kelly said the girl at her salon did really good hair, but I wasn't about to let a white girl do my weave. It was time to take these tracks out. They had been glued and reglued and I needed my hair touched up with a perm. Basically I need the works. I got the yellow pages and called a few salons. I asked the receptionist at each salon for the best stylist. The last one I called said this girl named Livia was the best. But she didn't have any openings for two weeks and she put me on hold. Then she came back on the line and said what do you need done?

I told her a straight natural weave. She asked if I wanted it sewn or glued in. She said, "We charge a hundred for glue and a hundred and fifty for sewn in." She gave me an appointment and said if I couldn't make it, to call.

I was a little skeptical about trying a new hair salon. I didn't want all that high hair with hard curls with a lot of spritz that I have seen on southern women. I know Miami was pretty fly and up to date on most things. I was ready to fly back home just to get my hair done.

I got to the hair salon and I was scared to let the girl Livia touch my hair. She had a bald head with little pencil tip curls at the top. On the side of her head she had pink hair slapped on with her track showing. My mom always said to beware of the hairdresser with no hair. She said she always wants to cut your hair and make you bald like her. I took that into consideration about the hairdresser with messed-up hair. She might have me looking like her. But I let her do my hair. She had a lot of clients. All of their hair looked nice. It was my time to get in the chair, and she didn't let me look in the mirror until she was done.

I looked in the mirror and my hair looked so good. She had layered it and made tight bouncy curls. I loved it. I gave her a thirty-dollar tip and made another appointment.

I shook my hair in the wind. I turned my radio on. I was getting tired of all that boom-boom bass music. So I put in a CD.

I met Kelly at her and Carl's house in the Coral Gables section of Miami. We were going shopping, then to the spa. The house was huge. Carl was getting money. Kelly said his sign-on bonus was a half a mil. Carl made like 1.5 million a season and he had a few small endorsements. Damon made a good salary, but only about a quarter of that. Kelly said James's and Stephen's salaries were in the millions too. Some people are just so lucky. Carl was doing the right thing with his money. The house was so big and nice. I walked in and saw a crystal-clear coffee table aquarium. All types of tropical fish were floating around in it. There was a white baby grand piano and white furniture. Kelly just walked around the house in her slippers like, so what, this is nothing. She said, you think this is nice, you should see Lisa's house.

"Girl, I love your hair. Where did you go?"

"Some place I found in the yellow pages."

"They did a great job, but aren't you going to ruin it at the spa?"

"No, I'm not going in the sauna room or Jacuzzi. I just want a massage and get my feet and nails done." We went to the mall and Kelly literally spent four thousand dollars in one store and she only had two bags. I couldn't talk; I had wasted money on things I didn't need like a plain Juicy Couture T-shirt for seventy dollars, Jimmy Choo sandals for three eighty-two, and a pair of Blue Cult jeans for a hundred and fifty two dollars. After our light shopping we drove to the spa. The ladies welcomed us in the spa. They had the soothing sound of water flowing playing softly in the background. We undressed and put our clothes in lockers. They had white robes and brown plastic slippers for us. I followed Kelly to the waiting room. She picked up a magazine, and drank lemon water. There were cucumbers chilling in ice. I picked two up and placed them over my eyes. I heard Kelly's name then mine. I took the cucumber off of my eyes and followed the masseuse to the massage room. She asked me what kind of massage I wanted. I told her a Swedish. She rubbed my back so good. I didn't get the full benefit because I went right to sleep. It was so relaxing. That was my first non-boyfriend massage. The masseuse tapped my shoulder and said, "I'm done."

"Thank you," I said as I awakened from my sleep.

"Drink a lot of water to remove all of the toxins," she said as I left the massage room. I felt so relaxed and rejuvenated. I was getting used to this life.

Chapter Twenty-nine

Natalie

Anthony has not come home yet. A whole month and some change has gone by. Either he is really not coming home or he is taking this too far. I have been looking in the paper and calling around looking for jobs. The baby has been staying home with me. I didn't pay his day care and I'm not until I know I'm going to have more money. I said as soon as I get a job I was going to pay my balance and send him back. He is my son, but I'm getting tired of him. I think he is getting spoiled being around me all day. He wants me to hold him and he won't let me put him down. At least when Anthony was here I had a break. Now I can't even go to the bathroom without him crying. I have to creep out of my bed to get five minutes alone. I guess he misses his dad and doesn't know how to express it. I miss his dad too. But life goes on.

I braided the baby's hair and got ready for the Fourth of July block party. My parents cooked out every year. I still hadn't mastered getting me and him dressed at the same time. It takes me like three hours. I had to bathe, dress, do my hair, make bottles, and check the diaper bag to make sure there were diapers inside it. Then wash the baby, dress him, feed him, and if I was lucky, I would make it out the door by 5:00 p.m.

I couldn't park on my parents' street because it was blocked off for the block party. Everything was set up in the street, the tables, chairs, and umbrellas. My mom saw me struggling up the street with the baby. She grabbed my baby bag off my arm and my dad grabbed the baby.

"You need to do something with that baby's hair. I don't like those braids. He looks like a little girl," my dad said.

"I got to keep it braided. I can't cut it," I said.

"No, you don't cut a baby's hair before they're one," my mom said as she took the baby out of my dad's arm.

"Why not?" my dad asked.

"You just don't. If you do, the baby will talk slow."

"That's not true. Cut this boy's hair. I don't want to see him with girlie braids."

While my dad held the baby I helped my mother put all the food on the table and set it. "Mom, you need a spoon for the potato salad," I said as I sneaked a taste, dipping my finger on the side.

She brought the spoons out of the house and said, "Natalie, I have been thinking. I think you need an older man. Your father is five years older than me," she said as she gathered serving utensils. "I was reading an article in the newspaper yesterday. It was about people getting married in their twenties. They called them starter marriages. They said the starter marriage prepares you for your real marriage in your thirties."

"Mom, that's the dumbest thing I ever heard!" I said.

"I just think Anthony is too juvenile for you. He was your starter marriage. Now you're free to meet someone new."

I had no response for my mom.

My dad was cooking barbecued beef ribs on the grill. All my cousins were sitting around with their men and husbands, so I felt really sad. I was sitting all alone. Then my little cousin on my mom's side came up to me, felt my stomach, and asked if I was having another baby. That made me feel sadder. No, I told him. I wasn't pregnant, but I felt like I was having another baby. I helped myself to everything at the table at least twice. If that wasn't bad enough, my uncle Charles came over to me and said he heard about everything that was going on. He said, "If you need me to go set your husband straight I will."

My uncle Charles is crazy. There is one in every family. He drinks too much, says off-the-wall things, and wears out-dated tight clothes.

After the cookout was over my mother and I went to see the fireworks. They are at the Art Museum every year. We parked off Spring Garden Street and walked to the parkway. I thought the baby would love to see the fireworks. But when he looked up into the sky and saw bright lights and heard the noise, he started crying.

I came home and put Anthony to sleep, took off my clothes and got into the bed. My stomach felt like a water bed. It was like you could push it in and it would bounce back out at you. There is a point in your fatness when you say if I ever get that big, I will just stop eating and starve myself. Today is that day for me. I had eaten way too much at the cookout. I examined myself in the mirror. I needed to go on a diet. Or I'm going to do something extreme like gastric bypass surgery or something to get this fucking weight off. I know I don't qualify for gastric bypass, because you have to be about a hundred pounds overweight. And I think they staple your stomach and make it the size of an egg. I don't want all that done. I'm only about thirty pounds overweight. I can lose weight the old-fashioned way. But in the past nothing has worked for me. I have bought into every diet plan. Weight Watchers, Slim Fast shakes, L.A. Weight Loss. Diet pills always made me sick and sped up my heart, giving me the jitters and I couldn't sleep. I would wake up and start cleaning the house in the middle of the night. I bought Tae Bo tapes twice and never used them. The weight wasn't going to come off by hoping. I really had to make a conscious effort.

* * *

The next day I went to the YMCA in my neighborhood and I inquired about their aerobics classes. I peeked in on the workout class. Ladies were doing aerobics. Fast techno workout music was playing. A short, feisty lady was running around the room with a headset on yelling, "Two and three and one more. Two more, three more."

I watched for a few more moments, then walked back to the front desk. The lady who was instructing came out of the class and jogged up behind me, asked if I was interested in taking a class.

"Yes, but I don't have anybody to watch my baby."

"He can sit on the side in the back in his car seat. It's time to get that baby weight off. Right?"

I gave her a glance like, excuse me? But she was right. The lady said her name was Gina and that if I'd like to start I could sign up and get a flyer from the front desk.

I started the class the next day. I went and bought new sneakers, a water bottle, and a yoga mat. The baby did sit in his car seat.

The music started and I was doing fine at first. Then it was time for crunches. Can you say "owie"? I did about twenty. Then she kept saying five more. She said that like four times. Oh, really. I just stopped doing them. Then she walked to the back of the class and said come on and do ten more. "I can't," I said.

"Yes, you can. Give me five more."

Out of breath, I curled my body up and did five crunches.

Chapter Thirty

Janelle

I was hungry and tired of eating healthy food. I wanted a cheesesteak or burger. Damon didn't have anything in his refrigerator but health stuff. We ate out all the time and the housekeeper brings in a few things, but I wanted some real food.

"Damon, we need real food. I can't eat all this health food stuff," I said as I looked in the refrigerator.

"Rita brings in everything we need."

"No, I want to go to the market and get some cereal with sugar on it. Like some Cocoa Pebbles or Honey Nut Cheerios. Baby, let's go to the market. I want some shrimp and salmon and maybe even a cheesesteak."

"You going to make me a cheesesteak."

"Yeah, okay. Let's go."

We went to the Publix Market to get groceries. I filled the shopping cart with cereal, milk, cheese, and all types of juice. I wanted some turkey breast lunch meat. There were a million and one people in the deli line. We took a number.

"Damon, I want some pizza too! You ever make a home-made pizza?"

"No."

"They taste good. I'm going to get the pizza and you wait for the lunch meat."

I walked over to the frozen food aisle. I was only gone about two minutes. I walked up behind Damon and this Hispanic girl was all in his face. She was bagging her oranges and rubbing them suggestively. I watched to see what Damon's reaction was going to be. The woman was like, don't I know you? You play for the Dolphins. I knew she was a groupie. Kelly had warned me about women like this. She said they hang around the practice sites, markets, places that they know the player eventually will have to go. I continued to watch as the groupie made small talk with Damon. He was cool. He didn't fall into her trap. I heard him say, "Thanks, but no, thanks."

That was my cue to walk right over to him and say, "Babe, what kind of cereal did you say you wanted?"

He turned around and said, "Baby, you know I like Cocoa Pebbles."

"And you are?" I said as I extended my hand out to her. She didn't say her name, she just walked away.

"Well, nice meeting you," I said as she walked away. "You're bad, Damon," I said. "What were you doing talking to that girl?"

"Please, I don't want her. I told her I was good."

"You better had."

We went home and watched *The Matrix II* on DVD. I don't know why he likes that stupid movie. I'll never get it. I still couldn't get over the aggressive nature of the woman from the grocery store. I was curious to know if Damon would have talked to her if I wasn't there.

"Damon, have you ever knowingly dated a groupie?"

"No, but if I wanted to it would be so easy. I just don't want no woman that is just about my money."

"What about a white girl?"

"No, why?" he asked.

"I just wanted to know."

"My mom told me since I was younger that she was going to whoop me good if I brought a white girl home."

"Really?"

"She is not prejudiced. She just said that a white woman couldn't understand me like a black woman."

"Yeah, I mean I feel like love who you love.

"But Carl love him some white girls. I never even saw him with a tanned white girl."

"That's 'cause he so black," I said.

"You wrong."

As soon as Damon went out the door I got on the phone and called Kelly. I told her everything that had transpired.

"Do you believe this bitch in the market?"

"Girl, get used to it. It is only the beginning, and no offense, but Damon is not the star player. Imagine if he was Ricky Williams before he retired. Or Bobby Akano. You know how many groupies a day Dana has to beat with a broomstick to keep them away? She is going through hell with all those damn groupies. And sometimes he talks to them. It's only a matter of time before he leaves her."

"You think so?"

"Of course. Basically most groupies think they are some kind of way going to turn into a wife, but usually all they do is get fucked and some money on the nightstand. Every wife or girlfriend is a groupie, just a groupie that the man decided to take personal. I never considered myself a groupie. I didn't wait outside hotels, but I did place myself in the right locations at the right time. I used to go to all the parties in every city. I used to date this ballplayer before I met Carl. His name was Faheem Staton."

"I heard of him."

"Well, when I met him he was sitting on the bench for the Hornets when they were in Charlotte. He was tall and really good-looking, but he didn't have any self-confidence. Which is cool, see; only a naive rookie goes after the star player on a team. Anybody knows that the star attracts too much attention, and I'm trying to shine. I can't deal with a man that thinks he is cuter than me. So I always try to find a guy that is not sure of himself. Faheem's pride was a little shot because he wasn't getting any money and wasn't getting any time. I pumped his heart up. Started making him think he was the man. He had more confidence, started making more shots and got more time. Now he is one of the best players in the league. It looks good on my behalf 'cause he felt like I was in his corner and was there for him before his name was in the papers, and reporters wanted to talk to him. We broke up because his head got too big and he wanted to date this girl in this singing group. I left him and moved down here.

"You know a lot of women never become a fiancée or wife. They usually get to hang out in the house for a month, at the most. Then they get kicked out."

"When I met Damon I didn't even know he played football."

"That's good. Damon knows you don't want him for anything. Damon is not like a lot of these guys. Most of them got two homes, one for the family and the other for friends, drugs, and girls. Carl is different and so is Damon. You have nothing to worry about."

Damon came in while I was still on the phone with Kelly. He didn't hardly say anything to me. He went straight to the room and went to sleep. I don't know what I did to him. He had an attitude about something. The next morning he made me breakfast in bed. His behavior was so strange. One day nice, one day mean. One day sweet, one day sour as a tart.

Chapter Thirty-one

Tanya

Deja ran into my room, woke me up, and said, "Mommy, can you take me to Brittany's tea party?"

"When is it?"

"Saturday morning."

"Sure," I said. I told Deja whatever she wanted to hear so she could let me sleep. I was so damn tired; me and Monica was out all last night.

Me and Monica had gone to this round-the-way bar in Germantown. I needed some new friends. Talk about salty. As soon as we entered I saw this dude I used to fuck with named Ty. He was smiling all up in Monica's face. I wondered if he remembered who I was. I tried to turn around so he wouldn't see me and be like "don't I know you?" Then I would have to go into how we knew each other. I wasn't going to walk up to him and say, "Hey, what's up? Remember when you fucked me and your girlfriend tried to bust down the door at the hotel? And you didn't call anymore. You gave me cab fare home?" I told Monica not to talk to him, but she decided to anyway.

"He looks all right. He just jumped out of a Benz."

"He's from West Oak Lane. Don't talk to him, he's broke. Trust me. I know him. Plus, he's drama."

He did recognize me. He turned from Monica and said, "Hey, girl, small world."

"What's up, Ty? I see you still about them dollars. Yeah, you got that hot shit on. You stay in that hot shit."

"You still charging niggas?" he asked.

"Yup, but I protect mine."

"Yeah, you got to, shit is dangerous. It's a lot of hot shit out here now."

I was so glad when he left.

"What was that all about?" Monica asked.

"Some guy I used to deal with for a quick minute."

Right after that guy walked away, I ran into this dude named Do; he was Barry's friend. He used to look out for me and my kids after Barry died. Then he got locked up and I didn't see him. I didn't even know he was out. I walked over to him and said, "What's up, Do?"

"What's up, girl? How you been? You know I just came home. How my godkids doing?"

"You haven't seen your godkids since they was like, I don't even know, like three years."

"How old are they now?"

"Seven and nine."

"Really? Well, give them this. Tell them it's from Uncle Do," he said as he gave me two hundred dollars. I put my number in his cell phone and tucked the money in my pocketbook.

"Yo, who's that?" Monica asked as she eyed a guy across the bar.

"That's Rell from back Brickyard. He used to get money with Barry. He's with Do."

Monica went over to him and introduced herself. I followed. She was talking to him when some girl with this little ponytail that needed another pack of hair came over to him and said, "What's up, Rell? Why you ain't call me? You in here talking to anybody?"

Monica said, "I know that bitch ain't talking about me. I will bust her in the head with a bottle."

The girl heard her and said, "Imagine that."

Rell told the girl to chill and he would holler at her later. They talked for a while and then Monica said she was going to hang out with Rell. She dropped me off.

Saturday morning came. Deja had her pink Easter dress on.

"Mom, are you ready to go the tea party?"

"Huh?" I asked.

"Remember, Mom? You promised to take me to the party."

"Okay, I'll take you to the party. Just let me go back to sleep for about an hour." I went back to sleep for exactly an hour.

"Mom, it's twelve-thirty. The party starts at one."

"Okay, I'll get up. Why do y'all have that dress on from Easter?" I asked.

"Mom, that's what you wear to a tea party."

I got up and took a quick shower and brushed my teeth. I put my hair in a bun. Deja gave me the invitation. The party wasn't far from our house. I called the number on the invitation to find out what she was supposed to wear. Deja's friend answered and said, "We all are dressed up."

We got halfway to the party when Deja announced that she had to go to the bathroom. After we took care of that problem she said, "Mommy, we have to bring Brittany a gift. Do you have any money? Can we pick her up a gift? I want to get her a Bratz doll."

I just wanted to put some money in a card and call it a day.

"Deja, we'll get her a Bratz doll later. She will like it if you give her a twenty-dollar bill."

"Mom, she said she wanted a Bratz doll."

"Next time, Deja."

We stopped at the pharmacy and got a card. I let Deja

sign it and we walked to the party. The house was comfortable.

"Hi, welcome to my home," a gray-haired woman said.

The tea party was like a little girl's ball. I felt bad, my daughter looked crazy. She did her own hair and the other girls were pressed and curled and they looked sweet. All the other little girls had their hair in Shirley Temple curls and ponytails.

"Are you Brittany's grandmother?"

"I'm her mother," she said, embarrassed. She was about forty-five with her soft gray hair cut short.

"I'm so sorry. I apologize, I just thought—"

"No, that's okay. I thought you were Deja's sister. Your daughter is such a sweet girl."

All the parents were making small talk. I tried to join in, but their conversations were not interesting. This one lady sounded like she had something stuck in her throat. Her voice just seemed fake. She was really Afrocentric and stuffy. She looked at me like *you have your hair curled and I have natural dreds; therefore, I'm a better person than you.* She asked the other lady, "Where did your do your undergrad at?" That hoity-toity bourgie party was making me sick. Brittany's dad walked around the party taking pictures. As soon as he said one word to me, her mom came over and asked him to do something. I didn't want her man.

The little girls poured tea and apple juice. There were these little cutesy sandwiches cut in triangles and circles. It was cucumber dip and just a bunch of other weird food. The children didn't eat anything.

Deja was hungry after the party, so I took her to get pizza. I still felt tired from going out last night. On the walk home from the pizza place Deja said, "Brittany's daddy came to her party. Mom, when is my dad coming back? Can he come back for my birthday? I really want all my friends to meet him. Is my dad going to be at my party?"

"Your daddy can't come to your party," I said.

"Why, Mommy?"

"Because your daddy is in a better place. He died."

"So he's never coming back?"

"No, never, baby."

When we got home my phone rang and it was Monica.

"Tanya, why didn't you tell me that bawh was crazy and broke?"

"What bawh?"

"Rell."

"I didn't know he was. Why, what he do?" I said as I began to laugh.

"I went home with him last night. He got this raggedy-ass car. Yo, I thought you said he is getting money."

"I said he used to get money with Barry. That was years ago."

"Well, he ain't getting no money anymore, that's for sure. He was acting strange. He was like, so what's up, pretty? I'm like, nothing's up. Then he just got on the floor and start smiling at me while he did push-ups and sit-ups."

"He was working out?"

"Yes, three in the morning drunk all high and shit. Girl, that nigga is crazy! We didn't do anything. He didn't even try to touch me and I'm glad."

"Well, that'll teach you. Stop going home with everybody you meet."

"But I didn't get to the good part yet. When I woke up I was like I'm ready to leave, I see this motherfucker was in the bathroom smoking the motherfucking pipe," she said.

"You are lying."

"No I'm not. Thanks for looking out, Tanya," she said sarcastically.

"You're welcome," I said, still laughing at Monica's dumb ass as I closed my cell phone.

Chapter Thirty-two

Natalie

I started going to the aerobics class three times a week. Gina put me on a low-carb, no-sugar diet. I could only have water, diet soda, fruit, lean meat, and no starches at all. It was kind of hard because I love bread and any kind of rice or pasta. I was committed though, I was going to lose this weight. And so far, I am doing okay. I bought a digital scale so I could see exactly how much I weighed. I was at one hundred and eighty pounds even. I wanted to see how much weight I was losing down to the half pound.

I got on the scale today. I had lost five pounds. I couldn't believe it; something was finally working for me. As happy as I was about losing weight, I still missed Anthony so much, and that made me so very sad. I came to the conclusion that I can't live without Anthony. Yes, he has some bad qualities, but then again he has a lot of good ones. He is a good provider, he has a job with benefits. He married me. He didn't make me his "baby's mom." We were married before I was even pregnant. He did buy me a car. He loves me. That's why he doesn't want me out. I understand that now. I called him and told him he was right. I wasn't supposed to be running the streets. I had a family. I had a good husband and child. Natalie and Tanya were searching for what I already had. Tanya wouldn't put me before her man if she had one. And look at Janelle. As soon as she got somebody interested in her, she left me easily. I got enough heart to call him again.

"Hello," he said.

"Anthony, I wanted to know if you wanted to come over for dinner."

"For what, Natalie? I can't play games with you anymore. You know what I need in my wife. I need her to listen and obey. If you are not prepared to do that, then I don't think we should talk. I don't want to even start the deception again. I can't make you a good woman. That's something you have to be already inside."

"I am a good woman, Anthony, and I want to be your wife. I don't want to get a divorce. So can you please come over and talk?"

"I'll see what I can do," he said.

"Okay, try," I said as I hung up the phone. He didn't say no, so that was good. That meant he was on his way.

Anthony arrived about an hour later. He came in and I tried to hug him. He said that it didn't feel right and for me to stop. He was so damn stubborn. He had a seat on the sofa. I offered him something to drink. He said he wasn't thirsty and asked me where the baby was. I told him the baby was taking a nap.

Anthony and I talked for about an hour. I cried, he cried, and when it was all said and done, he said he would try to make it work with me. We ate dinner and played with the baby. I made his bottle, bathed him and put him to sleep. By the time I came back down the steps, Anthony was sitting on the sofa flicking through the cable stations. I sat next to him and touched his hands. I gave him a hug and he hugged me back.

"I love you and I love our family. I am going to make it work," he said as he squeezed me tighter. I missed his touch and warmth. I even missed his smell. I was so happy to have him home in my arms. It was such a relief. My husband began to make love to me like he missed me. He laid me across the sofa and took my shirt off and unhooked my bra. He caressed my breasts with his hands as he entered me.

"Is the pussy still mine or did anybody else have it, Natalie?" he asked as he stroked in and out of my vagina.

"No, baby, it's still yours," I said as I exhaled.

"You sure?" he asked.

"Yes, I'm sure."

"You love me?" he asked as he momentarily stopped making love to me.

"Yes, Anthony. I love you."

"No more lies, okay?"

"No more lies," I said as he continued to satisfy me.

The next morning we went to IHOP for breakfast. Baby Anthony was so happy. It was like he missed his daddy too.

"What are you going to order?" I asked Anthony. He said he didn't know yet. The waitress asked if we were ready to order. I said yes and ordered an omelet and Anthony had French toast and sausage.

While we waited for our food to arrive, Anthony played with the baby. He was making him laugh. He looked at the baby and said, "Daddy's back. Yup, big guy, Daddy's back until Mommy messes up again." I knew what he was referring to, but I ignored him.

The first week of Anthony being home was *so blissfully sweet*. He was treating me good, like he actually didn't want to lose me ever again. Anthony did the dishes and helped me cook. I didn't have to tell him to take a shower after work. He didn't leave clothes on the floor. He even gave me a massage, and greased and scratched my scalp. It felt good. It felt perfect, like I was where I was supposed to be. I think Janelle was right when she said sometimes people just need to clear their head.

We went to get the rest of his belongings from Ms. Renee. Because Anthony was so happy, so was Ms. Renee. She spoke to me and to the baby. She acted as if she hadn't seen baby Anthony in years. There's something really wrong with this lady. Really. She was going to talk about some grandmom got some goodies for her grandson and asked us if we wanted to stay for dinner. I just looked at that bitch. The last time we were here she said she wanted a blood test on my child.

Chapter Thirty-three

Janelle

I called Natalie. We hadn't talked in a while. I got her answering machine and I left her a message. "Hey, Nat, this is Janelle. Call me when you get in. I hope everything is going okay." I called Natalie's mom, Aunt Sharon.

"Hi, Aunt Sharon."

"Janelle, how is it going in Miami?"

"It's okay."

"What do you mean it's okay? Girl, you got that little shape. I would be on the beach getting some sun every day. Let your aunt Sharon come down there. You won't be able to find me."

"You can come down whenever you want."

"Don't tell me that. I'll be down there. I don't know where Natalie is. She is running after that fool of a husband of hers."

"They got back together?"

"I think so."

"Well, I guess that's good."

"Janelle, I don't know. I just want my daughter to be happy and I think he takes her through so much." She sighed.

"Well, tell her I'm trying to get in touch with her."

"I will."

* * *

I love Miami. There are so many celebrities and stars, I mean big movies stars. I saw where Oprah Winfrey lives today. Some people are so fortunate. It really costs a fortune to live here. I guess right now I am fortunate too. I saw how much Damon is paying for this place. Whew! You don't even want to know. Four thousand a month. I am never going home. Never, ever. Who wants to go back to cold weather? Everybody is going to be buying fall clothes, boots, and winter coats. I'm going to be sipping on my margarita on the beach.

Natalie called me. I couldn't wait to hear how she got Anthony to come home. I know it had to be drama-filled. "What's up, Nat? Hold up, there is someone at the door. Hold on."

"Go ahead," she said. I went to the door and peeped out. There was a delivery guy with flowers. He brought in all different kinds of bouquets with sunflowers in them. The delivery guy asked if it was my birthday. I said no, then he asked did my husband do something wrong. I told him no again. Then he said I must be a lucky girl and asked me to sign for the flowers. I thanked him again and let him out of the house.

I picked up the phone again and Natalie said, "You have a good man. He brought you flowers?"

"Yes, a lot of them. Oh my God. Dame is so thoughtful." I read the card to Natalie. It said *Janelle, you have brought sunshine into my life when it was cloudy, and love into my heart when there was hate. I love you, girl. Damon. P.S., Look in the refrigerator*. I went into the refrigerator and saw a large black jewelry box. I opened it and it was a watch.

"What kind of watch did he give you?" Natalie asked.

"A Franck Mueller watch. It's pink with diamonds all around the wrist." I tried it on.

"I never heard of that. It must be real expensive. That girl Kelly that you hang out with will know."

"She probably will. She prices everything. So, what's up with Tanya?"

"Her usual partying."

"When is she going to grow up?"

"Um, I don't know."

"I got to go, Janelle. Anthony is on his way home."

I called Damon to thank him for my flowers and watch.

"Dame, I called to say thank you for the flower and watch."

"No problem, baby, just wanted to thank you for being my sunshine. I know I have been out of it lately. I wanted you to know it wasn't you. I just got a lot going on, okay?"

"Yes."

"We got to go to Lisa and Stephen's tonight."

"Why?"

"Amber and James got married over the weekend in Vegas," Damon said.

"Aw, that is so nice."

"They are having a get-together today at Lisa and Stephen's to celebrate."

"When?"

"At five."

"Do they live far?"

"No, right over in Coral Gables."

I didn't know what to wear. I had a lot of clothes, but nothing that matched. I had cute sandals that matched with a shirt, but no pants. Or really nice accessories that didn't go with anything. I decided on a salmon-pink dress.

You couldn't even walk up to Lisa and Stephen's house if you wanted to. You had to drive. I've seen nice houses before, but I didn't know people really live like this. Damon's house was my apartment compared to this. Lisa welcomed us into her home. She had a lilac orchid in her hair and a white dress on. Damon gave her a hug, and I said hello. They had a gigantic Olympic-size pool, winding stairs, a view of the ocean, and high ceilings. She told me to feel free to look around. She must have known I was amazed. I saw Kelly talking to Amber. I walked over and congratulated Amber.

"Nice rock, huh? And to think nobody thought he was going to marry her," Kelly mumbled after Amber left. With her champagne flute in her hand, Kelly ranted on, "Well, he had better give her something after all those kids."

Changing the subject I asked, "How many bedrooms in this place?"

"Seven bedrooms and six and a half baths. I told you this house was breathtaking."

Lisa walked over and said, "Are you okay?" I told her I was. "Did you eat?" Lisa asked.

"No, not yet, but I will," I said.

"You have to try my *pollo agridulce*. You'll love it, Janelle," she said as she offered me some from off her plate. I took a little and asked what type of meat it was.

"It is a Cuban-style chicken."

"It's good but very spicy."

"So you're the next one that better hear wedding bells, Kelly," Lisa said.

"Yeah, then maybe Janelle," Kelly responded.

"I'm not in a rush. We just met," I said as I walked away and located Damon.

We ate, mingled, said our goodbyes and then headed towards home. The sky was becoming dark and the palm trees were swaying from the blowing wind. It was about to rain. I could smell it. As soon as we drove in the driveway the rain began to pour. We didn't have an umbrella so we had to run in the house. Damon locked the door and came and sat on the sofa with me. I thanked him again for the watch as I held my wrist out to look at it. He said anything for my lady. I kissed him and sat on his lap. I pressed my body against his and began to slowly gyrate. He then glided his hands across my breasts. I took my pants and underwear off. He unbuttoned his pants and slid his underwear down. I sat on his lap with my back to him and inserted his hard dick into me. I began bouncing up and down, twisting my hips around and around in a wave motion. He was loving it. He moaned my name and said I was the best thing that ever happened to him. I told him I loved everything about him. We rested a moment then we ordered a sausage pizza and stayed in the bed snuggling the rest of the night.

Chapter Thirty-four

Natalie

"Anthony, what's in that case?"

"It's a gun."

"What are you doing with a gun?"

"I got it for protection. I started going to the gun range when we were apart."

"Well, I don't like guns and I don't want it around the baby."

"Shut up. The baby is not even old enough to reach the gun, and by the time he is, I will talk to him about it."

"Get it out of my house. Take it back to your mother's. I don't like guns. They are dangerous. My dad's partner's son found his gun when we were younger and accidentally shot himself in the neck. He is paralyzed now."

"I'll take it to my mother's."

Anthony paid for the baby to go back to day care. I could look for a job for real now or go back to school. And in the meantime continue to help my mom with the shop.

I want to look good for my man. I was still maintaining my weight by going to my aerobics class. I was down eleven pounds now. I could see it in my face and even my neck looked thin. I was on my way. I put on my 14 jeans and they were loose. All I want to do is lose like fifteen more pounds and skip over a size 12 and go right into a 10.

When I go to the market I have two lists. My diet food list and Anthony and the baby's list. When Anthony was not there, I didn't have to cook. I could eat healthy all I wanted to. Now that he is home, I got to make these big starchy dinners because that's what he likes. I make chicken breast, buttery garlic noodles, spinach, and rolls. I just eat chicken and spinach. I gave Anthony his plate in the living room and sat down with mine. We were watching videos on 106 & Park.

"Why don't you have any noodles on your plate?" Anthony asked.

"Because I'm on a diet."

"What diet you on that you can eat meat and no noodles?"

"Low carb, Anthony," I said as I changed the station.

"You know you hungry. Won't you eat some?" he said as he offered me some of his garlic noodles.

"No, thanks," I said.

"Why are you working out so much? You already look good, baby," he said.

I thanked him and gave him a kiss.

Chapter Thirty-five

Tanya

I went and signed Davon up for summer school. I was so mad it had to come out of my pocket for this shit. But I wasn't going to let him get left down.

"Listen, Davon, you are going to go here and you are going to listen and learn. If I get one phone call I'm going to fuck you up."

"Yes," he said.

"All you got to do is shut up and pay attention and you will pass. It is not that difficult. Don't make me waste my money on this if you're not going to do the right thing. Do you want to be in the same grade again?"

"No," he answered.

"Then go to class. You better fucking pass."

I had another dream about Barry. I was talking to him, telling him I loved him and wanted to be his wife. Then I asked him for some money and he pulled it out and this girl walked up and said, "How you going to give her money, Barry? I need that money to buy our baby stuff."

I turned around and looked at Barry. He said he didn't have no baby by her and he ain't buying her baby shit. "Is that your baby, Barry?" He didn't say anything and just as he was about to answer me I bashed the girl in the head with my fist, but only I couldn't hit her hard enough. My punches were weak. She kept laughing at me and when I looked up, Barry was gone. I got out of bed, turned on the light, went in my closet, and pulled out my photo album. I flipped through the pages and found the pictures of me and Barry. Sometimes I think I'm going to forget what Barry looks like. One picture we were at Davon's first birthday party at Chuck E. Cheese. Another was a Polaroid picture from the arcade when I was pregnant with Deja. I miss Barry so much. Why was he taken away from me? I think sometimes about the what-ifs. What if I was there and I could have made him duck the bullet or warned him? Or if we would have been out somewhere instead of him being with Moe? Then none of this would have happened and everything would be okay. He would be here and I wouldn't have to do nothing. I heard a knock on the door. I went downstairs and peeked out the window to see who it was. It was Ms. Tee for Mom-Mom.

Ms. Tee was my grandmom's best friend; she lived across the street. Ms. Tee was a light pecan color with jet-black, wavy hair. She had a solid thick build and a slight limp. Ever since I could remember she always wore a lot of jewelry. I thought she was rich when I was younger. She had a bunch of golden bracelets that sang a tune every time she walked. Gold hoop earrings and five necklaces that went from smaller to larger around her neck. I opened the door and said, "Ms. Tee, my grandmother's not here."

"Do you know where she went?"

"No, she didn't tell me."

"Well, tell her I stopped by. You know Nene just had her baby? That makes five."

"Five."

"Yup, I told her she can't come back and stay with me. She better try to make it work with this one's dad."

"Okay, Ms. Tee," I said as I closed the door. I don't know why she sat up here and told me about Nene. She knows we can't stand each other. I hated her granddaughter Nene. Me and Nene used to get into fights all the time when we were young. She used to dress and act like an old-fashioned grandmom was raising her. My grandmom kept my clothes up to date and in style because she was a little fly herself.

That little bitch gave me the roughest time when I first moved in with my grandmother. She kept bothering me all day at school. She kept telling people I started school in the middle of the year because my mom was on the pipe. She was so jealous of me because I had nice clothes and pretty hair. I kept telling that girl to mind her business, but she kept running her big mouth. She knew my business because of her grandmom. Next thing I remember I was at lunch and a boy name Jermaine said there was going to be a fight after school. I asked him who was fighting and that's when he said, "Nene and you, dummy." The time was 2:49. I was about to piss on myself. School was out and everybody was gathering to see the fight. I started walking and everybody started following me. The crowd got larger and larger. Kids that didn't even go to our school joined the fifty or more students in the crowd. Someone yelled, "Who's fighting?"

"Nene and some new girl," yelled another back in the crowd.

I was the one fighting and somehow had made my way to the back of the fight procession. I was ready to sneak off and run the other way. Before I had the chance the swarm of kids who needed to go home and do some homework, instead of watching a fight, parted. And from the other side came Nene punching her fist into the palm of her other hand. In fear, I dropped my book bag, just looked Nene in her face, and was trying to think of a plan. I didn't get a chance though. Someone pushed me into Nene. Then I recall closing my eyes and swinging really hard. I didn't feel or hear anything. Then I noticed I was getting help, but where was it coming from? I didn't know anyone, that is, except for this other girl from our neighborhood named Shaylene. She was like two grades ahead of us. I fell to the ground, opened my eyes, and saw Shaylene beating Nene in her head and pulling all her hair out.

The only thing that saved that girl was the whistling of the lunch aides' whistles. I located my bag and was out and so was everybody else. Wasn't nobody trying to get caught by those Lunch Aides so they could get suspended.

Somehow me and Shaylene made it to my house at the same time. We were both out of breath. We sat on the steps and caught our breath. I was huffing and puffing. Then that's when Shaylene said, "You was kicking Nene's ass."

"So, why you jumped in it?" I asked as I punched her in her arm. "Now everybody going to say I can't fight," I said.

"Nobody ain't going to say that."

"Yes, they is," I said. I didn't know a lot about fighting, but I did know you shouldn't get help, especially when you were winning.

"Girl, don't worry about me jumping in your fight. Be concerned about her telling your grandmother on you."

"How she gonna find out?"

"I don't know, but if she do, the lie is that she was getting the best of you. If you need me to tell your grandmother, I will tell her what happened. Just knock on my door."

"Okay, thanks."

I never thought twice about Nene telling, 'cause she was tough and the Lunch Aides didn't catch up with us, so we were cool. At least that's what I thought.

As soon as Mom-Mom got off work, Ms. Tee was at the door with Nene. And she had a black eye. I wondered who did that, me or Shaylene? Either way it didn't matter. She got her ass whooped. I ran into my room. Then I came out into the hallway so I could hear what was going on. Peeping downstairs, I heard Nene lying, saying I said her grandmother was fat, and she was defending herself when I punched her in the eye. Mom-Mom looked up the steps and saw me and said, "Tanya Lewis, get your ass down here."

I came down the steps.

"Now what happened? Why is this girl's eye black?" my grandmother asked as she held her hand in my face.

I was shaking, I thought Mom-Mom was going to hit me. She said get over here, right here. I came a little closer, but jumped back when I reached her. Then I told her the truth. "Mom-Mom, she's lying. She was at school all day saying my mom was a piper and smoker on drugs and that's why I started school in the middle of the year. Then she asked to fight me after school. Shaylene saw it and she broke it up."

Ms. Tee looked over at Nene and smacked her right in her lip. She had a red swollen lip to match her black eye.

"Why you do that, Grandma?" Nene cried.

"'Cause you don't be talking about nobody's mom when your mom is on drugs too! You want to make fun of some- one, make fun of the way your ass is on punishment for the next week.

"Sorry about that Henrietta. I'll call you later after the numbers go off." Ms. Tee walked across the street with her slight limp. I couldn't believe Nene's mom was doing drugs too!

After that day, I tried to be Nene's friend, but she was too mean. I asked her to play double Dutch with me and this other fat girl named Ieasha, who always had candy. Nene played with us. That is, until it was her time to jump. She didn't even get to "Big Mac Filet a Fish jumping." She couldn't jump, so she got mad at us. She snatched the rope and it almost smacked me in my face. She said, "This is my rope and I don't want to play anymore."

By then I would tell her, why don't she go across the street, her and her dumb rope? That's when me and Ieasha would start playing by ourselves. I would bring out my Barbies. I had the Barbie pool and dollhouse; my grandmom bought me whatever I wanted. Nene would usually just look at us from across the street with her lips poked out, looking mad. Then she would be back across the street about a half hour later and apologize and we'd play like nothing ever hap- pened. Until she got in my face again.

And now, to think she has five kids and still managed to get her shit right to be trying to go to school. And I thought I had too many kids. Well if she can do it I know I can. She is not as smart as me. Maybe one day I'll go to one of them schools.

Chapter Thirty-six

Janelle

I called home. My little brother Taron answered. "Where's Mommy? She didn't get home from work yet?"

"No, she's not here. I'm home by myself."

"Where's Jamal?"

"He went to his friend's house to do a project."

"You get the jerseys I sent y'all?"

"Oh yeah, I wanted to ask you, can you ask Damon if he can get Ricky Williams to sign my jersey? Because it will be worth a lot of money on eBay."

"No, I can't do that. Just be happy with what I sent you."

"Man, you make me sick. Don't nobody want no stupid jersey without an autograph on it."

"You are so ungrateful. Bye, Taron." I was looking for Kelly. I called her voice mail and I got this weird message. "Hello, you have reached Solel Flowers. Thank you for calling. Please leave your name and number and we will contact you as soon as we can." I called Kelly at home.

"Why do you have that flower message on your answering machine?"

"Oh, Janelle, I can't go to the mall with you. I'm doing an investigation right now."

"What are you talking about?"

"I found Carl's cell phone bill and I'm calling every number and girl on there."

"How do you know they all are girls?"

"Because every number I dial, I get a woman's answering machine."

"Really?"

"I even got a bitch talking in Vietnamese, somebody else that sounded French. I'll tell you one thing, he does not discriminate."

"Was there any black girls?"

"Not yet, but you know he doesn't date black girls, no offense."

"None taken. Dame told me that. Are you okay?"

"Yeah, I'm fine. I just . . . it's hard to say. I just tell you *men ain't shit, they ain't shit.*"

"So, what are you going to do?"

"I called the number he called the most and the latest at night. I left a message saying that Mr. Carl Stanton would like to send you a floral arrangement, and we need the correct address. When she calls back I'm going to go right to her house and tell her to leave him alone."

"You are crazy! Calm down. I'll come over."

I got to the house and you would have thought that Kelly was working for the FBI. She had bills strategically placed around the room. She highlighted and circled dates and times. She put one asterisk next to calls after 11:00 p.m. and two asterisks next to calls that lasted for over fifteen minutes.

"So what have you come up with?"

"I'm still waiting for her to call back."

"What even made you think to do all this?"

"I heard it on the radio once. The DJ called a man to see who he would send the roses to. And when the man was cheating he would always send them to the other woman."

Kelly's cell phone rang and she answered, "Hello, Solel Flowers." She put her cell on speaker. I heard a woman say, "I'm Marisol and you need my address."

"Hi. Yes, you are so lucky. The flowers are beautiful. What is your address? Eighteen twenty-two Northwest Terrance Drive? Okay, the flowers will be right there." She picked up her bag. I didn't know why I even went with her. I guess I went to make sure she didn't get mad and beat the girl up or anything.

We drove to the house. A young Spanish-looking girl came to the door. "Hi, are you Marisol?"

"Yes, who are you?"

"I'm Carl's girlfriend."

The girl looked startled then she began crying. "He said you were his housekeeper. I saw you ride by in his car. He said that he doesn't like white girls and that you keep his place clean for him."

"Well, he is lying. I am his girlfriend."

"Well, I'm sorry. I feel bad," she said.

We left the girl's house and Kelly called Carl. She screamed, "Who is Marisol? What? No, you listen! I will go home! I don't have to deal with this." She hung up her phone. She said that Carl said he was going to call her back.

"This shit is crazy. Are you going home?" I asked.

"Hell no! What do I look like? All of them cheat. It is what it is. Please, I'm just going shopping on his ass. I need a few bags and shoes. Don't you need a few things at my treat?"

"Okay."

"Let's go to the spa too!"

We went to this rooftop spa called Cloud Nine. I got a deep tissue massage and it put me right to sleep. Then I got a botanical pedicure, a foot massage, and an aromatic manicure. My facial lasted almost an hour. I felt so good. Kelly had spent about a thousand dollars on our services. She needs to get mad at him more often, so I can get more free services.

I went home and Damon was sitting on the sofa watching ESPN. It was freezing in the house. "Dame, why do you have the air so cold?"

He hunched his shoulders at me like he didn't know why and continued to watch the television. I went to turn the thermostat up and saw that it was on fifty degrees. Damon must have bumped his head. I shook my head. Too much working out, I thought. I started making dinner. All that pampering made me so hungry. I made us turkey chops, string beans, and mashed potatoes. I nibbled off the food. I put bread in the oven. Damon entered the kitchen and gave me a kiss on my neck.

"What you making, pork chops?" he asked.

"No, these are turkey chops."

"I'm hungry too! Hurry up and finish."

"I'm almost finished."

"And remember, Janelle, you have to drive with me to Orlando to go to my cousin's wedding this weekend."

"You never said anything about a wedding this weekend."

"I did tell you like a month ago."

"No, you didn't, Dame. I got to find something to wear. I don't have anything to wear to meet your family."

"Janelle, it is Wednesday. You can find something by Saturday."

"Dame, did you know Carl was cheating on Kelly?"

"No! Why would you ask something like that?"

"Because Kelly found all these numbers today and she called the girls."

"Stay out of their business, Janelle, I mean it," he screamed in this ultramean voice.

"Okay, damn, Damon, calm down, you don't have to get like that." I fixed his plate and Damon sat without saying a word.

"How is your food?"

"It's okay. It's hot in here," he said as he took off his shirt.

"I turned the air off."

"What! Don't turn the air down again," he said angrily.

"Damon, it was ice-cold in here." He got up from the table and began walking toward the door. "Where you going?" I asked.

"I'll be back."

Chapter Thirty-seven

Natalie

I got on the scale this morning and got the shock of my life. I had gained back five of my eleven pounds messing around with Anthony. He always wants to order out and feed me. He got me eating bad again, chilling, not going to workout class, and just being lazy.

I had to get back on my missions. One with this diet situation and the other with really posting my resume online. I wanted to get on the Internet and check employment Web sites. The minute I signed on to AOL, baby Anthony began to cry. "Anthony, could you get him out of his crib until I get off the computer?"

"No, I'm watching television," he yelled.

"Anthony, please."

"Bring him here," Anthony said.

"I'm on the computer. Come get him, Anthony," I said.

"Man, I'm tired. If you want me to watch him, come down the steps and bring him to me."

I brought him downstairs into the living room and then Anthony said, "Can you get me some juice while you're down here?" He turned back toward the television. I curled my lip up at him. I went into the kitchen and poured him some juice, slammed it on the floor by his foot, and went back upstairs. *Oh, he gets on my nerves,* I thought.

I got on the computer and I posted my resume to a few sites. I hope somebody calls me for a job, because I don't know how long I can deal with my mom and her clients. I hated washing those women's hair. They wanted me to wash three and four times. They complained too much, aggravated me. They brought their own special shampoo to the shop and would tell me to use a little. Or another didn't want too much perm on their edges and wanted me to use a big-tooth comb or their hair was going to fall out. Sometimes I wanted to say shut up and do your own hair.

I continued to search through job listings and temporary agencies. I wasn't even sure what kind of work I was looking for. I just wanted anything that paid money. I heard my cell phone ring. I looked around the room for it. It was Tanya.

"Hey, Natalie, just wanted to check on you."

"I'm okay. What have you been up to?"

"Nothing much. You know Deja's birthday coming up at the end of the month?"

"July thirtieth, right?"

"Yeah, I might need you to take me shopping for the party, okay?"

"Yeah, just call me when you're ready. What's Davon been up to."

"His ass is in summer school."

"Call me when you need me," I said.

"I thought you were on the computer," Anthony yelled as he entered the bedroom.

"I am on the computer."

"No, you're not. You're on the phone running your mouth."

"Tanya, I'll talk to you later," I said as I ended the conversation.

"Yeah, I know, your slave master is back. Bye."

Chapter Thirty-eight

Tanya

Deja's birthday was next week and I was still undecided on where and what kind of party to give her. At a hotel party the kids could go swimming and jump on the bed. And in the morning all I had to do was walk out the door. I didn't have to clean or any of that. Monica had given her daughter one last year. I went onto the porch and called Deja from down the street.

"Deja, what kind of party do you want?" I asked her.

"I want a tea party."

A tea party was out. I couldn't get into all that. "What kind of party do you want other than a tea party? How about Chuck E. Cheese or Fun Zone?"

"Mommy, I want a skating party."

"Okay, I'll call the skating rink." She ran back down the street. My mom-mom got mad at me for letting them play outside before twelve. I didn't care as long as she didn't go into anybody's house or run into the street. Davon was outside and was watching her. They weren't going off the block.

I called the skating rink. I had to pay ten dollars per kid. They said I couldn't bring my own food and I had to buy their cake and two pizzas. I didn't care what they said, I was still bringing my own food in. What are they going to do, take the food away from me? Later on when I get dressed I'm going to go down there and pay.

I kept all my money in a shoe box under my bed. I didn't have a bank account.

I pulled out three hundred. My stash has never gone under a thousand dollars. When Barry was alive he would say you have to have a savings, and then you got to have a backup savings fund. It was something his grandmother taught him. It's something I have lived by.

Walei took me shopping today. He was easy money, but he also was a headache. He kept calling me all day long. I wanted to tell him not to call me anymore. Instead I got him to take me and the kids to Great Adventure. He paid for everything. We spent the entire day in the water park and the evening in the regular park. Deja was scared and too short to get on the roller coasters. I had to take her to the kid part of the amusement park.

Walei was good with the kids, talking to them and buying them whatever they wanted. We took pictures and Davon won three teddy bears. The kids fell asleep during the ride home. They had a really good time. I was really being a good mom. I was nodding off myself, when Walei nudged me and said, "Tanya, I have to talk to you."

"Walei, I'm sleeping. What?"

"I have to talk to you."

"About what?"

"I might be leaving. Going back home. I was here on a student F-1 visa. It was an extension visa, good for one year. Unless I find a job and get industrial experience or a petition H-1 visa from an employer or get married, I might be going home. They are going to deport me."

"Just tell them you are looking for a job."

"Ah, Tanya, no, it's not that simple."

"What do you want me to do?"

"Nothing, Tanya. I just wanted to let you know."

Well I'm not marrying you, I thought.

Chapter Thirty-nine

Tanya

I had to go shopping for Deja's party. I wanted everything to be perfect. Natalie took me. I had a few stops to make. I told her I would give her a couple of dollars. She said that she didn't have anywhere to go. I went to the market and then the dollar store. I ran into Nene. She gave me her number and told me to call her 'cause she had something major to tell me. I finished up my shopping and for some reason Natalie had an attitude with me. I gave her twenty dollars and fed her baby; she better get out of my face.

I went to Monica's house. She wasn't home, so I sat and waited for her. Alexis said she had gone to make a run with her old head. He was this married dude that gave her money. Her daughters were upstairs doing each other's hair and practicing dance moves. They were both home because they got in trouble for fighting the day before.

The phone rang. I answered it and heard a recorded message saying you have a collect call from Derrick. If you wish to accept, press one. If you wish to deny this collect call, please hang up or press two. Then the recording said the same message in Spanish. I pressed one and accepted the call. I heard a pause and Derrick was on the line. Derrick was Monica's twin brother. He had gotten locked up for a gun a couple of years ago.

"What's up, Tanya? Where's my twin at?" Derrick asked.

"With her friend."

"How you?"

"Fine," I said.

"Yo, I have been trying to call. Y'all always ain't home or her line always be busy. She need to get herself some call waiting. So how's the kids?"

"They doing good."

"Where my nieces at?"

"Upstairs doing each other's hair in their room."

"Well, I need you to do me a favor. I need you to get one of your cute girlfriends to write me, and I want you to write my bawh, Darnell."

"I'm not writing nobody unless they are about to come home."

"I know, I know, here he go." Before I could say no, he had put him on the phone.

"Yo, who this?"

"What you mean who this? This is Tanya."

"Tanya, where you from?"

"North Philly."

"Where at?"

"Off of Twenty-ninth Street."

"By Lehigh Ave?" he asked.

"Yeah, why?"

"I know you." I got a little scared and asked him how he knew me.

"You used to go with my brother Jay."

"Yeah, we used to deal. How's he doing?"

"You know he got killed about six months ago?"

"No, I hadn't talked to him in so long. I didn't know he was dead. Sorry to hear that."

"I'm sorry, I thought you knew."

"How did he die?" I asked.

"In a car accident. This guy he was hanging with, this

young bawh, was high on some wet and the cops tried to pull them over. The dickhead tried to lose the cops and hit a pole on Girard Avenue."

"I heard about that."

"Yeah. Well, maybe you can drop me a line or come see me."

"I don't do the jail visits, but I'll see you when you get home. I'll hook you up with somebody," I said.

"All right then."

Derrick got back on the line. "So what's up, Tanya?"

"Nothing."

"Barry's brother Moe is upstate tripping. They then put his ass in the psych ward. He lost his fucking mind. He be swinging at shit that ain't even there."

"Moe been crazy. I don't give a fuck. That nigga killed Barry."

"I heard that. I get out in a few weeks."

"I didn't know that."

"Yup, I'm counting my days down. I'm going to cut hair when I get out."

"I'll tell Monica you called."

I hung up the phone and thought about Jay being dead. Everybody I know is dying or getting killed. Shit is fucked up out here. And Moe fucking swinging at shit. He is only getting paid back for taking Barry away.

I fell asleep on the sofa. Sabrina and Alexis were still upstairs. One of them was in the shower and I heard keys jingling in the door. I thought it was Monica, but it was Lil' Ron. I was startled.

"You scared me," I said.

"Where is Monica?" he asked.

I made up a bullshit lie and said that Monica went downtown. He said okay and then walked straight up the steps. He went into Monica's room. I heard some movement and fumbling above my head. I heard Alexis scream and then the bathroom door slam. Then he came down the steps and said, "All right then," and left out.

I locked the door, went upstairs, and knocked on the bath-room door.

"Did he see you naked?" I asked.

"No, he almost did. He always just walks right in the bathroom without knocking. The door be closed, so I don't know why he still come in."

"I don't like Lil' Ron," I said.

As soon as Monica walked through the door, I said, "Lil' Ron should not be able to run in and out of your house. You shouldn't be letting him leave shit here either, especially with your daughters. They are getting big. He almost walked in on Alexis today. You holding his shit?"

"No, it's not like that."

"Watch your shit, Monica."

"I'm good. Lil' Ron is not keeping anything here and me and my daughters talk. They know if a man tries to touch them they would tell me. He didn't know they were home today."

"Is he still dealing with his baby's mom?"

"I don't know and I don't care."

I saw that Monica was getting upset, so I dropped the subject.

"Um, you dumb-ass bitch."

"Mind your business, bitch."

"Oh well, when one of your daughters be pregnant and Lil' Ron is the pop, don't get mad at me," I said as I laughed.

"Yeah, whatever," she said.

The skating rink where I had the party was the same place Natalie got her earrings stolen when we were young, like fourteen or fifteen. We were on our way home and these guys pulled up to us in this decent car. We thought they were trying to get with us, 'cause we looked good. We were all happy and thinking we were grown. They asked us if we needed a ride home. We said no and kept walking. Then one of the guys got out and said, "How you doing, baby?" to

Natalie and then he snatched her earrings out her ears. The guy jumped back in the car and they pulled off. Natalie's ears were bleeding really bad. She still has the scars on her earlobes. We used to have some good times. We used to cut school and run home to answer the phone before the school's automated system called our house.

Everyone showed up on time. Mom-Mom, Monica with her daughters, Natalie with her baby, all the kids on my grandmother's block, and Davon and his friends. Everybody ate pizza and skated. When the kids weren't skating, they were playing games and getting on the little rides. Deja was having a good time. She told me that it was her "bestest" birthday ever.

Natalie was still a little mad at me for almost making her baby choke. Deja enjoyed herself and all the kids had fun. Davon's birthday is coming up in September and he said he wants a Spider-Man or Sponge Bob Square Pants party.

Chapter Forty

Natalie

Tanya needs to buy herself a car. She asked me to take her shopping for Deja's party. I didn't have anything planned and she said she had one stop, which was Pathmark. I told her I was going to sit in the car. I didn't feel like getting out, it was too hot. I had my air on. She said fine, I'll be right out. I was sitting for an hour, waiting in the parking lot for her to come out of the market. I was about to cry. I hate when people take advantage of a good thing. Then her ass went into the fucking dollar store and the party store, and took another thirty minutes. Then last but not least she got back in the car, asked me to pop my trunk so she could put all her bags in, and asked me to take her to get a cake off Twenty-second Street. She made me so mad.

I said, "Tanya, I didn't think I was going to be out this long. I need to feed Anthony and change his Pamper."

"Okay, pull over. I'll get him something to eat." She went into this corner store for ten minutes and came out with a damn cheeseburger.

"My baby only got four teeth. How the hell is he going to eat a burger, Tanya?"

"You can feed it to him by chewing it up for him; that is how I use to feed Deja and Davon."

"How is that going to happen? I'm driving. I can't feed him while I drive."

"Well, I'll feed him," she said as she crawled in the back of the car with him. I was cool with that. She did buy him some Pampers. She changed him while she was back there. I looked at her through the rearview mirror.

"He can't eat that," I said as she gave my baby a big piece of bread.

"Yes, he can."

"No, he can't," I said as Anthony began to gag. I pulled over again because I thought he was choking. I took him out of his car seat and patted his back. He began to cry and I knew he was okay. And all Tanya's selfish ass could offer me was a "sorry."

"Bitch, you sorry you almost killed my son."

"Come on now. You getting too excited about nothing."

"What? All you can think about is yourself. I'm not your personal chauffeur. You had me waiting for you all day. The world does not revolve around you, and don't ask me to take you anywhere ever again in life."

"I gave you money, so shut up and drive me home," she said.

I really didn't want to bring Anthony to the skating party. He couldn't skate and I just was basically out of it. But I wanted to be supportive of Tanya. I bought Deja a Barbie doll and a Dora the Explorer book bag and books. I couldn't disappoint Deja or Tanya, so I dragged myself out of bed and went to the skating rink.

It was noisy and crowded with a bunch of kids pushing, shoving, and falling. I didn't get any skates. I walked over to Tanya's table. She had party favors and was handing out food and soda. I said hello to everyone.

"Hi, Ms. Henrietta."

"How you doing, Natalie? Look how big that boy got.

Come to me, baby," she said as she held her arms out. "Your coming down nicely, baby."

"Thank you. I'm trying," I said as I went to get a slice of pizza off the table and pour from the pitcher of Sprite. I was cheating on my diet again. I would work if off later.

I was proud of Tanya, she was really being a mom. Davon had come up to me and patted me from behind. I turned around and said, "Hey, Davon, how you doing?"

"Okay, your baby's getting big." Then he skated away and played with his friends. There wasn't much for me and Anthony to do. I put him on a car ride. He seemed like he liked it okay. He wasn't scared. I wanted to put him on some other rides. I dug in my pocket and pulled out two twenty-dollar bills. Anthony leaned over and almost fell. I caught him just before he reached the ground. I turned back around and in my hand I only had one twenty. I looked around on the ground. I dug in my pocket to see if I had put the money back. I lifted Anthony to make sure it wasn't under him. I didn't see it. I looked everywhere. I couldn't believe I had lost my money. Just as soon as I was going to chalk it up as lost, I heard a little boy say to another boy, "Look, that's a twenty-dollar bill." I walked over to him before he could pick it up all the way and said, "Thank you, that's my money, I just dropped it." The little boy gave me a look like *bitch, please.*

"This my money. I found it," the watermelon head boy said.

"Excuse me, little boy. That's my money. You just picked it up. I was standing right here."

"No, I didn't. Man, you better get out of here," he said.

His little friend next to him said, "He been had that money."

"Where is your mother?" I asked.

"Man, we out."

The little boys ran to the other side of the rink. I asked Ms. Heniretta to watch the baby and went to find the little boys. I wasn't even mad about the twenty dollars. I was mad that this little boy thought he was going to take my money. I walked across the rink to the other side. I spotted the little boys sitting at another birthday table. I saw an adult. I said, "Hi, is that your son?"

She said, "No, why?"

"He just picked up my money."

"That's his mom over there," she said as she pointed to this tall lady.

The lady turned around as I approached her and the little boy said, "Mom, that's the lady that try to take my money from me."

"No, I did not," I said as I looked over at the little boy. I couldn't believe he was lying on me. "Listen, your son just picked up my money."

"Yeah, well, once it touch the ground it didn't belong to you anymore." A few kids had started gathering around to be nosey.

"Excuse me?" I said.

"You heard me, I teach my kids finders keepers. If it is on the ground it's not yours anymore. Plus, he been had that money. I gave it to him."

Tanya walked up and asked me what happened and I told her. She was ready to take it to the lady and get my twenty dollars back. I reminded her it was her daughter's birthday. The lady walked away with her son. Tanya called her a broke bitch and she didn't say anything.

After the skating party I cooked Anthony a great big dinner of stuffed chicken, greens, and macaroni and cheese, even though I had already eaten. You would think his ass would be like "my wife cooked, let me do the dishes." No, he didn't think that way. He finished his plate, left everything on the table, and went to his home on the sofa.

"Anthony, can you clean the table off and do the dishes? I'm washing the baby and putting him to sleep."

"I'm tired," he whined. At first, I didn't say anything. I wasn't trying to start. But Anthony had slowly reverted to the same old good-for-nothing, lazy, funky-ass Anthony I had left. I fucking cooked and cleaned, and this motherfucker won't even do the dishes? *I hate him,* I thought.

"Anthony, why can't you do something around this house?"

"Because I pay bills and work hard. So I'm not lifting a thing."

"What?" I just took Anthony out of the tub, dried and lotioned him, and brushed his hair. I turned the television on and slammed the door. I picked up the phone and overheard Anthony talking to his mother about me. It was never going to end. She would always be in our business. Anthony was dumb. He didn't even hear me pick up the phone. I pushed the Mute button. I could hear Ms. Renee crystal-clear, saying, "I told you not to go back to that girl. She is nothing but a whore. You don't need a whore, son, you need a good Christian woman. A good woman will do the dishes and clean the house." Anthony said a few okays, and yeah, Mom, I know. She said, "Anthony, I love you and I'm telling you the truth."

I was pissed the fuck off. I came down the stairs and yelled, "Anthony, why are you telling your mom our business?"

"What, I didn't tell her anything."

"Anthony, I heard you. Don't tell your mom about what is going on in this house. Choose me or your mom."

"Get out of here with that. She is my mom, you're my wife. I don't have to choose."

"Oh yes, you do."

"I'm not choosing."

"You will choose. You don't have a choice, Anthony!"

Chapter Forty-one

Janelle

The Pro-Player Stadium was large and loud. Everybody had blue, green, and orange on. The wives and girl-friends sat at club level. We were close enough to see the players, but far enough so that they couldn't see us and we weren't a distraction. My seat was really good, but I couldn't see everything because I didn't have my contacts in. I have to go get new contacts.

"Welcome to the Pro," Kelly said.

"It's nice in here," I said.

"I hope Amber does not bring her kids. They are so annoying! She thinks it's just adorable when they say rude things," Kelly said as she looked in her compact and touched up her makeup.

"That's not right."

"No, really, I'm not in the mood for bad kids."

I laughed at Kelly.

The game started. Everyone was excited when the players ran onto the field. Damon wasn't on the starting lineup, so he didn't get his name called. I knew a little about football. I watched the game and listened to all the other women yell at the refs and say how good somebody's butt looked in tights.

I wasn't looking that hard. The cheerleaders ran onto the field in their skimpy aqua-colored shorts and half shirts.

"Look at those airheads. All they are is groupies with pom-poms and too much makeup on." Everybody starting laughing at Kelly's comment.

"Everybody knows they don't make any money. They need to get a real job and stop trying to entice players," she continued.

"This one girl I know, she used to cheer for the Chargers and now she is married to one of the players." Amber said.

"They are not supposed to date," Lisa said.

"Well, they kept it a secret until they got serious. Then once they became engaged she quit the squad," Amber said.

"Like I said, groupies with poms-poms," Kelly said again as everyone laughed.

At halftime I finally got to meet the infamous Dana. She had on sexy high-heeled sandals. Her legs were perfect. I could see why everybody hated her. She was gorgeous. She was at a game dressed as if she were in a nightclub. She came up to me and said, "Hello, you must be Damon's new girlfriend. Nice to finally meet you. I heard so much about you."

I wanted to know what she had heard. I couldn't come out and say, "What have you heard?" So I teased and said, "Like what?"

"Don't worry, it all has been good. I heard you were from Philadelphia. I'm from D.C."

"Really?" I said.

"You guys get cold winters like us."

"Yeah. I hate any weather under thirty degrees."

"I bet you won't miss the cold this year."

"No, I won't."

Dana looked around and said, "I hate it up here. It's really not like being at a real game. It's more like being at a social event. I like sitting outside and really getting into the crowd and game, ya know?"

"This is my first game. It's okay so far," I said.

"Before Bobby I hated football too. I didn't know the difference between an interception and a field goal. I hated Sundays because any guy I was dating just wanted to watch football, then they wouldn't listen to me."

Everything they said about Dana was wrong. She seemed really nice and friendly. Kelly, Lisa, and Amber had said that she was a bitch.

Out of nowhere Dana said, "These women want to be your friend when everything is going right in your relationship. If you're not careful they will introduce their sister or cousin to your man. Kelly did it to me. I went home for the weekend. The next thing I know she has her sister down here going on double dates with my boyfriend. It's crazy. Then you have these women that want to be your friend because they want you to hook them up with a teammate. It's so much bull, ya know?"

"That's crazy," I said as I continued to listen to Dana ramble on and her "ya knows." Then she said, "And if you are not married, they think you're just a fling that is hanging around, and you can go at any point. I disagree, but like I said, watch your back. Damon's last girlfriend, Alicia, was good for telling them off. That's why they are so happy she's gone. You know she was a bisexual, that was a scandal. Damon got teased in the locker room for that one."

"He told me that," I said. Dana saw Lisa coming, so she changed the subject.

Lisa came over all smiles and said, "Janelle, I wanted to know if you wanted to volunteer at our celebrity auction coming up. We auction off the men for charity. It's a few weeks away."

I told her I would let her know. She cut her eyes at Dana. Dana turned the other way and ignored her. We won the game 16–5 over Jacksonville.

Chapter Forty-two

Tanya

"Tanya, I got a job offer in San Diego. We could get married and your children could go to school out there. Think it over, okay? We would have a great life."

"No. There is nothing to think about." Walei was leaving and I didn't care. He just gave me money. He was upset, ready to cry and shit. I told him to call me when he got settled and good luck with his job.

I called the girl Nene to see what was up. She had said she had something major to tell me. "Hello, can I speak to Nene?"

"She ain't here. She's at work."

"Ms. Tee, is that you?" I asked.

"Yes, who is this?"

"This is Tanya."

"Nene's at work. She got a job that pays her eighteen bucks an hour, a good job at the hospital."

"Really?"

"Yes, she finally graduated from that school after the baby was born. Took her long enough. You should try to go, Tanya."

"I'll ask Nene about the information. Tell her I called

her." Dag, she got all those kids and she still went back to school? That is what's up.

Nene returned my call later that afternoon.

"Hey, Tanya, what's up?"

"Nothing."

"My grandmom told me you called."

"Yeah, I did. I wanted to see what was up. You said you had something major to tell me."

"Oh yeah, right. You still be with Monica?"

"Yeah, we all right." I said I wanted to see what gossip she had on Monica. She always had dirt and stayed in some bullshit, some things never change. I listened as she said, "I heard she fucked with the bawh Lil' Ron. I'm friends with his baby's mom's cousin, Sheena. Sheena said that he be talking about Monica like a dog. He said she a stank pussy bitch. He said that she's a freak that just likes to suck dick, take it in the ass, and fuck everybody. She supposed to be pregnant, right?"

"I don't think so."

"Well, she told him she was and he said that it wasn't his baby, and that it was a south Philly baby."

"Really?" I said as Nene fed me more scoop.

"Yeah, girl. He be telling her I just leave my guns and shit at her house."

"Well, I don't know about all that. Let me call Monica and get her on the line."

I tried calling her and her answering machine came on. I hung up and said to Nene, "Well, if it's true, that shit is on her 'cause I warned her. That nigga do be over there all the time. And I don't like him around her daughters." She was about to get evicted. He didn't even pay her rent. Nene tried to change the conversation and asked me if I go out.

"Yeah, I go out, but I'm slowing down a little right now."

"Well, maybe we can go out sometime."

"Maybe. Oh yeah, Ms. Tee said you have a new job and you went to a nursing school."

"I did, I'll give you the number. Hold on, let me find it."
Nene came back on the phone and gave me the number to
the school. I called right away. It was a nursing assistant program, the woman said over the phone. I needed a high
school diploma or a GED and their next class began in
September. I knew Nene didn't have a high school diploma.
She had dropped out before me. Maybe she did go back and
get her GED.

I took a nap and decided I would call Nene later. I didn't
want her to think I was sweating her for information. Mom-
Mom said that Monica was downstairs. I told Mom-Mom to
send her up.

Monica walked into my room and said, "Let me tell you
one thing, bitch. The next time you want to try to play me
and talk about me behind my back, at least turn your cell
phone off."

"What are you talking about?"

"I'm talking about everything you said about me to Nene.
I heard you all on my answer machine talking dirty about
me. You said that I was warned. And I was stupid for letting
Lil' Ron stash his shit there. And he don't pay my rent and
I'm about to get evicted. And he be looking at my daughters.
You need to worry about yourself."

"I did say it. Somebody needs to tell you, bitch. Your shit
is getting sloppy. He talks about you, saying you're pregnant
and you fuck with all these dudes. He's not giving you any
money and you're about to get evicted."

"Tanya, you fuck with a lot of dudes too!" she said
loudly.

"Yup, but every dude I get with gives me money."

"Bitch, you still live with your grandmother and you
don't have a car!"

"So what? If I wanted a car I could get one. You know I
get money, Monica, so why you going to try to sit here and
play me?" Monica put her funky French-manicure-need-a-
refill finger in my face. The situation was about to get critical
if Monica didn't get the fuck out of my face. Me and Monica

had fought before and I beat her ass. I wasn't in the mood today; plus, my grandmother was downstairs, otherwise I would knock her the fuck out and make her take back every word she just said. Stupid bitch. Her mouth was about to get her hurt. I stepped away from her and said, "I told you to your face that I don't like him. And that's on you if you keep dealing with him." I got up out of the bed.

"Well, I am going to keep dealing with him."

"Well, that is on your dumb ass."

"Whatever."

"Don't ever come in my grandmother's house and act like you want to say something to me. One, I wasn't trying to talk about you. Everything I said I told you to your face. You need to listen to all the shit Nene said Lil' Ron being saying about you." I walked her to the door.

Monica called me the next day like nothing had happened. I didn't say sorry to her and she didn't mention what had gone down. She wanted to let me know about Derrick's party.

My grandmother was playing her gospel music real loud and was on her way to church. She had cooked breakfast. I could smell the beef scrapple, pancakes, and eggs she makes every Sunday. Every so often, she comes into my room and asks me to join her. I always say I'm tired and maybe some other time. Occasionally she will take the kids with her. She came into my room this morning and said, "Tanya."

"I'm asleep," I said. Me telling her I was asleep still did not stop her from walking into my room.

"Mom-Mom, I'm asleep."

"Wake up! I have something I want you to do around the house." She had a list in her hand. I got out of the bed, looked at the list, and said, "I'll do it when I wake up."

"It's nine o'clock, you are up, and nobody sleeps past nine in this house. Tanya, I want those dishes done by the time I get back."

"Huh?"

"I didn't stutter. I want the dishes washed and the refrigerator cleaned out because I'm going to buy food after church."

"Mom-Mom, I can't do all that."

"You can and you will. If you don't clean up this house by the time I get back I'm going to put you out. Tell Deja and Davon to do the rest."

She walked out of my room. I got up and looked at the list again. It read *dishes, clean the refrigerator out, vacuum, dust, clean the bathroom, and take out the trash*. She is tripping! She won't have to put me out. I'll just spend a couple of days over at Monica's house and I'll be right back. I couldn't take the kids there because of all the drama. No matter how mad she gets she will never put the kids out.

Chapter Forty-three

Natalie

I put up with a lot of shit over the years with Anthony and his stupid mom. I used to let shit shake off me like okay, that lady is insane, she don't know any better. But she has gone too far. Today I came home and there was a message from her saying, "Anthony, call me when you get home. I was at church earlier today and I met a few nice decent wholesome ladies. I told them about you. I think you should meet one of them. I'm sure they wouldn't run away to Miami for the weekend. Well, call me when you get in and remember what I said, we need to get a blood test on that baby. That boy dark as the dickens and you light and that girl brown. That baby shouldn't be that dark."

I called my mother and let her hear the message. She said that Ms. Renee left that message for me to hear and for me not to fall into her trap. I wasn't going to fall into her trap, but Anthony better call her up and put her in her place once and for all. I'm sick of this mess.

Anthony came in, listened to the message, and said there was nothing wrong with it and I was overreacting.

"She said she wanted you to meet a new woman."

"She means well. I'll talk to her."

"Talk to her now, Anthony. I'm your wife. You going to let her disrespect me like that?"

"I'll talk to her," he said as he unwrapped a new game for his PlayStation.

I'm just done with Anthony. Maybe a divorce is the best thing for us. I have tried to make it work and he is not making any effort at all. I don't want to grow old with regret. I think Anthony's just not the man for me. I think he is feeling the vibe too. He looked at me this morning and said he had a feeling that I was going to start acting up. Sometimes I feel like he can read minds. Because how does he know I can't take his ass anymore? What was I thinking about when I got back together with him? Why did I want his ass back? I shouldn't have ever gotten back with him. There was a reason I snuck away to Miami, because I was not happy. He was making me miserable then and he is making me miserable now. It's not working out between us. I can't take him. The other night we were in bed and he farted. Then he dug up his nose and flicked it into the air. Then he went to rub my leg and I turned my back to him and pushed his hands away. I was not interested in him. I was tired of living a lie. This is never going to work, never, ever. We are too different and don't want the same things in life. He is satisfied with being a mechanic playing with his PlayStation 2 and car. And I want more out of life. Much more. I want to have another baby and go to school and just be happy. I know all marriages are not happy all year-round, but they're not supposed to be sad nine months out of the year either.

I sat down and wrote a list of all the reasons I wanted Anthony out of my life. So in case one day, when I get lonely and want him back, I can remember why I let him go. I hate the way he looks, and acts. I hate his mother. I hate the way he just wants to sit and watch television all day. He doesn't help out with the baby. He wants his way or the highway, spoiled motherfucker.

When Anthony comes home today I'm going to have his shit ready for him to leave.

I need to get on with my life. The one thing I learned from Janelle is that there are good men out there and I deserve one. She got a good man giving her the world and he is not even her husband. I'm going to find someone to make me happy, make me laugh, and love me. Here I am sitting around with this asshole for what? What the fuck do I need him for? Starting today, I'm going to change. I'm going to keep losing weight and I just have to get myself together for myself and my child.

I waited on the steps for him.

"Anthony, I want a divorce!" I screamed when he came through the door from work.

"Don't say that. You don't mean that," he said as he tried to hold me.

I pushed his hands off me and said, "No, I'm serious. I thought we could work all of our problems out, but it is obvious we can't. I can't take it anymore, I don't love you anymore. You make me miserable. I'm not the woman for you. The only woman you will ever love more than yourself is Renee Grant."

He tried to plead with me. Once he saw it was no use, he went upstairs and began moving. He hadn't even been home a full six weeks. Some of his boxes were still packed from when he moved back in. I didn't care, I couldn't take it anymore.

Chapter Forty-four

Janelle

Kelly and I made the four-hour drive to Raymond James Stadium for the game against the Tampa Buccaneers. I still hadn't figured Kelly out. She seemed like she was in love with Carl at times, other times just his money. This time we were going to sit in the crowd with all the fans. I had an extra set of tickets that Damon gave me.

"You have tickets. Give those away," she said. She pointed to these white guys in the ticket line. I saw a black man in the next line with his son. I gave them the tickets. The man said, "Thank you" and offered me money. I didn't accept the money and the man thanked me again.

I didn't really follow the game. There were so many different plays. Special teams, field goal, interception, punt return, it just didn't make sense and was boring. Especially if I didn't see Damon on the field. The one thing I was certain of is that we lost.

"This is the second loss. Carl is going to be in a bad mood," Kelly said. "They are always in a bad mood when they lose."

After the game I was prepared for Damon to be mad, but he was cool. I waited outside the visiting team locker room for him. Reporters were everywhere. He came out in a black tailored suit and light blue shirt. My baby looked good. Damon wasn't upset, he said it was only preseason and that it didn't mean anything. It was a Friday evening. "Let's go to the movies," he said. I was tired. I just wanted to go home.

When we got in the house Damon started screaming, "Janelle! Why don't you clean up around here?" There were only four dishes in the sink.

I looked at him like he was crazy. "There are only a few dishes and I'm not cleaning the bathroom. Damon, that's why we have a housekeeper."

"Man, you can clean up after yourself."

"Okay, Damon. I don't know what is going on with you, but you need to calm down. You're getting mad at me for no reason."

"Look, don't tell me what to do. As a matter fact, I need to leave for a while."

"Damon, calm down."

"No, you calm down," he said as he went into the bedroom and shut the door. I didn't know what I said or what was going on. And I didn't like it. I didn't do anything to him and he was snapping on me. I guess Damon was mad about the game and he needed somebody to take his anger out on.

Chapter Forty-five

Natalie

With Anthony gone I now had time to fantasize about my new man. I made a list of all the things I wanted him to be. I want a man that is not going to be up his mother's ass, that would be good. I want him to be loving and comforting. I want my man to be sweet and good. But I guess they all are good in the beginning. Anthony was so good at the start. Ms. Renee wasn't even a bitch until he asked me to marry him. That's when she went crazy and she said I was taking her son. I just hope one day I will fall in love again.

I was sitting watching *Brown Sugar*. I love that movie. The guy Boris Kudjo looks so good. He is tall and sexy. That's another thing I added to my list, I want a tall man. A man that can tower over me and make me feel secure. He also has to be able to fuck Anthony up if he gets out of line. My favorite part of the movie is when Boris Kudjo sends Sanaa Latham all of these roses. He also shut down the restaurant and cooked for her. A man that can cook. How *sexy* is that? I need a man to treat me like that, but maybe that's just in the movies. I don't think there are any sweet men out there like that. And if there are, his name is not Anthony Grant.

I fixed me and baby Anthony something to eat. He was walking, crawling, playing with his little truck. I had to go to my parents' and break the news about me and Anthony. I called their house and my father answered.

"Daddy, you going to be home?"

"Yes, why?"

"Because I got to come over and tell you and Mommy something."

"Your mother has clients downstairs and I'll be here."

I drove over to my parents' house. I called my mom from out of the basement. They both sat down at the kitchen table.

"Mommy, Daddy, it's not working out with Anthony. We are getting a divorce."

"Thank *God*. I thought you were going to say you were pregnant again," my mother said as she put her hands together.

My father looked over at my mother like *cut it out*, then back at me and said, "But you just got back together."

"I know, Daddy, but we just aren't compatible."

"Well, baby, we are here for you and baby Anthony."

My mom hugged me and said, "Natalie, I told you. You were too good for him."

"Okay, here's the problem. He might kick me out of the house," I said.

"That's not going to happen. You can take him to court and get alimony, child support, and that house."

"Well, if he kicks me out, can I move back in, Dad?"

"Of course, baby."

Chapter Forty-six

Tanya

Monica gave Derrick a coming-home party. All his friends came in and out. It was more like a get-together than an actual party.

Derrick looked like a different man. I hate to say it, but jail must have done something to him. His skin was clear, he had gained a few pounds and had muscles. He looked a lot better.

"I got a job already at the barber shop on Woodland Avenue. You should bring your boy down there," he said.

"I will," I said.

"My probation officer is cool as long as I'm working. I'm good. These streets are deadly. I'm good. All I want to do is raise my boy and live my life. I don't want anybody telling me when to eat, sleep, and drink. I'm never going back to jail."

"That's what's up," I said.

"This food tastes good," he said. "Somebody must have taught you how to cook, Monica, while I was away."

"Shut up, boy. I've been cooking for you your whole life."

"Where you working at, Tanya?" he asked.

"I'm not working right now."

"Yo, you need to get a job. When you don't work you get in trouble."

Between mouthfuls of macaroni, Derrick changed the subject and said, "I don't like the dude Lil' Ron, he is sneaky. He came up in my face on some what-up shit. I was like nigga, get the fuck away from me."

"Yeah, he ain't my favorite person either."

"My sister don't need no bad-news-ass nigga around her."

"I told her that."

"That's all right, I'm going to have my man step to him. He ain't running shit no more now I'm home. And he ain't going to fuck up my probation."

"You are crazy, Derrick." I said as I finished my plate.

I took Derrick up on his offer and went to get Davon's hair cut. I walked into the barbershop, and all heads turned as the bell on the door jingled when I opened it. One guy was sweeping, two others were cutting, but I didn't see Derrick. I asked one of the barbers where Derrick was.

"I don't think he's coming back, but if you want I can cut your son's hair. I have one more person."

I thought about it for a minute and decided to stay and get Davon's hair cut. He needed a haircut in the worst way. His hair was nothing like mine, his had a deep thick wave. Him and Deja take after Barry's side. I'm going to have to keep them little girls away from my son. He has smooth dark ebony skin, he's going to be a heartbreaker.

The guy had just started working at the barbershop. He was light brown, about six two, and looked good. His arms were nice and shapely. His name was Buc.

Buc finished cutting his client's hair. He said that Davon could have a seat. Davon got in the chair.

"How you want your hair cut, shorty?" he asked. Davon just shrugged his shoulders. Then Buc looked at me and asked me how I wanted his hair cut.

"Just low, but not a baldy."

Buc made small talk as he cut Davon's hair. He asked where I lived, was Davon my only child, and was I still with Davon's dad? He kept asking me so many questions. I had to tell him to mind his own business.

Then he looked down at Davon and said, "Why your mom got a smart mouth?"

"My mom don't have no smart mouth." Everybody in the barbershop started laughing.

He cut Davon's hair and I thumbed through a few sports magazines.

"You're all done, shorty," he said as he sprayed oil sheen in his hair and took the hair cape off him.

"Thank you for cutting his hair," I said as I stood up and gave Davon the money to walk over and pay Buc.

I washed me and the kids' clothes while Mom-Mom was at her bingo game. I know she would have told me to go to the Laundromat. She tries to say I'm not allowed to use her washer because I broke the last one by overloading clothes. I wasn't going to anyone's Laundromat. I emptied out Davon's and Deja's pockets. I got in the habit of emptying pockets. The last time I didn't, Deja left a crayon in her pocket and it ruined all of the clothes. I pulled Davon's pocket inside out and a ten-dollar bill dropped out. There was a white piece of paper balled up inside it. The paper read *The cut is on me and when you call me, so is dinner, Buc.*

Thanks for the free haircut, but I'm not calling you, I thought. Then I came up the stairs and called Monica's house to see if Derrick was there. She put him on the phone.

"What's up, Tanya?" he asked.

"Nothing. Why weren't you in the barbershop earlier?"

"I went to see my son. You know my baby's mom be tripping. Bring your boy through tomorrow."

"He already got a cut."

"Who cut his hair?"

"That guy Buc. Who is he anyway."

"Some bawh from VA. He is cool peeps, he's up here helping his grandmother out 'cause she sick."

"Oh."

"Why?"

"No reason. He just cut Davon's hair 'cause you wasn't there."

"All right then, I'm going to sleep, I'm so tired."

"Tell Monica I'm going to get with her later." I knew Buc sounded like he had a little drawl. I should call him. No, I ain't calling him, but I will keep his number just in case.

Chapter Forty-seven

Janelle

"**O**h my God, you don't have my size? Call one of your other stores," I cried out to the saleswoman.

"Our other store is in New York."

"I don't care! Call and see if they have them and have them sent to me." I wanted these Giuseppe Zanotti black, red, and yellow, calf-high, patent leather, and stiletto-heel sandals. The lady made some calls and said she would have them for me in two days. I had to pay for them and give her my address. Besides that dilemma, I didn't have anything to wear to meet Damon's family. It was the first time I was going to meet them and I didn't have anything presentable to wear. I had been in every store in the mall looking for the perfect outfit. I wanted something that said *classy*, but I still wanted to look youthful. I didn't want to come off as whorish either. We were going to a wedding. His cousin Benny or somebody was getting married.

I really couldn't find anything to wear. I called Damon and told him that I couldn't find anything to wear and that we would have to leave a little later.

"Janelle, you're becoming a little spoiled shopping diva. 'It's the end of the world Damon. I can't find anything to wear,' " he whined in a feminine tone.

"Shut up, Damon, this is not funny. I don't have anything to wear."

"Girl, please. You go shopping with Kelly every other day. I see about twenty-five things in the closet with tags still on them. So what are you talking about? I have to go. It's almost a four-hour drive and I'm in the wedding."

"Fine, Damon."

"I will leave you, Janelle."

"I don't care. Bye, Damon." If he leaves me, I don't care. He won't leave me.

I got home and saw Damon had actually left me. He had taken the train to Orlando. I couldn't believe it! He left me a note saying *If you change your mind, Janelle, call my aunt Blondell. She will tell you how to get here. Damon.* I was so angry about Damon leaving me I began to cry. I called Natalie. I knew she would understand.

I explained everything to her and she said, "Well, you have changed a little, Janelle."

"What do you mean?" I said with an attitude.

"Well, I mean every time I talk to you it's about what a great deal you got on a pair of Jimmy Choo shoes or Manolo Blahnik. Whatever they are. The only other person I heard talking about those shoes was Carrie from *Sex and the City.*"

"So, I have changed?"

"Yeah, I think so, Nell. You better go get your man. You know how many women will be after him trying to become Mrs. Damon Scott at the wedding? Woman are always looking for a husband at weddings."

"You're right. Let me go put these women in check. Well, it's going to be a long drive, so let me call you back when I get in the car. I'm going to try to charge my phone."

I called Damon's aunt Blondell and she gave me directions. I asked her not to tell Damon I was on my way. I wanted it to be a surprise. I made the long drive in about three and a half hours. It was supposed to be a four-hour drive. I walked into the reception and saw the bride. Her dress was nice and she was cute. The groom was skinny and

tall. He kind of favored Damon. You could tell they were related. I saw Damon from across the room, standing in a cir-
cle with a group of guys. He looked so good in his tuxedo. I
walked over to the huddle of guys Damon was standing in. I
tapped him on his shoulder and said, "Damon."

He jumped and said, "Janelle, what are you doing here?"

I could tell he was startled. His hand was tracing this
girl's back. She was a fat, young chick, no more than nineteen. He pulled me to the side, and the group dispersed.

"How did you get down here, Janelle?"

"Damon, don't worry about that. What the fuck were you
doing touching her back?"

"Janelle, that is my little cousin."

"If that is your little cousin, why were you all up on her?"

"I just said, 'Little cousin, you got big. Why you got that
big tattoo on your back?' "

"Whatever, Damon."

Here it is, I had driven all the way from Miami to Orlando
and he had me down here looking like the jealous girlfriend.
I wanted to go home. I was pissed off.

The wedding itself was tacky. They had a buffet with
family members that were in the wedding fixing plates and
plastic plates and utensils. Then they had cheap champagne
that cost three dollars a bottle. I knew Damon was guilty, because he was all up on me asking me if I was okay. Then he
kept getting me glasses of champagne and trying to make
me a plate at dinner. His sister came over to the table we
were sitting at. He introduced us. He said, "Londa, this is
Janelle."

I said hi and she said hey halfheartedly. She was rolling
her eyes at me. *Fat bitch,* I thought. Damon's sister's hair
was tied up in a bun with hard shiny ribbon curls swooped
over her forehead. Her pink dress was heavily creased from
her bulging stomach and waist. The rest of the bridesmaids
had on red dresses with pink gloves. She acted as if she was
Damon's woman. Her name was Yolanda. She was divorced
and had a son and a daughter. Damon said he was going to

be right back and left the table. Yolanda made small talk for a moment. Then she asked me what college I went to.

"I didn't go to college," I said.

"Are you from Miami?"

"No, Philadelphia."

"Oh, where do you work?"

"I don't. I used to be work—"

She cut me off and said, "It must be nice not having to work. I guess you all are the same."

"What are you talking about?"

"The last girl he had didn't work either; then she went off with another woman."

"Yeah, that was crazy. I'm not like that. Well, excuse me, I'm going to find Damon." When I got up, I heard her murmur something about how I was probably leeching off her brother. I wanted to say something, but this was Damon's family and I didn't want to cause any more scenes. I found Damon as he was getting glasses of champagne. He introduced me to the rest of his family. His mother, Mrs. Scott, was sweet. She was real country. She had yellow-blond braids and red lipstick on. His father said a brief hello. He was too busy dancing with the bride to pay me any attention.

I felt like I should have stayed home. This family was country and didn't care about me. They treated me like I wasn't nothing special. Just like one of his many girls. I was calming down, the glasses of champagne were starting to take their toll. I had to go to the bathroom really bad. I walked as fast as I could. Once I was in the bathroom I saw Damon's so-called little cousin kissing one of the groomsmen. She was lying all the way back on her back. She jumped up and the guy ran out of the bathroom. I went into the stall like nothing happened. When I came out, I looked at myself, washed my hands, shook my hands dry as I looked around for a paper towel. The girl was fixing herself up trying to brush out the wrinkles from her dress.

"So, how are you related to Damon?" I asked as I stepped in the girl's face.

"I'm his cousin," she said meekly.

"His cousin. Are you on his mother's side or father's side?"

"I'm his cousin Benny's cousin."

"So y'all not really related?"

"Well, not technically, but we consider each other cousins. I would never deal with him like that. I have a boyfriend. The guy that just left."

I wanted to say, *I didn't ask you that, you little bitch!* I looked her up and down and walked out of the bathroom. I guess I was wrong. She was really his cousin and I needed to go and apologize.

I found Damon and said, "I'm sorry that I didn't believe that was your cousin."

"It's cool. You know I'm happy, baby girl. I wouldn't do that to you. Why would I invite you? Let's get out of here."

Chapter Forty-eight

Natalie

My doorbell rang. I couldn't imagine who it was. I had just come in from dropping the baby off at day care. I looked out the door and a lanky young white guy with glasses on said, "I have a package for Natalie Martin-Grant."

I opened the door said, "Yes, I'm Natalie Grant."

"Mrs. Grant, this is a petition for divorce. I need your signature." I grabbed the papers and read them.

"What?"

"Your husband sent these to you."

"Is he asking for the house?" I asked.

"Mrs. Grant, I don't know. You can read through it."

I called Anthony as I looked through the documents and told him.

"Okay."

"Are you putting us out?" I yelled to Anthony on the phone.

"No, you put me out. You can stay there." I looked over at the guy. He was looking at me like *sign the papers*. I signed the copies. He handed one of the copies back and said, "That is your copy."

He walked away and I said, "Excuse me, how do I know when everything is finalized?"

He turned around and said, "You will receive a notice in the mail in thirty-one days if neither of you contest."

"Thank you," I said as I closed my door. That was it, my marriage was over. It was really over. *I don't want to be divorced!* I screamed as I tried to call Anthony back. *I want to be married.* Oh God, I got to call him back and tell him this is a big mistake. I just wanted Anthony to do right, be a good man, tell Ms. Renee to chill. I don't want this. This is a mistake. I don't want to get a new boyfriend or husband. New boyfriends are always molesting or beating their girlfriends' kids. I can't take that. I'd rather work it out with Anthony. I want Anthony back. I had him back before and I let him go. This time I'm not going to let him go. I know he is a mama's boy. I know everything about him. I know that he doesn't like chocolate, but he loves hot cocoa. I know he doesn't lie and cheat. I'm not even thirty yet! I can't be divorced. I got to make it work with Anthony.

I drove to Anthony's job. I ran to the front counter and asked for Anthony. They said he wasn't in. I walked back to my car. Adrenaline pumping, I called Janelle.

"Janelle!" I screamed, I was so happy she answered the telephone.

"What's wrong, Natalie?"

"Anthony sent divorce papers for me to sign. And I signed them."

"Natalie, I thought that's what you wanted. Right?"

"No, I thought that, but I don't want that. Janelle, I don't know, I'm so confused. If I lose Anthony I will have nothing. My son won't have his father. I won't have a family," I said, out of breath.

"Nat, calm down, you can't live your life for baby Anthony. He is your son, and you are his mom. But moms need to live their life. If you try to get back with Anthony to make it work just for the baby, you will die early and live a miserable depressing life."

"I'm not going to find another husband. It's statistics saying so. It's been researched and proven. I'm about to be divorced now. You know how much harder it will be for me to find someone again? Only one in every twenty women marry again after divorce. And the rate for black women remarrying is even lower. It's true! I read it in *Essence.*"

"Well, you'll be the one out of twenty. You'll find somebody else to love, Natalie. Nat, listen. You are pretty, you only have one child. You can move on."

"I can't move, I got to call Anthony. I'll talk to you later." I hung up on Janelle. She didn't understand. I called Anthony back. He answered the phone.

"Anthony, I don't want a divorce. I want you back. Please listen to me. I want you back. I need you back. I'll do anything," I said.

"What, Natalie, are you crazy? No, Natalie, absolutely not. You got me to move all my stuff back in there, and then once I came back, you showed your ass. You started disrespecting me. No, it's over. You don't want me. You proved that several times."

"I love you, Anthony."

"It's over, Natalie," he said then.

The phone went dead.

Chapter Forty-nine

Tanya

Davon and Deja were with Mom-Mom and I was chilling over at Monica's house. I thought of calling that guy Buc. He could take me out somewhere. I dug around in my handbag and found his number. I dialed and an old lady answered the phone. "Hello, may I speak to Buc?"

"Who you want? Walter?"

"No, Buc."

"You mean Walter. Walter, the phone."

I heard him pick up the phone and say, "Hello."

"Hi, this is Tanya. You gave my son your number."

"Yeah, I remember. What's going on with you?"

"Nothing much. I wanted to see if you wanted to do something."

"Well, I'm a little busy right now, but I'm going to call you back," he said.

I gave him my number and then hung up. He didn't *ever* have to worry about me calling *him* anymore. He gave *my son* his number and he is going to tell me that he has to call me back? *I don't think so.* I turned on the television and began watching some stupid reality show. The phone rang. I answered it and someone said, "Is Monica, that whore, there?"

"Who is this?" I said.

"Your worst nightmare, bitch. Tell that bitch that she better stop messing with my man or her ass won't have no way of making money after I cut off her leg."

"What? First, get off this phone. Second, get a life. Third, Monica ain't here. She probably with your man right now while you arguing with me, and if you call here again I'm going to whoop your ass, bitch."

"Who is this?"

"Bitch, you don't need to know who I am."

"I know this ain't Tanya! That's why you ain't got no baby's father and your kids are bastards." All I heard was laughing and somebody saying ha, ha, ha! That was a good one! Then she said, "Now give that bitch my message and find a baby's father."

I hung up the phone and called Monica to tell her that somebody was playing on the phone. She said it was probably Lil' Ron's baby's mom. She couldn't find him and had been calling him all day. Monica and him were chilling in a room in Wildwood, New Jersey.

The phone rang again. I thought it was Monica again. "Monica?" I said.

"No, it's me bitch, ha, ha, ha. Tell that Monica I'm going to put a hit out on her and her kids."

I hung the phone up again, and then it rang again. This time I picked it up and said, "Bitch, stop playing on the fucking phone." Then I heard a man's voice say, "Uh, hello, can I speak to Tanya?"

"Who is this and what the fuck do you want?"

"Um, this is Buc from the barbershop and I want to know if I can still take you out."

"How you doing? Sorry about that. Somebody is playing on my girlfriend's phone."

Buc asked me to come and meet him at the barbershop. He said he had a head to cut. I didn't feel comfortable sitting around all the guys. He said it would only take a minute, so I went.

I walked to the barbershop. The door was locked. I knocked a little and he came and opened the door.

"What's up, Ms. Tanya?"

"Nothing." I walked in and had a seat. All the other barbers were looking at me and whispering, "Who is that?" to Buc. He just laughed at them. I know he called me down here to show me off.

Buc gave this young guy a shape-up and said, "See you next week." The guy paid him and gave him a pound by slapping their fist together.

"Where you want to go?" Buc asked.

"I don't know. We can go to Red Lobster or something."

"I'm allergic to seafood," he said.

"I don't care, I'm not allergic," I responded.

"What? What am I'm supposed to eat? Don't be selfish."

"Well, maybe a steak place then."

"I know a place." Buc cleaned up his station and counted his money. I was counting it with him. I think Buc might be my Walei replacement. He named this place we could go to. We got in his big black truck. And I don't mean SUV! I mean truck, a big workingman's pickup truck. It was new, but I don't like trucks. They are not roomy enough.

Buc's idea of a nice place to eat was a Chinese buffet. I was not feeling it at all. There were kids running around and babies crying, an old man was coughing all loud. I was not eating there. It was just not a nice first-date restaurant at all.

"I don't want to eat here," I said.

"Where you want to go?"

"Anywhere but here." We got back in the truck and went to Bilal's Garden on Wadsworth Avenue. The food was good and Buc was okay. I don't know what it was, but there was something that I didn't like about Buc. He was nice and everything but wasn't accommodating enough.

After we ate dinner, we walked back to his truck. He opened my door and closed it for me. I got in and waited for him to open his door and get in. He started the truck and I turned the music up. I pulled down his sun visor vanity mirror and checked myself out.

Buc flicked the visor back up. He then turned the music down and said, "Yo, listen, I know you used to dudes falling head over heels for you and doing whatever you say. But I'm not that dude, all right?"

"What are you talking about?"

"About your whole attitude."

"Whatever, take me home," I said.

"Look at you. You ain't that cute. You didn't even say thank you."

"What was I supposed to say thank you for?"

"You didn't even say thank you for me taking you to dinner, opening your doors, or any of that."

"You only did what a man is supposed to do."

"Is that right?"

"Yeah, that's right. I didn't think you had to say thank you for every little thing. But if it means so much to you, thank you."

"You're welcome," he said.

I got him to take me to Monica's house. She was sitting on the steps when we pulled up. I said good-bye to Buc and he said, "I'll call you and, Tanya, you are that cute."

I smiled and stepped out of the truck.

"He is cute," Monica said as he pulled off.

"He's all right."

"What does he do?"

"Cut hair. That's the guy from Derrick's barbershop."

"Really? He's what's up." I'm glad she thought so, because I sure didn't think so.

Chapter Fifty

Janelle

Damon was in the shower getting ready for his last pre-season game against the New Orleans Saints. I took off my clothes so that I could get in the shower with him. I unsnapped my bra and began to slip off my pants. I walked into the foggy bathroom. The shower was running and it was steamy. I walked in and saw something I could not accept. It just didn't make sense. *I just couldn't believe it.* Damon was sitting on the toilet nodding. His body was swaying back and forth like he was about to tilt. He had a little mirror with lines of cocaine. I nudged him, he didn't move, and then I gently smacked his face.

"Damon," I said.

"Huh, yes, what's up?" he said as he dropped the mirror and everything fell on the floor.

"What are you doing, putting that shit up your nose!" I screamed.

"Nothing, I'm tired. Watch out," he said and jumped up like nothing was wrong. He wiped the fog off the mirror and the powder off his nose. "I'm cool, hey, baby girl," he said as he tried to hug me.

I didn't want to be his baby girl right now. I was so upset. Cocaine and Damon, it didn't make any sense. He was re-

spectful and mannerly, neat and clean. He was an athlete and
he was messing up his body. I didn't know what to think. He
told me he didn't do drugs because his uncle died from an
overdose. Cocaine, that's why he always is changing his
mind, being nice, then ice-cold.

"You got to go to counseling," I said.

"I can't. People know who I am."

"There are confidential places where nobody would know
you."

"I can't go. I tried to go before. It wasn't for me. The people in the class were homeless and drugs addicts that had
lost everything. They had real addicts in that class. I wasn't
on crack or heroin. I'm a casual user."

"Well, you got to do something. Damon, don't they test?"

"No, not all the time, not for street drugs. Since I have
been in the NFL, I only got tested once and they give you
like two months' notice. They test more for steroids. I have
to go. I got a game. I have to make the plane."

"This is serious, Damon," I said.

"I don't have time right now, Janelle. Help me get ready
and we can talk about this when I get back."

I packed his clothes and drove him to the airport. Damon
was acting like nothing happened, like it was cool and normal. At the moment something was telling me to leave. I
knew it was about to get worse. I told myself, *Janelle, it's
only been a few months. Get out now while you can.*

After I dropped Damon off at the airport I couldn't get the
image of what I saw earlier out of my head. I needed to talk
to somebody. I didn't feel comfortable calling Kelly. I felt
lonely. I even thought about going home. He won't even
miss me if he is always on the road. Damon needs help and I
don't think I'm the person to help him. The real season is
about to begin and if he is not in practice, he'll be on the
road. He doesn't need me. Maybe he needs his space. I could
just meet him in the city he is in, but that won't work be-

cause I wouldn't be able to stay in his room. I would have to stay on another floor and we won't have a chance to be together.

I continued to drive around, then decided to stop and pick a few things up from the market. I just wanted to get into a hot bath and relax. I needed to make sense of everything that was going on. I pulled up to the driveway at home and got out of the car. A figure came from the side of the car and I screamed. Kelly grabbed me and said, "It's me."

"What are you doing?"

"I needed to talk to you."

"Where is your car? How did you get here?" I asked as I looked around.

"He took it."

"Y'all got in a fight? You can stay here if you need to," I said as I grabbed my bags out of the car.

"No, I'm going home."

"What! Why are you going home?" I asked while I opened the house door.

"He found somebody else. That's how it goes down."

"What are you talking about?"

"Carl has found a replacement for me. I need a ride to the airport and I don't need everybody in my business," Kelly cried.

"I wouldn't tell anyone. Are you okay?" I asked.

"Let me take a shower. Please, don't tell anyone. Okay?"

"Never. You got my word on that."

"Janelle, you're the only person I could trust," she said as she sat down and began telling me what happened. Then she stood up and started to pace.

"I was at the gym, you know, doing my Pilates class. I was tired, sweating, and ready just to take a shower. I come into the house and Carl had another woman in there. I'm looking at him like, are you crazy? He acted like he didn't do anything wrong! He acted like he didn't know me. He wouldn't even let me get my stuff. The girl was in the other room sipping wine in my glasses, while me and him were arguing. I had to catch a cab here. I know he put the word out to everybody not to talk to me because Amber didn't answer her phone and Stephen said Lisa wasn't home."

"He would do that! Why didn't you just call my cell? I would have come and got you."

"I don't know. I just need to take a shower. I have to call my dad. Carl took my phone, everything. My mother is going to wire me money when she gets off work."

"You look like shit too! What's going on with you?" Kelly asked.

I didn't know if I should tell her what I saw. I had to confide in someone. "Damon is snorting coke."

"That's it? Girl, they all having *something* wrong with them. Nothing is how it appears. You had better be glad that's all that is wrong with him. Damon is a good guy. All these other guys think women are disposable."

"I don't think they all think like that," I said.

"Don't you get it? It's about them. Let your ass spread a little, your boobs sag, and it's all over."

"Kelly, I can buy your ticket home."

"Would you please? Janelle, I will send you the money as soon as I get home and get everything situated," she said as she placed her hands together.

"Girl, please, whenever you get it."

Kelly called Delta Airlines and she was lucky, the next flight was in two hours.

After I dropped Kelly off, I came home and I watched the game at home by myself. It was going okay until I saw Damon didn't get up from the pileup. I was scared and then I saw him limp off the field. I hoped he wasn't hurt. That was the last thing he needed, to be hurt. My mother called me. They were watching the game too! She asked me if he was okay. I told her I didn't know and I would call her back when I knew something. I tried calling Lisa, but she wasn't home. Amber wasn't home either. I found Dana's number. She called me back and said that Damon was fine. He called me as soon as the game was over. I could hear all the others guys in the locker room.

"Baby, are you okay? I saw you limping."

"I'm fine. I pulled a muscle. Let me shower and get dressed and I'll call you back." He sounded like he was upset.

I waited by the phone for him to call me back. I waited half an hour and called him back again.

"Are you on your way home?" I asked him.

"Yeah, I'll get there in a few hours. We are about to get on the plane."

I shouldn't have said it and it may have come out the wrong way, but I was mad and Damon needed to hear it. "Damon, maybe you were off because of what happened."

"What, Janelle? I don't need this right now. Do you play?"

"No."

"Well, don't tell me why my game was off. I'll call you back."

As soon as I put the phone on the hook I began crying. Damon was being so mean. I didn't need this. He could be with somebody else and cheating like Carl, I don't know. He's not going to play me and end it first. I am going to end it while I'm up. While everything is working for me. He was in a different city and he was mad at me. I didn't do anything to him. He is the one that has been keeping a secret. For the first time in four months, I wanted to go home.

I started packing all my clothes. I had to get out of here before he got home. I didn't want to see Damon. I called the airport and reserved my flight. I could just sit in the airport. I didn't want to be here when Damon got here. I left Damon a Dear John letter. I told him in the letter that I loved him but he needed help and I wanted him to get himself together and he didn't need me distracting him.

The cab pulled up. I was dragging my luggage out the door. I left a lot of my clothes and shoes behind. I didn't have enough room for everything. Just as I sat in the cab, I saw headlights coming toward me. Damon jumped out of the car. I went to shut my door, but Damon pulled it back open. I asked the driver to hold up for one minute. He said that the meter was going to be running. I got out of the cab. Damon was standing with his face buried in his hands.

He looked over at me and said, "So that's how it's going to go, Janelle? Fine. I'm used to people walking out on me when things get hard. Bye, see you. I got you. It was fun while it lasted, huh?"

"Damon, it's not like that. I love you, but I can't take you and the drugs. It's too much."

"Go ahead, Janelle. I know you heard. Somebody called and told you. You think I'm down and out."

"I know you're not down and out. You pulled a muscle. Big deal, that's not anything."

"I'm not talking about pulling my muscle. I got cut today too! C-U-T. I'm not in the NFL anymore. So go ahead and walk out on me. It wouldn't surprise me."

"What are you talking about, Damon? You can't get cut, the season has already begun."

"I'm a free agent. They can cut me and they did, Janelle."

"I love you, Damon. I'm not leaving because you got cut. I'm leaving because I'm just, I'm not prepared for this. This meaning drugs. I didn't know you got cut today," I said as I walked closer to him. I turned around and went to get back in my cab. The fare was running. I tried shutting the door again.

Damon opened the car door and was on his knees crying. He said, "Janelle, please don't leave. I need you. I'm not into that. That bitch Alicia started me on this shit. When she left I used it more. I'm an athlete. I take care of my body. I'm not touching that stuff. I can do it. I will stop, I promise."

"Damon, I can't. I don't know how."

"You love me, don't you?"

"Yes, Damon, I love you."

"Then stay in my corner. Just stay in my corner. I need

you in my corner. Help me, Janelle, don't leave me," Damon begged me, still on his knees. "Pray with me, Janelle, please."

I stepped out of the cab. He grabbed my hand and I stood as he kneeled. We closed our eyes and prayed for him to get over his addiction. For things in his life to get better. After we prayed I paid the driver and Damon took my luggage out of the cab and into the house.

The next day Damon went to go return his equipment and clean out his locker. For the first time I saw Damon's bank account statement. He had left it on the kitchen counter. By his standards he was broke and now unemployed. He only had seventeen thousand dollars in it. The house was at least four thousand a month. Damon had made $325,000 a year for the last three years. The only thing he had to show for his money was his house in Orlando and his two cars. I felt bad for him. Were the drugs to blame? His old chick? Was I to blame? I had spent thousands of dollars on clothes, shoes, and everything in between. My spending habits had gotten out of control fucking around with Kelly, and now look where she is. I couldn't sit back and do nothing. I had lived rent-free for months and shopped every time I got a chance.

The next day I searched in my closet and saw I had shoes that I hadn't even worn yet. Then I saw another pair and another. All ranged from three hundred dollars to nine hundred. I put them in a box and placed them in the bag to take them back. I found three shirts and two pairs of pants I didn't even like. I put it all in a bag and took it back to each store I'd bought it from. There were bags, belts, things I bought just because I could.

I looked in the dresser drawers and found receipts then I drove to the mall. I had three bags from different department stores. The first store I went into the salesgirls looked at me like I was trash for returning something for cash. I didn't care. We needed money. Times were about to get hard. Tomorrow I will look for a job.

A few days had passed. I wasn't sure what to expect so I was going to ask him what was going to be next. Were we moving, staying here or what. He was sitting on the sofa eating a bowl of Honey Combs cereal and watching television. I took a seat next to him, and said, "So, what's next?"

"We wait. My agent is going to make some calls for me. He said he can get me some tryouts with a couple of teams. Somebody will pick me up, I'm not worried. We'll be okay. Don't worry," he said.

Chapter Fifty-one

Natalie

I haven't talked to Anthony since I signed the divorced papers. He still been paying for the baby's day care and leaving diapers and milk there. I'm now down twenty-one pounds. I weigh 159 pounds. I have nothing to do but lose weight, eat right, and exercise.

I didn't make it to the aerobics class to work out as much. I have been keeping the weight off by using my old Tae Bo tapes. My mother called me as soon as I started exercising. I said, "Hello" and was gasping for air.

"Why are you out of breath?" my mother asked.

"I was doing Tae Bo."

"Natalie, don't you know you're never, ever going to be skinny? Your dad's side is big. My side got big thighs and hips. When you have a daughter, she's going to inherit it too."

"Mom, what's up? I'm working out."

"My client Jerri. You remember her, you washed her hair a couple of times."

"I don't remember?"

"Well, anyway, she needs someone to help her at her catering company. I told her you used to do catering work before you had the baby."

"How soon?"

"Immediately. I gave her your number. She is about to call you."

"All right."

Ms. Jerri called me and asked if I could work Friday the third. I said yes. She said she had a uniform my size and just meet her at her business. She gave me the address. I hung up and finished working out.

Friday I helped her cater a retirement party. I walked in and everything was chaotic. I did remember the lady Ms. Jerri. She said hi and gave me my uniform. I went and changed into it. She introduced me to two girls, Nadine and Ketora, her nieces. They were younger than me, like nineteen or twenty. Ketora was petite with a short flipped haircut. The other, Nadine, was the real silly one, she still had braces on and was real tall with a shoulder-length wrap.

Ms. Jerri told me to start setting the tables with them and assist them if they needed help. We had to place the silverware, napkins, plates, salt and pepper shakers, and flower centerpieces on each table. Then we had to make sure the Sweet and Low and sugar containers were filled. After that I had to bring out water glasses and fill them up. The guests started arriving and I served on the buffet line. After they ate and began dancing, I started clearing the tables and serving coffee. I then cleaned the tables and started to break them down. Ms. Jerri gave me a hundred dollars for the night.

The last couple of times I weighed myself I noticed my weight had stabilized. I hadn't lost any weight and I had been working out like crazy. I went online to look for some low-carb recipes and diet tips. As soon as I found a low-carb-recipe Web site, a pop-up menu came onto my screen. It kept flashing. I hit the X on the screen and it took me to findloverightnow.com. It was a dating Web site. I kept trying to push X, but all these screens kept popping up. There were testimonials about the site and it had a 90 percent success rate. There was a free compatibility test. I answered the questionnaire just for fun. It asked me questions about my personality, goals, and what I was looking for in a partner. I filled out the entire fifty questions. The site prompted me to post a message about myself. I typed in *divorced twenty-something woman seeking friendship from professional male 25–33 for friendship.* After I completed the questionnaire, another link appeared and said that I had five perfect matches. I read the matches to my profile. It was funny, I wasn't even thinking about meeting a man. I looked at the profiles and pictures. One guy's picture was ugly. Another guy was forty-seven with glasses that made his eyes look big. One didn't have a picture. The fourth was a fat white guy and the fifth was a man that looked a little too feminine for my taste. So much for my perfect match. I logged off.

The next event I did with Ms. Jerri was a big city council luncheon. My coworkers, Nadine and Ketora, had me set up the tables by myself. I had forgotten what order the knife, spoon, fork, and soupspoon went in. I poured water in every glass and ran around folding napkins and placing plates on the table. Just as the guests began to arrive I finished.

Now I had to go and get the hors d'oeuvres out of the oven and start serving them. I saw that Nadine and Ketora were in the back having a smoke break. I mean, a fucking smoke break? That pissed me off. I don't know why people that smoke cigarettes think they can have more breaks than people that don't. "Ladies, the guests are arriving," I said. They put out their cigarettes and came in and served the food.

Ms. Jerri called me on a regular basis. I was happy to be working steadily. Most of the events were luncheons, and for the ones that weren't, my mom or dad watched baby Anthony for me. I liked working for Ms. Jerri, but Ketora and Nadine were another story.

But I had something for them. The next event we did was a white couple's wedding. They seemed so in love, just like me and Anthony were. We had had a big wedding, sort of. But now all that had been for nothing. Since it was over, if I had to do it all over again, I would have taken that money and put it in the bank. Me and this older woman, Sue, were busy setting up everything by ourselves. Ketora and Nadine went on another convenient smoke break. So I made sure I didn't get stuck at the end of the night cleaning. When they started cleaning, I took a smoke break. I didn't even light the cigarette. I just stood there with it in my mouth. Ketora walked out in the front of the catering hall and was about to light up until she saw me and asked, "Since when did you start smoking?"

"Since I see you can get more breaks if you smoke."

She frowned, put her cigarette in her bag, and went back into the building.

Chapter Fifty-two

Janelle

I wanted Damon to go to rehab, but he said he could do it on his own. He didn't want anyone else involved. He said if the news got to any teams, nobody would pick him up. I didn't tell him I had told Kelly, even though she already knew. Damon was going through withdrawal. He was so irritable and his muscles were hurting him. He was doing a lot of whining. I went on the Internet to learn his withdrawal symptoms. The site I went to said that Damon might shake or spit up and be restless. It also said his muscles could be in pain.

I was getting tired of Damon and wanted to go home, but I didn't want to turn my back on him. He was waiting for me to do that. I couldn't prove him right. I can hear him now. "I'm not in the NFL, so you don't want me no more." If I left now he would think I was just with him for the money. The money was nice, but I really loved Damon, or did I? I just wasn't ready for this. This is too much even for me. I don't know how much more I can put up with.

"Damon, get out of the bed and take a shower."

"I don't feel like it, Janelle. Leave me alone."

I walked out of the bedroom and into the living room and watched television. I hadn't watched the soaps in a while.

Damon had the air blasting. I got a blanket out of the closet and watched *The Young and the Restless.* I called Natalie. I couldn't call my mother. Then I decided against telling anyone else Damon's business. I needed to talk to someone. I heard the phone ring and ring. I didn't bother answering it. I knew it wasn't for me. The phone stopped ringing. Damon must have answered it. I heard him talking. Then he ran into the living room and yelled, "My agent called, babe. He got me a tryout with Green Bay and the Giants!"

"Baby, that is so great!"

"My prayers were answered."

"Where is Green Bay?"

"Wisconsin. I leave tomorrow. I just called my travel agent." Damon began to pack his bag. I thought about how it might be to live in Green Bay, Wisconsin. I don't know if I would be able to do it. It was cold there and snowed. There was *no way* I was moving my black ass to Wisconsin. I hate the cold. I love the heat. Living in Florida was a no-brainer. Wisconsin? I don't think so.

Damon had left this morning for the tryout. He called while I was in the shower and left a message to call him. He didn't sound too good.

I called him right back and he picked up on the first ring and said, "Baby, they didn't pick me. I'm not coming home. I'm going to head straight to New York and see how that works out." Damon was trying not to cry, but I could hear him.

"Baby, it's okay. Do you want me to meet you?" I asked, trying to comfort him.

"You don't have to. I'll call you when I get to New York."

"What time do you get in?"

"Around eleven."

"Call and reserve my ticket. I'll pack now."

* * *

I met him in New York and we stayed for a couple of days waiting to hear if he had made the team. We went to see the Broadway play *Rent.* I wanted to try something different. I had never been to a Broadway play and neither had Damon. In the middle of the performance Damon's phone started to ring. He said that it was his agent, John, and he had to answer it. I kept watching the play. I waited for him to come back to his seat. When he hadn't come back in fifteen minutes, I figured it was bad news. I walked into the lobby.

"What did he say?"

"I'm going to start off as a third string and have a one-year contract. It's less money than what we anticipated, but they're willing to work with me."

I hugged Damon. I was so happy for him. "Baby, it doesn't matter. You are still in the NFL. I can get a job, you know? I used to manage a store. There's plenty of retail jobs in New York."

He grabbed me, hugged me again, and said, "That's why I love you."

"You love me?" I asked.

"Yes, I love you," he said.

"I love you too!"

He grabbed me with his big arms and said, "There is one problem. I need you to go pack everything up for me. I only have a couple days to get out here before the season starts. They have an apartment for some of the newer players in Montclair, New Jersey. They set me aside one."

Chapter Fifty-three

Tanya

I didn't feel like hearing Natalie's mouth. She was a pain in the ass. Always talking about going to jail. She is so scary it is ridiculous. I had her take me to buy some weed. I was going down to Monica's house. We were about to go out to this bar and have some fun. I had done my motherly duty for the day and taken the kids out. It was time for me to have some fun now. I might go out again with the dude Buc. We have been keeping in touch, going out to get drinks and stuff.

I went to the Chinese store around the corner from Monica's house to buy a blunt. The small Chinese store menu was hanging on the wall. There were kids everywhere and these women were arguing over a loose cigarette. Young guys were outside gambling and a grown man was drinking a kids' red bug juice. I ordered three chicken wings and fried rice. I called Monica on my cell to see if she wanted anything. She told me to get her a beef and broccoli. It was hot inside the store, so I went outside and started splitting the blunt in half.

I walked to Monica's house, passing by girls on the step braiding hair and little girls jumping rope. Monica was in the window. I walked in her apartment, set the food down and pulled our food out of the plastic bag. I took a spoonful of my fried rice and pulled out the blunt. We smoked a little, then ate our food. Monica's daughters were gone and we had the house all to ourselves. I took a nap; the food had tired me out. We were rested and ready to walk around the corner when my cell phone rang. I looked at it. It was my grandmother's number, so I didn't answer. It was probably Deja or Davon wanting to know where I was. I turned my ringer off. Then I saw the light flashing again that I had a call. I answered.

"Come home, Tanya," Mom-Mom said.

"Why? What's wrong, Mom-Mom?"

"Just come home." My grandmother sounded like she was worried and had been crying. What was wrong? What was going on? I asked.

"Tanya, just come home now."

"Why, Mom-Mom, what's wrong? Please tell me," I said as I began to cry. "Take me home. I got to go home, Monica," I said.

"What's wrong?"

"I don't know, my grandmother said for me to just come home."

We got in Monica's car and my mind began to race from bad to worse. What was so bad that my grandmother couldn't tell me over the telephone? Did something happen to Deja or Davon? Were the cops at my house? They could have found out about me stealing that credit card. Was something wrong with my grandmother? She was always so strong. Why was she crying?

I got home in less than ten minutes. My heart was racing. I didn't see any detective or cop cars. No cars were parked on the block with city or state government license plates. We still parked at the corner.

"Everything is okay," Monica tried to assure me before I went into the house. I ran in and I saw my grandmother. She was still crying.

"Mom-Mom, what's wrong?"

She turned to me and said, "Your mother is back."

I looked over at the sofa and saw Saundra Lewis, my

mother. I never knew what death looked like until I looked into my mother's face. She weighed about a hundred pounds at the maximum. She looked old and worn out. Drugs had fucked her up bad. She looked so sick. But I didn't have shit to say to her. She was laughing and talking with my kids.

"Mom-Mom, I know you didn't call me home to see her. I thought something was wrong with you or the kids."

Saundra tried to come up to me and hug me. I didn't want to hug her.

"We need to talk," she said.

"Saundra, we don't have anything to talk about," I said. I ordered Deja and Davon upstairs.

"Why, Mom?" Davon cried.

"Because I said so. Go to bed."

The kids pouted and went upstairs. My grandmother was still in her seat. Monica had walked outside and Saundra was still in my face saying she was sorry.

"I'm sorry, Tanya. I'm sorry for leaving. I hope you can forgive me."

"You're sorry. I can't forgive you. I can't forgive somebody who left me for more than half of my life."

Saundra approached me and tried to put her hand on my shoulder. "I know what I did was wrong. I'm sorry, I've lived with it every day of my life."

I wasn't feeling Saundra. I snatched away and said, "Look, you can't just show up and say sorry after all these years." She is just going to show up after all these years? No way! Was I supposed to be happy and welcome her with open arms?

"I have nothing to say to that woman, Mom-Mom," I said as I turned to my grandmother. I walked out of the room like Saundra wasn't even there. I went upstairs to make sure the kids were okay.

"Mom, who is that lady?" Deja asked.

"Your grandmother. Your stank, crackhead-ass grandmother."

"That's your mom? The lady from the pictures?" Davon asked.

"Yes, that's her. I want y'all to be good and go to bed, and tomorrow I might take y'all to the toy store."

I went downstairs and walked right past Saundra. "Mom-Mom, if you need me I'll be over at Monica's house. I made the kids go to bed."

Saundra attempted to say something to me again. I turned around to her and said, "What do you possibly have to say to me? Whatever it is, I don't care."

"Tanya, these are my last days."

"And save your story for somebody that cares—I don't give a fuck," I said.

My grandmother interrupted me and said, "Don't talk to your mother like that. She is your mother. And she is sick. She has AIDS. She is dying, Tanya."

"She should have died. I hope she dies now. I don't care what happens to Saundra right now."

"Tanya, you don't mean that! Don't say that, Tanya!" my grandmother cried.

"I do mean it."

"Child, stop being so mean."

"I do mean it. And, Mom-Mom, if you ever left me like she did for years at a time, I wouldn't care what happened to you either. She left me. I was the child she left on you, re-member?" I said as I broke down and tears began running down my face.

"Remember when she stole your jewelry and the watch Pop-Pop bought you for your birthday? She stole your tele-vision and used to steal your mortgage money from under your mattress. If you don't remember, I do."

My grandmother was crying too! She said, "Tanya, I re-member, but that was in the past."

I couldn't take everything that was going on. I headed for the door. Deja ran down the steps crying. "Mommy, please don't leave! I want you to stay here with me."

"Go to bed, Deja."

"Mommy! Don't leave, Mommy! Please don't leave."

"I'll be back," I said as I wiped away my tears. Deja held on to my leg and sobbed. I grabbed her and told her to go to her room.

"Tanya, just go with your mean ass. I'm tired of you upsetting these kids."

I bolted out of the door. My grandmother held Deja back. I walked to the corner and opened the car door. Monica was smoking a cigarette, listening to music in the car.

"You all right?" she asked as I got in the car.

"Yeah. Fuck that bitch. That bitch left! She fucking left me," I said as I began crying uncontrollably. Monica started the car and began patting my back.

"She said she has AIDS and these are her last days. I don't give a fuck! What about me, bitch? What about how you left me!" I screamed.

"I don't care what she did. That is your mother. She is still living and you need to spend her last days with her. She is already paying for leaving you. Look at her life. My mother is gone, you know I don't give a fuck about anything. Not a nigga, only God, my kids, and money. But I wish my mother was here."

She stopped and then started crying with me and said, "I wish I had somebody to watch my kids or take to dinner on Mother's Day. You got your grandmother. I don't have anybody. Me and Derrick were in and out of homes our whole life. Your mom is sick. God brought her back to you for a reason. You need to help her."

We got to Monica's house and she was still talking to me about my mom. I was sitting on the sofa telling her everything Saundra did to me when I was growing up. Monica went to get me a tissue and Lil' Ron ran into the house and shouted, "Monica, the cops are chasing me. Get rid of everything."

I heard sirens in the distance. They were getting louder by the second. I jumped off the sofa. For a moment I didn't know what to do or which way to run. Should I hide under the bed or in the closet? I looked out the window to see if the cops were on the block. They were coming down the street. I could see the red and blue flashing and hear the sirens.

"What do you want me to do?" Monica asked.

"Help me get rid of this shit. If you don't, then I'm going down. Take the car and take everything to my mom's house."

Me and Monica ran out of the back of the building. I was not staying in the apartment with Lil' Ron. I was out too. I saw a cop and I was about to panic. Monica was cool. The cop looked at us and he got on his radio and said something. I couldn't quite make out what he was saying. We walked down to the next landing. And another cop ran past us and up the steps. They didn't know what apartment we were coming from, so they didn't stop us. I was so nervous. Monica got in the car.

I started walking away from the building.

"Get in the car, Tanya. If you walk away from me, we are going to look suspicious."

"I'm not going to jail for a nigga I don't even fuck with. I'm not getting in your car." I kept walking. Monica got mad, but fuck that shit. I was almost off Monica's block and she was halfway down the street when a police car flew past me, going the wrong way up the block. That police car blocked Monica in. She backed up and another car came from behind her. Another unmarked came from the side. Monica tried to run out of the car, but the cops grabbed her as soon as she got out. I wanted to turn around and help her, but I couldn't. I had to get away. I saw a bus coming and I was about to jump on it. Another police car came and jumped the pavement in front of me. The cops told me to put my hands up above my head and get against the wall.

"What did I do?" I yelled.

They patted me and handcuffed me and put me in the wagon. The cop I saw from the stairway radioed in, "We have the other one."

They put me in the car. They had Lil' Ron coming out of the building and put him in a separate car. I didn't have any drugs on me and I was not in the car with Monica. What were they trying to charge me with?

They took us down to the police station. I was scared as hell. I didn't know what to think. The uniform cops took me into a dimly lit room. There was a green table and steel chair in it. The cops took the handcuffs off me and ordered me to sit down. An old white detective with stained cigarette teeth and grayish brown thin hair entered the room.

"Whose bag is it?" the detective asked me in the interrogation room.

"What bag?" I asked.

"The bag your girlfriend was carrying."

"I don't know about any bag," I said as I stared at the wall.

"Listen, if you don't tell me about Lil' Ron and the gun and the coke she had you are going to jail for attempting to distribute an illegal substance and a gun charge."

"I don't know what you are talking about," I said again.

"There are a lot of girls up at Muncy Prison that are going to love you."

"I don't know anything," I repeated.

"It's like this, you and your girlfriend tried to hide drugs for her boyfriend. She put you in danger and she won't tell on him. And you won't tell on her. Both of you can just split the jail time. Sit here and think about it."

They kept me and Monica separated. I tried to rest in the cell, but I couldn't. It was hot and the bed was a hard metal. I closed my eyes and then I would look at my watch and only fifteen minutes had gone past. I didn't know what to do. I needed a lawyer. I couldn't call my grandmother. Not after what I just did. She would pass out. I didn't belong in jail. I wasn't a ride-or-die chick. I needed my kids. I needed to be home with them, not here. I shouldn't have left Deja when she was crying for me.

Chapter Fifty-four

Natalie

When I woke up this morning, there was a message from Ms. Jerri on my machine saying something about "effective today, there are no more smoking breaks." She wanted to let me know. I didn't like her message. She didn't say anything to her little nieces. So I said fuck it and kindly called her and said I wasn't going to be able to work today because the baby was sick. I hope she doesn't get mad and tell my mom I called out on her.

I continued to listen to my messages. There was a message from Tanya. She wanted me to drop her and the kids off at the movies. I dialed her number and she picked up on the first ring.

"You're lucky I'm home. I didn't go to work today. I can drop you off. I have to go to Wal-Mart anyway," I said.

"Okay, the movie starts at two."

"I'll be there by one-thirty." I hung up the phone, dressed Anthony, and then myself. I threw on a pair of sweats. That was the only thing that fit since losing all of my weight.

I picked Tanya up. She and the kids got in. Deja was happy to see the baby.

"Hi, Anthony," Deja sang. Davon was so handsome, he got in like a little man and said, "What's up?" as he got into the backseat.

"Where's your mother?" I asked.

"She said she will be right out."

Tanya came out to the car fifteen minutes later.

I dropped Tanya and the kids off at the movies, and then I went to the Wal-Mart. I needed to buy the baby undershirts, sleepers, and diapers. I grabbed a cart and was headed inside when I heard someone say, "Hey, sexy." I turned around to see that an attractive man was talking to me.

"Yo, Ma. What, you don't know you sexy?"

"Thank you," I said, surprised. My working out was finally paying off. Someone had called me sexy. Nobody had really tried to talk to me since I was in Miami, and before that I can't remember.

"Can I have your number?" the guy asked.

I looked him over. He looked too gangsta for me. I said, "No, I'm married."

He said, "No, you're not" and started walking in the other direction.

After I did my light shopping, I felt like being nice, so I waited for Tanya and the kids to come out of the movies. I didn't want her to have to catch the bus. I waited outside in the car. When I saw them I beeped my horn. They all got in and smelled like popcorn and hot dogs.

"Did y'all have a good time?" I asked.

"Yes," Deja said.

"No. It was corny. I knew what was going to happen," Davon said.

"Thanks for waiting for us, Nat. I'm going to go out Southwest with you, all right? You're going home, right?"

"Yeah."

"I'm just going to drop them off. That's cool."

"Yeah," I said.

We dropped the kids off and Tanya was quiet the whole ride. Then out of nowhere she said, "Hold up. Take me to Sixtieth Street. I got to meet up with somebody."

"Who? Girl, I'm tired. I want to go home."

"Nat, it will be real quick. It's important."

Reluctantly, I changed my direction and headed toward Sixtieth Street. As soon as I pulled over, I saw this guy with a scruffy beard and bad skin. Tanya got out and started talking to him. I locked the car doors. The guy Tanya was talking to looked dirty and the block looked suspect. I kept glancing through my rearview mirror to make sure nobody walked up on me. I saw Tanya laugh with the guy, then give him some money.

She got back in the car and said, "I need you to take me around the corner." The guy Tanya was talking to hopped in my backseat next to Anthony. Tanya said, "That's Mal. He's cool."

He said, "What's up?" by nodding his head. He closed the door and I drove him around the block. I glanced at him through the rearview mirror. He ran out of the car into a house and then came back over to the car. Tanya rolled down her window and he put something in her hand. He said, "Holla," and she said, "I'll probably see you later on to-night."

I don't claim to be the toughest, downest girl from around the way, but I know Tanya did not just have me take her drug man to his drug house, to go pick up her drugs.

"Bitch, I know you didn't have me go and take you to buy some drugs with my baby in the car."

"Calm down. It's only weed," Tanya said nonchalantly.

"It's only weed? How about if we got caught in a drug sting or something?"

"That would not have happened. I know him. He only sells to people he knows."

"Then you let that nigga in my car! I don't know him!"

"I told you I know him. He is cool."

"Whatever, that's not cool. I can't afford to get locked up

and have my son taken from me, or have my car taken, because you want to buy some drugs!"

"You tripping, girl. I'm getting out at the next corner," she said like she didn't care.

I was so furious. I wanted Tanya to get her life together so bad. I'm tired of trying to talk to her. I can't help her if she won't help herself. She knows what she's doing.

When I came into the house I got on the computer. I hadn't check my e-mail for a long time, so I opened it and saw that I had two messages. Before I got a chance to read my messages, someone instant-messaged me and said *Hi.*

I instant-messaged the guy back. At first he seemed very nice. He said *What's up?*

Nothing, I typed back.

So what are you wearing? he asked.

None of your business, I typed in italics. Then he instant-messaged me back. *You bitch.*

I immediately logged off the instant message with him and blocked his name.

I read my second message. It was a guy named Troy from the Philly area. He liked children and was thirty-two. I saw his picture, it was nice. His message was simple and plain. He said *I liked your introduction. Maybe we can chat or e-mail, Troy Sloan.*

I e-mailed him and said maybe we can chat sometime.

The first e-mail he typed was *How are you? What are you doing?* I told him right away I had a son and was recently divorced. He said he had a daughter that was seven and he had divorced two years ago. We instant-messaged back and forth for about an hour. It was time for me to log off. Anthony started whining and his skin was hot. I told Troy I would talk to him later because my son was sick.

* * *

I gave Anthony Tylenol. That wasn't reducing his fever, so I called my pediatrician, Dr. Mosely. He said that he would call in a prescription for Children's Motrin for me. I went to the pharmacy to go pick it up. I usually have to sign and that is all, but after I signed my name, the pharmacist said, "That will be seven ninety-eight."

"I didn't know I had a co-pay," I said.

"That's not the co-pay. That is the full price. Your insurance expired at the end of the month."

Immediately I called Anthony. "Anthony, why in the hell would you take your son off your insurance?"

"Natalie, the only way I can get over you is not to have any communication at all with him or you."

"What? That is the dumbest thing I ever heard. We are divorced so you're going to divorce your son too and not provide him with medical insurance?"

"Yup, I'm tired of being the nice guy."

"The nice guy, please," I said.

"And this week was the last time I'm paying day care. My mom said I give you too much by letting you stay in the house for free," he said.

"What? Fuck your mom and what she say!" I shouted.

"Don't talk about my mom, Natalie!" he screamed.

"I'll talk about that stupid bitch all I want, and fuck you too, Anthony! I'll take your ass to court and you'll have to pay me a hundred dollars a week. Keep playing with me."

"No, I won't. Take me to court, I don't care. I'll make you move out of my house."

"We'll see about that!" I said as I disconnected the call. I tried to call him back, but Ms. Renee kept picking up the phone. I decided to go over to their house.

I pushed the bell and Ms. Crazy Renee came to the door and asked me why I was in front of her house.

"I need to see Anthony," I said, ignoring her last comment.

"Anthony doesn't want to talk to you."

"Ms. Renee, this is your grandchild. He is sick. He needs insurance. He also needs a father."

"What do you want me to do? I can't make him take care of your child. I know one thing, he's not giving you any money so you can go and spend it on yourself!" she said as she closed the door.

I rang the bell again and demanded for Anthony to come to the door. I banged some more and some more.

"Anthony, get your ass out here! Come to the door. I'm not going to take care of baby Anthony by myself. You're going to help me." I kept banging on the door. I knew eventually he would have to get tired of the noise. Ms. Renee peeked out the window and the next thing I knew I saw red and blue flashing lights. I turned around to see a patrol car and a white light shining up on me. I tried to shield the bright light from me and baby Anthony's face.

Ms. Renee opened the door and said, "Officers, she will not leave. I asked her nicely. She is my son's baby's mom. He doesn't want her anymore and she is upset."

I had had enough! I blurted out right in front of the police and the neighbors peeking through their windows to see what all the commotion was about, "I'm not his baby's mom. I'm his fucking wife, Ms. Renee, I'm his fucking wife, bitch."

She corrected me and said, "You're his ex-wife."

"Young lady, calm down," one officer said.

"No! I'm tired of this bitch. I'm tired of your fucking, lazy-ass son being up your ass. Anthony, you need to grow the fuck up. Take care of your son, your fucking bastard!"

The officer grabbed my arm and said, "Miss, go home."

"No, I'm tired. I have been putting up with his trifling ass for too long."

It was obvious the cops were not on my side. They were on theirs. They kept telling me to go home. I didn't. I continued to cuss Anthony out. He came to the door and I tried to spit on him. Then he said I had brought all this on myself.

"I can't believe you, Anthony," I said as I went to lunge at him. The cops grabbed me and took baby Anthony out of my arms and I screamed and started hyperventilating. Where were they taking my baby?

"Don't take my baby!" I screamed. They pushed me up against the patrol car and put handcuffs on me. They gave the baby to Ms. Renee. The cop told her if she didn't take the baby they would have to call the Department of Human Services. Out of the corner of my eye as I was being led into the wagon, I saw Anthony grab the baby.

The police took me to the police station. As soon as I came in, a cop approached me and said, "You're Sergeant Martin's daughter, aren't you?"

"Yeah."

"What the hell is wrong with you, causing a disturbance? Do you know how embarrassed your dad would be if he knew all this was going on? Don't go back over there. Handle things the right away. Take your ex-husband to court."

The cop that knew my dad convinced the arresting officers to write me up a citation for disturbing the peace. They gave me a court date and the citation and I was free to go. I didn't want my dad to find out, so I called my mom. She came down to the station to pick me up. She picked up the baby before she came and got me. I was humiliated and I had had enough of Anthony. I was finally done with his ass. And I meant it.

I was watching Dr. Phil on one of those talk shows. I don't remember exactly, but they were talking about moving on with your life. On the show they said to get over something you must confront it. I needed to confront Anthony and be at peace with our divorce. I couldn't call him or talk to him, so I wrote him a letter. It read:

Anthony, I love you. But right now, I am hurt. My mind is boggled just thinking about all that we went

through. I have your son and I love you. I love you. I
really just wanted us to be a happy family. Right now,
though, I don't think you love me or care about me at
all. The last few times we broke up it was always me
coming back after you. I am always running behind
you and wanting you. I wish we were together. I wish
I was the one to make you smile and you still loved
me. I wish you looked at me like you used to. You used
to look at me like I was the best thing ever.

I wish we would have gotten along. But I guess it
wasn't meant to be. I'm really going to leave you alone
this time. I don't know what awaits me. I don't know if
I'll ever be able to replace you. You're a good man. I
want you to be happy.

I don't know what is going to be worse, being mis-
erable with you or without you. I am so sad. I miss
you. I want to call you, but I won't. I always come back
to you. I always call you. I refuse to call you. I'll never
call you no more, Anthony. No fucking more. I won't
accept no more hurt. No more disrespect. I'm going to
find someone that loves me, someone who will be a fa-
ther to the baby. Someone who will make me feel like I
am so special. Right now, I have to prepare for him be-
cause I wish I could change you, but I can't.

Getting it all out felt so good. I needed that. I was going
to mail my letter off to Anthony tomorrow. I got ready for
bed. I had to go to work tomorrow. I watched *Judge Mathis*
and nodded off.

Chapter Fifty-five

Janelle

I got the yellow pages and called to see how much it would cost to move from Florida to New Jersey. The first place I called said they only did local jobs. The next company would take me, but they weren't available until the end of the month.

I had to be in New Jersey as soon as possible. I was packing Damon's things and I found everything. There were letters, thongs, and pictures from half-naked girls in his closet. I called him and said, "Dame, do you want any of these pictures I found in your closet?"

"No, baby. Throw them in the trash. I am so sorry you had to see that."

There were some pornos and magazines. Those I didn't mind. The ladies in the magazine didn't have a phone number and letter describing everything they were going to do to him. I labeled and numbered each box. Boxes were everywhere. Damon had called me back and said he found a company his friend had recommended, and they would be here first thing in the morning.

I had to make the long drive from Florida to New Jersey. I followed the moving trucks. I could have caught a plane, but

I didn't trust the movers with all our stuff. I drove straight up 95 until we got to Delaware Memorial Bridge. Then I got on the New Jersey Turnpike to go home.

When I arrived at the condominium it was three in the morning. I called Damon to tell him to come to the door.

"Come to the door? I'm not home," Damon said.

"Where are you?"

"I went out to the city and had a few drinks with my teammates. I know a few guys from Syracuse. We're at this club called Lotus."

I was so mad at him. I had taken this long journey, gotten a flat, followed behind the movers, and dealt with the movers trying to talk to me at every rest stop up the East Coast. I felt funky and needed a bath. And after all that, his ass was not home.

"Janelle, I'll be right there. Maybe tomorrow we can come to the city and do something."

"Yeah whatever," I said as I waited for him to arrive.

We went to eat dinner at a steak house in Manhattan. I ordered a steak and mashed potatoes. Damon had fried catfish and rice pilaf. Our food was delicious. I was eating my potatoes and bit down on something hard.

"Baby, there is a rock in my food," I said as I pulled the hard substance out of my mouth. Damon called the manager over.

We explained to him what happened and he said, "Sorry, miss."

"Sorry? Is that all you can say? I could have choked on a pebble," I said, as I became angry.

"It must have came from the dirt on the potatoes."

"So you should have washed them off. Let's go somewhere else," I said.

Damon was still trying to eat his fish as we got up, paid our checks and left.

"Let's go to Harlem," I said.

"For what?"

"I want to see the Apollo and I want to see what 125th Street looks like. I never been there."

We went to 125th Street and it was crowded. There were big billboards on the side of buildings. There were street vendors selling books, pocketbooks, and mixed tapes. We saw the Apollo and people waiting in line to go to a show.

After Harlem we drove to Times Square. I had only seen Times Square on TRL, on MTV, or in a movie. Damon was acting like a little kid, looking up at all the moving billboards. They were the size of tall buildings. There were different-colored lights flashing. It was like a continuous light show. Advertisements for musicals, artist, and designers.

Chapter Fifty-six

Tanya

Twenty-four hours without a bath or a call home. The cops wanted me to talk about Lil' Ron. I would talk if I knew something, but I didn't. Nothing was making any sense. I hadn't even been arraigned yet. The cops wouldn't tell me what was going on. I knew they had to at least let me make a phone call home or to an attorney. If I had to say something, anything, to get out of this place, now I was going to say it.

In all those hours I had had a lot of time to think. I didn't have the distractions of kids, niggas, television, or the radio. The only voice I heard was mine. I kept asking myself, *Where the fuck is my life going?* My life was not supposed to turn out like this. I should have been a model or an actress. I should have done something with my life, anything. I could have gone to somebody's school, got a job. I was headed in the same direction as Saundra. Living off men, and going from man to man. My mom never had a job. I never saw my mother get up in the morning and go anywhere. Now look at me, I'm following right in her footsteps. I never had a job. Anything I wanted, a man always bought it for me. I need to make a change in my life. I need to do something with my life. I ain't got shit. Not a motherfucking thing. Nothing, not a car. I live with my grandmother, I don't have a job, and I ain't got shit. I ain't got shit. I don't want to be my mother. I don't want to end up like her. She is an ugly mess and I hate her. I hate that bitch for all she did. I know I don't always have my kids, but I never left them. I wouldn't ever leave them like Saundra did me.

I was angry that they had me in this cell. I started yelling and screaming, "Let me out, I didn't do anything. Let me the fuck out."

The cops paid me no attention at first. Then these two mean lady cops came into the cell and put handcuffs on me. They chained me to the bed. There was nothing I could do but sit. I sat for another four hours. I was tired and just wanted to go home.

The same lady cop who chained me to the bed began to unlock my handcuffs.

"What's going on?" I asked.

"Your girlfriend confessed. It's her boyfriend's guns and drugs. She told us where all the rest of his drugs are and that you had nothing to do with it."

They released me and I didn't have anyone to call. I didn't have any money. I just began to walk. I was going crazy. Too much shit had happened to me. They kept Monica. She had to be arraigned and had to go to a bail hearing. I wish Walei was still here. I could have called him to come and get me. I never even had sex with the nigga and he really loved me. He gave me whatever I needed. I should have went with him to San Diego. I didn't have any money and my cell phone was dead. I didn't know who to call. I felt like I didn't have a friend. I couldn't go back to Monica's and I definitely was not going home. The only person that might come and get me was Buc. I called him from a pay phone. His phone rang and rang. I was about to hang up when he answered.

"Hey, Buc, listen, can you come and get me?" I asked.

"Who is this?"

"It's Tanya."

"Where are you at?"

"The Round House on Eleventh and Vine."

"Hold tight. I'll be right there. Give me fifteen minutes."

I waited for Buc in a little coffee shop. I got a cup of black coffee. I saw Buc and I walked out to his truck. "What's up, Buc? Thanks for coming and getting me."

"What's going on with you? I pick you up from the Round House?"

"Nothing. I just need to chill. There's a lot going on."

"You look like you need a friend. Are you okay?"

"Yeah, I'm fine," I said as I broke down again. I let it all out. I gave Buc a brief summary of what had happened in the last two and a half days. He said I could stay with him if I didn't want to go home. I took him up on his offer. We went to his house and I took a shower. He gave me a T-shirt to sleep in. He just held me and let me cry. I poured my heart out to him. I just wanted to scream. Instead I started talking aloud about my problems.

"My mom was in and out of my life and now I'm becoming her. She shows up now and tells us she's dying. Then I go to Monica's house and she almost got me a case. Why have I got to have it so bad? My kid's father got killed. Shit is just fucked up for me. Life is not right."

"I understand everything you're going through. My mom and my dad were doing drugs when I was growing up. I didn't even have heat in my house or water. I would take baths at my friend's house."

"For real?"

"Yeah, Tanya, you not the only person that went through something. At least you had your grandmother, I didn't have anyone. I went away to the Job Corps at fifteen and learned how to cut hair. I know how it feels. My parents are doing okay today. They're not together anymore, but my mom is married and my dad just had a son. I know you hurt, but you are going to have to forgive your mom. People can change."

"I can't forgive her. I just can't."

"You got a lot to think about, Tanya, but family is important. Think about that."

I didn't want to think anymore. I wanted to rest my mind. I yawned. My eyes were watery and my head was pounding. I closed my eyes and temporarily I became dead to the world.

I woke up in the middle of the night and asked Buc to take me home because my kids needed me.

Chapter Fifty-seven

Janelle

Our condo wasn't as big as the house in Miami, but it was nice. It was spacious and had a fireplace. I was happy I got to decorate it the way I wanted to. Damon gave me money to go to Bath Bed and Beyond, Target, and Wal-Mart and I bought everything we needed. I did our bedroom in a creamy white. I wanted to do a purple or pink, but Damon would not go for that. The kitchen only had one window, so I bought yellow curtains and accessories. He has been practicing so hard and is never home. I'm glad I stayed with Damon. I love him and he loves me. I just didn't want him to mess up his career by doing coke. I didn't share his drug habit with anyone besides Kelly. I didn't want my mom or my uncle to think badly of him or me.

Ever since that night I tried to leave him, I don't think he has touched it again. I know because I have been checking everything: his clothes, wallet, gym bag, searching in the condo and his car when he is asleep or out. As far as I know he has been doing great. But temptation is always right there. So I decided I was still going to try to find him help. I called information and came across an outpatient facility a few miles from the condo. The lady on the phone was very pleasant and told me the cost and their confidentiality policy.

When Damon came home he said, "The place looks nice. You are doing a good job, baby."

"Sit down, Damon."

"What's wrong?"

"Listen, I know you said you want to do this yourself, but I found a private outpatient drug rehab."

"I told you I can handle it myself," he said as he got up and grabbed a Gatorade out of the refrigerator.

"No, Damon, I want you to go. I'll go with you. Nobody will know who you are or what you do. I already spoke to someone."

"I haven't touched it since we prayed, Janelle. You don't have to worry, I'm not going to touch any drug again. I asked God to help me and He has."

"I believe you, Dame, I just—"

He stopped me in the middle of my sentence and said, "Janelle, I'm not going to jeopardize you or my life. I promise you I will never touch that shit again."

"But, Damon, I just think it would be better. Forget it." I sighed.

"Janelle, I got it under control. But if it will make you happy I will go to counseling, okay?"

"Okay."

Damon tenderly picked me up off the floor and kissed me.

Since we were right in New Jersey, we decided to take the two-hour ride to Philly. I missed my mother and brothers. I never thought I would say that, but I did.

My mother had gotten reemployed with a law firm in Cherry Hill, New Jersey. Her salary was good and she had benefits, all the important things. I told her I was bringing Damon home. She was so excited. She had never met him in person because of his schedule.

As soon as I entered the apartment, I smelled smoke. I walked into the kitchen and my mom was taking a burned chicken out of the oven. She was trying to put barbecue sauce on it. Damon sat in the living room with my brothers. They asked him a lot of questions. I was giving Damon a tour of Philly. He wanted to get a cheesesteak and see the Art Museum where Rocky had raced up the steps in the movie. I then took him to meet my Uncle Teddy.

Chapter Fifty-eight

Natalie

I read my e-mails and that guy Troy had e-mailed me, *I hope your son is feeling better. P.S., e-mail me your picture when you get one.* I went into my photo album to find a recent good-looking picture. All of my pictures were with the baby or when I was pregnant. I had to take a new picture so I could e-mail it to Troy. I thought that was nice he asked about baby Anthony. I told him Anthony was fine. We instant-messaged back and forth for an hour. I told him I would send him a picture tomorrow.

Troy asked me to call him on the telephone. We had become pretty friendly. He said he wanted to hear my voice. I was curious about his too. I blocked my number by dialing *67 so if he was crazy he couldn't call me and find out where I live and come and kill me.

"Hello," a voice said. The voice was smooth and deep.

"Hi, this is Natalie."

"Hey, Natalie, about time I got to hear your voice." We stayed on the phone until 1:00 a.m. He ended the conversation saying that he had to get up and go to work in a few hours. I would have stayed on the phone and talked four more hours. His personality seemed so genuine. I hadn't been on the phone like that since I was a teenager. I was so excited I had to call someone and tell them.

"Janelle, I met this guy!" I said.

"What? That is so good. Why didn't you tell me?"

"I didn't want to spoil a good thing."

"That's so good. I told you just take your time and you would meet somebody. So where did you meet him?"

"Online."

"Online where?"

"The Internet."

"Are your serious, Natalie? Natalie, only desperate women and psychotic men meet people over the Internet."

"That's not true. I'm not desperate and Troy is really nice. He wants to meet in person. And I think I'm going to meet him."

"I don't think that is a good idea."

"Why?"

"He could be crazy. How long have you known this guy?"

"I know him about two weeks. Is this the same girl who met a man and moved in with him three days later?"

"Shut up."

"No, but for real, he e-mailed me from his job. He is an analyst for an insurance company. His name is Troy Sloan. I'll give you all his info. I feel comfortable. He seems so nice. Plus, I have talked to him on the phone. We are meeting up at a restaurant. I'm not leaving with him, so I'll be okay."

"Well, if you're comfortable, I'm comfortable. At least call Tanya. Be careful. Who does he live with?"

"His mother."

"Not another mama's boy, Natalie."

"No, he lives with his mom because he just got a divorce like me."

I went to the hair salon to get my hair styled. I bought a new outfit and makeup at the mall. I was dressed to the nines and

I wasn't scared when I walked into the restaurant. I didn't play any dumb game, like tell him I'm going to have on black and wear red. I just showed up. I walked in, looked around, and didn't see anybody that matched the description he had given me. I looked down and saw his number calling me on the screen of my cell phone. I picked it up and he said, "I see you, Natalie. You look even prettier than I anticipated." I looked up and he was standing across from me. He came over and gave me a quick hug. He was tall, with a light complexion and was almost a baldy. He was in a suit jacket with khakis and brown lace shoes.

"I'm glad you could make it," he said as we grabbed a table and he pulled out my chair. "This is a nice place."

"Yeah, me and my husband used to come here. I mean my ex-husband." I looked up to see his reaction.

"Look, I understand. How long has it been?"

"Not long, but it is definitely over."

"How do you know?"

"Because I know. He is really through and so am I. You know how you can't make a person change who they are? I didn't want to change him, but I couldn't understand him and he didn't understand me. I love him. Well, I'm not in love with him, but he just has a weird way of thinking."

"What was weird about his thinking?"

"Well, his mom messed him up mentally. She tried to teach him how to be a man. Instead, she turned him into a conservative 1950s-thinking man. Do you believe he thought I should be home with the baby and he really didn't want me to work? He also thought I shouldn't have friends. He told me every woman I knew was a slut, with the exception of my mother."

"I don't see anything wrong with a woman staying home with her child, if it's her choice. I know many women would love to stay home."

"Well, it wasn't my choice. He was always telling me what to do. And just being spoiled. It just irked me so bad.

And then he wouldn't help me with our baby." I took a sip of my water. "I'm sorry for rambling on about him."

"It's okay to vent. That's how you get over it."

"Okay, now you are a psychologist."

"No, but I know. I have been there. My ex-wife didn't know what she wanted to do with her life. She knew she didn't want to work and she liked to shop. One day she was taking classes for massage therapy and the next she was talking about starting her own day care. I had my daughter by somebody I dated before I got married. She would argue with me about me going to get and see my daughter."

"That's not cool."

"Yeah, I felt like she was jealous of my daughter and I couldn't take her indecisiveness anymore."

"She seems a little crazy. Jealous of your daughter."

"Yeah, I know. Let's not talk about our exes and our past. Let's talk about setting up our next date."

Our food was good and Troy's conversation was better. When dinner was over he walked me to my car and told me to call him as soon as I got home. He was really nice. I could see us being really good friends.

I talked on the phone to Troy all week. I could not wait to go out with him! I was thinking about him all week. He e-mails me every day. It feels so good to look forward to something and have someone to appreciate me in a romantic way. He has been sending me cute e-mails. I was going out with him tonight. I was so excited. I packed the baby's overnight bag and started running the water for my bath. I washed and then took my clothes off the hanger. I found my shoes under the bed. All I had to do was my hair. I called my mother to let her know I was on my way to bring the baby.

"Mom, we'll be there in about forty-five minutes."

"Okay, you can come over, but I'm not going to be here," she said.

"Where are you going to be? You said you would watch the baby."

"Damn it, I forgot you asked me to watch the baby. I have my women's meeting tonight," she said.

"Mom, you promised me you'd watch him. You can't go back on you word."

"I know what I said, but I'm sorry, I can't. I have to go to my meeting."

"Mom, that's not fair," I said as I hung up and threw down the phone. I didn't know how I was going to call Troy and tell him I couldn't go. It made me so mad. Here I had a nice guy that wanted to take me out, and I couldn't go. On a Saturday night I had to sit in the house and watch television. I took Anthony's clothes off him and put him in his crib.

I called Troy and luckily his answering machine came on and I didn't have to talk to him. I left him a message.

"Hey, Troy, it's me, Nat. Um, sorry I'm going to have to cancel. Talk to you later." Five minutes after I left the message for Troy I heard the phone ring. I didn't want to answer it. I knew it was going to be Troy. I picked up the phone reluctantly and said, "Hello."

"Hey, what's going on? Why are you canceling?"

"I don't have a babysitter."

"Oh," he said as he took a long pause. Then he said, "Let's take the baby with us."

"No, not to dinner."

"Why not?"

"Because it's only our second date and I don't want to bring my son. I'll just talk to you later." I hung up the phone. I was really mad. I started to take off my clothes. I looked in the mirror and began to cry. I looked really nice and I wasn't going anywhere. Troy called back again and asked me what my favorite food was.

I said, "Why?"

"Because I can come over and bring something to eat and we can watch a movie or television."

"No, that's really nice of you, but I'm just going to go to sleep." I finished taking off my clothes and went to bed.

I awoke I brushed my teeth and walked in to Anthony's room. He was standing up in his crib waiting for me. "Good morning big boy," I said. He reached his arms out to me. I picked him up and took him downstairs. I let him crawl around while I made his breakfast. I turned the television on and put his oatmeal in the microwave. The phone rang and I answered it.

"Can you see if you get a babysitter today?"

"Hey, Troy," I said.

"If you can't we can take your son somewhere."

"That sounds good. Let me call my mom and then I'll call you back."

I called my mom and she told me to bring the baby over. I called Troy back and we were going to meet up around three.

I dropped the baby off and my dad was sitting on the sofa. "Hi, Daddy," I said as I entered the house. "Where's Mommy? She is watching the baby."

"She left out," my dad said.

"What? She's supposed to be watching him."

"Natalie, I know. I got him until she comes back. Where are you going anyway?" he asked.

"Out, Daddy, nowhere special. Maybe to the mall," I said. I hated lying to my dad but I didn't need a lecture about how I was dating too soon or any of that. "Okay, Daddy, I'm out of here," I said as I sat Anthony on the sofa next to my dad. I gave Anthony a kiss and left.

I met Troy in the strip mall parking lot near my house. The lot was filled with people and cars. He wanted to pick me up at my house. I didn't feel comfortable enough for that yet. We went to the movies and then ate at a small Italian restaurant. Troy was interesting and a very good dad. He talked about his daughter Jaine a lot and she kept calling his cell phone every five minutes. He didn't turn his phone off. I wished he would have though. We were just seated when Troy said, "So what's up Ms. Natalie?"

"Nothing."

"What do you want to do next?" he asked

"Uh, I don't know." I said as I hunched my shoulders. The waitress brought us our salads and a breadbasket.

"When do you have to pick up your son?" he asked.

"My mom is keeping him overnight."

"So I get to keep you the whole night."

"No," I said as I blushed.

"I'm only playing. I'm just happy we had the opportunity to get together again."

"Me too!"

On the ride back to my car I wanted to ask him if he wanted to do something else. I didn't care if we just sat in his car and talked, because I didn't have anything to do when I got home. Nothing but maybe watch television and fold clothes. But I didn't have the heart. I didn't want to come off as desperate, even though I really enjoyed his company. We pulled up next to my car. The parking lot was nearly empty. Troy got out of the car and came around and opened my door. I said thank you.

"When are we getting together again?" he asked.

"Just call me," I said as I searched for my car keys. Troy then leaned me against my car door and kissed me. "We're outside, somebody might see us," I said. In the back of my mind I felt like I was betraying Anthony. But that was my problem; I was always thinking about Anthony and needed to start thinking about me. The moment I leaned to kiss him back, his phone rang. At first he didn't answer it. Then it rang again. He decided to answer the phone and it was his daughter Jaine again.

"I'm out. . . . Yes, I'll come and get you, sweetie, tomorrow. . . . I love you too. Good night."

While he was on his phone I got in my car and started it. He told me to call him when I got in the house. I told him I would and pulled off.

Chapter Fifty-nine

Tanya

When Buc dropped me off, everybody was sleep.

"Are you okay, Tanya?" Mom-Mom asked.

"Yes, Mom-Mom."

"Where have you been?"

"Thinking," I said.

"Well, I hope you been thinking about doing the right thing with your life."

I sat down next to her. She grabbed my hand and said, "Tanya, I'm not always going to be here. I love Deja and Davon to death, but they're not my children and you can't keep burdening me with them."

"Mom-Mom, I'm going to get myself together."

"You see what the fast life will get you? Nothing. Look at your mother, my only child." She wiped away her tears with a napkin. "She is sorry, Tanya. She didn't do any of this to you. The drugs did it. She started that mess right after she had you."

"I can't forgive her. She said she wanted to kill me when I was a baby."

"Tanya, please find it in your heart. She is going to stay here. I'm giving her the middle room."

"Where are Deja and Davon going to stay?" I asked, shocked.

"I guess you will be getting your own place. Or we will all live together," she said unapologetically as she sipped her coffee.

"When is she coming back?"

"She is asleep in my room now."

I couldn't believe my grandmother was putting us out for Saundra, I thought as I walked away.

"Tanya."

"Yes, Mom-Mom."

"I would never put you out, but I can't turn away my daughter either."

I would not have my kids around a crackhead. Once a crackhead, always a crackhead. I peeked in the room to see that the kids were still sleep. I went into the bathroom and took a long, hot bath. I had so much on my mind. My mom comes back, I get locked up, Monica in jail, how much can one person take? I grabbed a towel and walked into my room and went to sleep.

My cell rang and woke me up. It was Buc calling me to see how I was doing. "You okay?"

"Yeah, I'm fine. My mom is staying here now, so I got to move."

"Where are you moving to?"

"I don't know yet. I have to find somewhere and fast."

"You hear anything 'bout your girlfriend yet?"

"No, I'm waiting for her to call me now."

"If you need anything let me know. I'm down at the shop. I can bring you something to eat or we can go and talk."

"Thank you. I'll call you later." I hung up the phone and called Derrick to see if he'd heard anything about Monica yet.

Sabrina answered the phone. "Who's this?"

"Tanya. Where is your uncle?"

"I don't know," she said.

"Did your mom call there yet?"

"No, they said she got to get arraigned or something. They trying to find out her bail."

"Do you know your uncle's cell number?"

"No. Do you know Uncle Derrick's number?" I heard her ask her sister.

"Listen, write down mine and when he calls tell him to call me." She said okay and my other line beeped.

I clicked over and it was Monica. "Yo, Tanya, it's me."

"You okay?"

"Yeah, I'm cool. I'm trying to get in touch with Derrick. I keep calling my house and my line is busy."

"I just called there and talked to Sabrina. She said he wasn't there."

"He must be trying to get some money together."

"How much is your bail?"

"I don't know yet. Tanya, I'm not trying to be a snitch, but I'm not going to jail for him."

"You better not, he wouldn't do it for you."

"I can't. I been talking to girls up here. They telling me I don't want to go upstate. They said it is so rough. I am scared. Girl, who gonna take care of my kids? I'm too old for this shit. I'll be thirty-one soon and I'm in jail. I'm not being down for no nigga that ain't down for me. But, um, try to get in touch with Derrick and tell him to wait by the phone. I'm going to call him by two."

"So what is the worst-case scenario?" I asked.

"I don't know yet. I might get probation or I might have to do some time. I don't know. I don't want to talk about it. Derrick said he going to try to hustle me some money up."

"I got a few dollars if you need it."

"Thanks. I got to go. I got to call this lawyer. He said he won't even go to my arraignment unless I get him eight hundred by four p.m. I'll call you later."

I went into the kitchen. Deja and Davon were eating cereal at the table. Deja gave me a hug and said, "Mommy, where you been?" Davon just looked at me, waiting for an answer.

"I was out looking for a house."

"We're moving, Mom?" Deja asked.

"Where to? I don't want to move," Davon said.

"I want to stay here with Mom-Mom," Deja said.

"Well, Mom-Mom's daughter is back and there's not enough room for us, so we have to move."

"Tanya, tell the truth, there is enough room. You want to move. If you want to leave, you leave. The kids can stay with me," Mom-Mom said.

"Mom-Mom, as long as that crackhead is here, we will not be here."

"Don't talk about her like that." My grandmother started crying and then Deja ran over to her and was hugging her. Davon ran upstairs and my mother, Saundra, walked into the kitchen. She was weaker than yesterday. She looked bad: she was frail, her eyes were puffy, and she was walking slowly.

"You don't have to leave. I'll leave," Saundra said.

"No, she is not going anywhere. You leave, Tanya."

"You saying fuck me for this bitch? Well, fuck you, Mom-Mom," I said as I raced up the steps and started packing my shit. I didn't even have anywhere to go, but I was not staying here. I got my suitcase and started filling it. I dragged it down the stairs and slammed it up against the door, then ran upstairs and grabbed a duffel bag and filled that up then I brought it down the steps.

"Deja and Davon, get your shit now!" I yelled.

"Mommy, I don't want to go," Deja said again. The kids hurried and dressed. I headed for the door and Mom-Mom was in front of it, blocking it.

"Please, Tanya, please don't leave me. Please," she whimpered. "I just got one daughter back. I can't have another leave. Please, Tanya, it is just us. Please, we going to work this out. We family."

"No, move, Mom-Mom, or I'm going to move you."

"Then move me, Tanya. Move me."

I put the bags down and just got so frustrated I began to kick and hit the wall. I was making holes, but I didn't care, it felt good.

My mother came over and stood next to me and said, "This house didn't hurt you, I did. I'm sorry, beat me. Hit me, you can fuck me up. Beat me. Do whatever you got to do to me. Don't beat this house."

I slouched down on the floor and began to shake. Saundra hugged me. Then Mom-Mom came over to me and hugged me. The kids were clinging to me. "We're going to work through this," my mom-mom said as she patted my back and I let out years of anger, tears, and pain.

Chapter Sixty

Janelle

I was looking for a job and this time I was going to keep it. Damon said I didn't have to work, but I needed to. Plus, I really would be bored. I don't know anyone here. I'm happy that I'm close to my family. New York traffic was always the pits. I was in the Lincoln Tunnel for at least forty-five minutes. Next time I'm going to catch the train over. I don't like traffic. I'm not used to it on this extreme level.

After I got out of traffic I found a parking lot. I gasped at the parking prices. I thought it was that one parking lot. But I rode around some more and all of them were thirty dollars or more for a few hours of parking. I finally valet-parked. I stepped onto the sidewalk. My plan was to try to find a job in retail as a manager, or an assistant manager. I could have sent my resume, but I thought hands-on might be better. I could actually see what the stores looked like. I wouldn't mind working in a high-end store on Fifth Avenue or a boutique.

The moment I hit the sidewalk I felt the fast pace of New York life. Everything was on a different level, the fashion, the people, the lifestyle. Yellow cabs were everywhere beeping their horns. I saw men in Wall Street attire to a homeless woman. A girl with doorknocker earrings from the eighties to a woman in a high-fashion dress right off the runway. New York was so busy. I kept thinking I was going to get mugged, like in the movies. Every street I crossed I turned my head both ways. I kept my bag close to my side. I looked up at the street sign and tried to understand how you could be on Fifth Avenue between Tenth and Eleventh. The numbering of the streets was crazy. I just tried to remember where I parked so I wouldn't get lost. I had the whole day to find my way around the city and possibly find a job.

I came home and Damon asked, "Where were you all day."

"Looking for a job."

"Janelle, my girl don't have to work, I told you that."

"Damon, listen. I'm your girl but, I need a job. I need my independence."

"Are you coming to the game this week?"

"I don't know, why?" I asked.

If you are you got to let me know by Wednesday so I can get the tickets."

"You didn't have to do that in Miami."

"Janelle, new organization, new rules."

"I'm coming. It's just going to be so weird sitting alone in the stands."

"Invite your mom, brothers, and uncle up."

I called my mother and brothers, but they already had plans. The boys were spending the weekend with their dad. "Hey, Uncle, I got tickets for the game against the Redskins. You want to go?"

"Tell Damon I said thanks but no, thanks. E-A-G-L-E-S. I would be betraying my team plus I have to work."

"I understand. Well, I'll see you soon. Bye, Unc."

If nobody was going to the game with me I wasn't going. I stayed home.

Chapter Sixty-one

Tanya

I have been trying to deal with my mother and everything that has been going on. I still feel like I hate my mom, but I have been asking God to help me forgive her. I don't want to end up like her. I have my kids under me. I haven't been anywhere. I was gradually forgiving her. The kids were getting used to having her around. My grandmother was just happy to have her child around.

I was in the kitchen eating breakfast when I overheard my grandmother asking my mother how she knew she had AIDS.

"Because I was dealing with Billy and he got it," she said.

"Did you go to the doctor?"

"No," she answered.

"You don't necessarily have it," Mom-Mom said.

"I know I got it," she said.

"Well, maybe you should still go to the doctor. I'll take you to get tested."

My grandmother called me into the living room and asked me to drive her to the closest clinic.

* * *

I went with Mom-Mom and my mom to get her test result. We had to wait a week for it. I was just as scared as she was. I did a lot of dirty shit in my time; all the niggas I fucked for money. Nights I got high and didn't remember what happened. It was scary. I don't want to die. I want to live. I want to see my kids grow up and see them become somebody.

My mind was drifting when the doctor came and told us my mom was wrong. She didn't have AIDS yet. She had HIV, the infection that causes AIDS. I asked what the difference was.

"Well, once you get the virus it slowly begins to attack the immune system. The weakening of immune function leads to AIDS," the doctor said.

"So she has HIV."

"Yes, she has HIV, not AIDS. If she takes care of herself she can live for many years."

I turned around and began to shake my head and cry. I cried and Mom-Mom cried. Saundra held us together. She didn't shed a tear. The lady at the clinic put my mother in touch with a social worker and the department of welfare. My mother had to be put on medication immediately.

Chapter Sixty-two

Natalie

Me and Troy have been dating regularly, going to the movies and dinner. It is just fun having someone of the opposite sex to date and talk to. He asked me if we could get a hotel room this weekend. He says he just wants to lie next to me and be able to hold me all night. All of our dates have been outside and it is getting cold. I wouldn't mind lying beside him.

We went to the hotel and he checked us in. We parked and went in at the side door. He kissed me. I felt so nervous. This was the first time I was going to have sex with someone other than my husband. I secretly always wondered if I was any good. Now I guess I would see; at least that's what I thought. Troy didn't touch me the entire night. He was a perfect gentleman. I was so upset. He held me all night. I was waiting for him to make his move, any move, something. I wanted his hands all over my body, holding, sucking, and caressing me all over. I went to sleep disappointed. I woke up mad.

I got out of the bed and went and took a shower. I thought he might invite himself into the shower with me. I took an extra-long shower, asked him to bring me my pocketbook. This would give him the perfect opportunity to see me or say something, and then I could encourage him to come into the shower with me and love me down. He did just the opposite. He didn't look in, he just reached his arm in without looking and handed me my bag. Okay, that was it, he was not trying to do anything. I couldn't get any more desperate.

I put my clothes on. I started doing my hair and spraying my body spray. I guess he really wanted to chill, I thought as I applied my lip gloss. Oh well.

He said, "I got to get in there."

"Okay, give me one minute," I said. He don't want to give me any and now he is rushing me out of the bathroom, I thought. I gathered my lip gloss, body spray, and comb.

I brushed past him and he did what I was waiting for, he took control. He pulled my hair back and kissed my neck and then bent me over the sink. He removed my shirt and began twisting my nipples. They became so hard they were hurting. He placed me directly in front of the mirror so I could look at myself. The same mirror I had stood in front of moments earlier and didn't think I was going to get any. And now not only was I getting it, I was getting it good.

"Was this what you were waiting for?" he asked as I kissed him back.

"No."

"Yes, it was. Be honest, Natalie. It is okay to want it, Natalie. You don't have to wait for the man to be the aggressor."

He spread my legs open and toyed with the opening of my vagina.

"Are you ready, Natalie?" he asked.

"Yes," I said as I rubbed my body back and forth against his fingers and kissed all over his neck.

He then placed his middle finger inside of me. "Your shit is so tight. Natalie, you ready?"

"Yes, I'm ready. Give it to me," I said as he kept gliding his finger in and out. I couldn't take it anymore. He pulled down my pants, unzipped his pants, put a condom on, and began to fuck me like I had never been fucked before. We went at it two more times before we left the room. We called the front desk and asked for an extended checkout.

We checked out at 1:00 p.m. I was sore and tired. I had to go home and soak and lie down before I went to pick up the baby. I couldn't even walk straight when I picked up the baby. I left my car running. I didn't want my mom to see the way I was walking. I called her and told her to have him ready because I wasn't feeling well, and I wanted to hurry up and get home. She met me at the door with his car seat and baby bag.

"You okay, Natalie?"

"Yeah, Mom, I just need to get some rest. I have to go to work in the morning."

I came home and washed Anthony's body, hair, and clipped his little toes and hands. I read to him and played with him until he got tired. As soon as he dozed off. I took my clothes off, got into the bed, and began to recall my morning and afternoon with Troy.

The phone rang and rang. It woke me up. I groggily answered it.

"Hello," I said.

"Natalie," Anthony said, sobbing my name.

"Anthony?" I said, unsure.

"Natalie, my mom is not going to make it."

I thought I was dreaming. I sat up in the bed and looked over at the alarm clock. "It's four in the morning. What are you talking about, Anthony?" I asked him.

"My mother is in the hospital. She has cancer. She never told me about it. She is not going to make it. They are giving her one week to live."

"Where are you, Anthony?"

"At Jefferson Hospital."

"Anthony, I am on my way." It was cold. I didn't want to get the baby dressed, but Anthony was crying. I had to go be with him. Ms. Renee was so strong. I can't see her being sick. She just cussed me out and now she's dying, I can't believe it. I called my parents. My dad answered the telephone.

"Daddy, Ms. Renee is in the hospital. They gave her one week to live. I'm going to meet Anthony at the hospital. Can you watch the baby?"

"Of course, come on." I heard my father wake up my mother and her saying oh my God. My mother got on the phone and asked if Anthony was okay.

"Yeah, he is really upset. Mom, they only give her a week to live." I hurriedly dressed in the dark. I got the baby dressed and dropped him off. I still hadn't had a chance to think about what was going on.

I saw Anthony. He was sitting in the hospital hallway. There were nurses and doctors walking past. An older man was mopping the floor. He was placing a WET FLOOR sign on that half of the hallway. I went up to Anthony and hugged him sideways.

He broke down and cried like a baby. "I don't know what I'm going to do without her."

"It's going to be okay. It's going to be okay," I said as I hugged him tighter

Anthony was crying uncontrollably. I tried to calm him down and soothe him. "I mean, how long has she been sick?"

"I don't know, the doctors won't tell me anything."

"You are her next of kin. They have to tell you something."

"It is some kind of confidentiality thing. They did say she has edometrail . . . endomen . . . fuck it. She got cancer."

"Are you certain, Anthony?"

"Yeah, the nurse was trying to explain it to me. Here, she gave me this." He handed me a pamphlet. I read the form. It was endometrial cancer, tumors in the lining of the uterus.

"Can she speak?"

"No, not really. I can't take seeing her like that. I can't lose her, Natalie."

I walked into the room and saw Ms. Renee. She was

hooked up to all kinds of monitors and machines. Her hands looked swollen and her hair was all over her head. She looked weak. "Hi, Ms. Renee," I whispered. I didn't want to wake her. She would die instantly if she saw me standing over her.

Anthony came into the room and grabbed her hand and kissed it. Ms. Renee didn't make any movement. She didn't open her eyes. I pulled a chair up for Anthony and one for myself. It was really chilly in the hospital. I asked the nurse if they had any blankets. She brought us two. I wrapped one over Anthony and the other over my shoulders. Anthony wept in my lap. I patted his back and we sat next to Ms. Renee's bedside the rest of the night.

When it got to be eight o'clock I knew I had to call Ms. Jerri and tell her I wouldn't be able to make it in. I couldn't call out on her again, so I had my mom call her. My body was stiff from sitting in one position for so many hours. I had to check on the baby and get some real rest.

I woke Anthony and asked him if he wanted anything. He said to get him a coffee. I got his coffee and told him I would come back later. I felt bad leaving him at the hospital alone. But Ms. Renee's fate was in God's hands and all we could do was pray for her.

I showered, ate, and fed the baby. I briefed my mom about Ms. Renee's condition. She said it was a shame and that she would pray for her. "Natalie, hurry up and go back down there with Anthony. He needs you."

On the way to the hospital I stopped and got Anthony a cornbeef sandwich. He was still next to his mother's bed. I told him I had some food for him. He said he wasn't hungry. Seeing Ms. Renee like this hurt me. Before, her eyes were closed and she looked like she was sleeping. Now with her eyes open and her barely being able to speak, it dawned on me that Ms. Renee was really dying. I started thinking of my own mortality and if my mom or dad were lying in that bed. I couldn't hold back my emotions. A tear streamed down my cheek. Then another one came. Before I knew it I was crying. I grabbed a tissue and waited in the hallway for Anthony.

He came out, grabbed me, and said, "My mom doesn't hate you, Natalie."

"I know that. What made you say that?" I asked.

"I just wanted to tell you that. She loves the baby and you. She just always thought you were taking me away from her."

"That doesn't matter right now, Anthony," I said.

"I just wanted to tell you that. When you were gone the doctor came and told me my mother is going to keep going in and out of consciousness."

"For how long?"

"They don't know. That's why I have to stay here. So she can see me every time she opens her eyes. I wish she could see the baby."

"Here, show her this picture," I said as I gave Anthony a picture of the baby from my wallet. I stayed in the doorway as Anthony showed the photo to Ms. Renee. She smiled a little and then closed her eyes again.

Chapter Sixty-three

Natalie

I haven't heard from Anthony today. The last time I spoke to him he said they were giving her morphine to ease the pain. He said after they give you morphine it usually is the end. I checked my messages and Anthony was on there. He left a simple message. *Call me, my mom just passed.* I couldn't believe it. Anthony was my ex-husband and I didn't know what to say to him. I didn't want to call him back. What could I say to him, "I'm sorry. Hope you feel better?" I just called and said, "Anthony, I got your message. I'll be right over."

Ms. Renee would have been fifty-seven in three days. She had been fighting cancer for six years and she didn't tell anyone. Anthony found a letter that she had written to him in detail of how she wanted her funeral planned. She had an outfit picked out, the deed to her house, and all her insurance papers together. She left Anthony a hundred-thousand-dollar policy and the baby a fifty-thousand-dollar policy.

I haven't spoken to Troy or checked my e-mails. I told Troy everything that was going on. He was real understanding and said he was going to give me some time.

Ms. Renee's two sisters flew in from Texas to help Anthony plan the funeral. I had only met them once before at our wedding. Mary Ellen was Ms. Renee's older sister and Ms. Dolores was the baby sister. Ms. Renee left a red dress with gold beads and mule pumps with red and gold beading to be buried in. Her sister Mary Ellen looked at the dress, then up at the sky, and said with a country drawl, "Sorry, Renee, you are not getting buried in that scandalous red dress!"

They went out to find her a white suit and white shoes to wear. I typed her obituary and wrote a grocery list of all the things I needed to buy to help prepare the food. My mother was going to help me with the cooking.

"My sister was a mean, evil somebody. Was she mean to you?" Ms. Dolores asked me.

"Not really," I lied. They didn't know how much Ms. Renee had hated me.

"She was just crazy. One day she was my friend, the next my enemy," Ms. Mary Ellen chimed in. "She spoiled that boy rotten. We told her and she didn't listen. Why you think she moved all the way across the country? 'Cause she was crazy."

I tried not to laugh at Ms. Dolores and Mary Ellen, but they were funny.

We gathered all her pictures and finalized her obituary. Ms Renee had a real interesting life. I didn't know Anthony's father was her second husband and she divorced her first husband and moved to Philadelphia. She went to school for nursing but never practiced because she had Anthony.

Her funeral was small and nice. I sat in the first row with the family. I knew she was there in spirit like "get out of this church." Ms. Renee had a polished oak casket. Her makeup was very light and she had a short gray wig on. Her white suit and shoes her sisters picked for her suited her well. There were bouquets of flowers everywhere. Her congregation had sent flowers, as well as neighbors and the auxiliary she belonged to. Her pastor spoke and said that Sister Renee was a beacon of joy to everyone that knew her. Her own sister Ms. Mary Ellen whispered to me, "Now why he lying? May God bless her soul, but my sister was a hell-raiser. He is going to get it for lying in church." I almost began to laugh, but instead I held my composure and kept a straight face. After the service we went to the cemetery and then back to her house. Everyone was sitting around reminiscing about Ms. Renee and eating. Anthony came up to me and hugged me. "I don't know what I would have done without you, Natalie. Thank you for being here for me."

"You're welcome," I said as I hugged him back.

Chapter Sixty-four

Natalie

A nthony started staying with me and the baby. It was like old times. I never gave him my letter. He was really making an effort to do the right thing. I was happy him and the baby were bonding again. It felt so good to have help and not to do everything on my own. He had a new emphasis on family with Ms. Renee passing on. We weren't intimate, but we still had a very close family bond.

Anthony wanted to sell his mother's house and move back in with me. I didn't know if I wanted him to do that. He said he wanted us to get remarried, wanted to buy a new house, and he was going to go back to school. He said he would pay for me to go too. Everything sounded so good, but just a few weeks ago, before Ms. Renee had died, we were at war. I felt strange, like in the time we were apart I grew up. I started a new relationship, a new job, and have been making progress in my life. I don't know if we are supposed to be back together. I mean look at all we have been through. I don't know if Anthony wants to come back because he really loves me or if he doesn't have anyone else. I don't know. I really don't know. When I'm with Anthony, it is not about me anymore, it is about him.

"I thought long and hard about it, but I don't think we

could be together," I told Anthony. I just didn't want to take all those steps backward. He understood he was the one who was adamant about the divorce. He thanked me for being by his side and said he was going to have to accept we were not married anymore. He said he couldn't live in his mother's house, so he was going to definitely sell it and move to Houston with his aunts. I had to live my life for me and my son and unfortunately Anthony was not a part of my new life. I was a little concerned about Anthony being apart from the baby. I didn't want him to move all the way to Houston, but I couldn't stay with him either, just for the baby's sake.

Chapter Sixty-five

Tanya

I did not want to end up like Monica or my mom. I enrolled in a GED class at Community College. I didn't really want to go. I feel like I'm too smart for some stupid GED prep class. I had dropped out in tenth grade, but I wasn't a dummy. The first day I went to GED class I almost walked out. We were in this little room in the basement. Our classes met every Tuesday and Thursday evening for twelve weeks. There was an old lady in the front row. In the back making noise were young kids that must have been kicked out or left school, and they thought a GED class was easier than the real thing. The old lady had a cane. She kept asking dumb questions. The teacher, an older white man with a twitch, had to answer them. If he didn't, it would seem like he was discriminating against her because of her age. It felt like I was right back where I was eight years ago when I dropped out. The teacher gave us an overview of what we would be doing. Everything on the paper looked so simple. There was no way I could sit in this class two days a week for twelve weeks straight. He said you could only be absent twice and being late three times would count as an absence.

I wanted to get into the nursing assistant program, but in order to get there I was going to have to get this GED.

When the next class was over I talked to my instructor. "Hi, Mr. Palmerton."

"Are you having trouble with the class?" he asked.

"No, not at all. I wanted to know, is there any way I could just take the GED test? I know this stuff already."

"Sorry, no, in order to take our test you have to attend class."

"Thanks," I said as I turned and walked toward the door.

"But I do know of another program you could go to in Center City. They give tests every month on Saturdays. If you wait a moment I'll give you their number." I waited for him to talk to a few other students. He then went in his tattered tan briefcase and gave me the number and I called as soon as I got home.

"Our next class doesn't start until November," the man said.

"Okay, can I sign up?" I gave the man my information. That meant I had to sit in that stupid class another month. I didn't want to chance failing and I'd already dropped out of the first class. I bought this book that was supposed to help me study for the test. It was so strange studying. I can't remember the last thing I'd read other than a fashion magazine.

I was still attending my GED class. I took the test and was waiting to see if I had passed so I could leave this dumb-ass class. The class was stupid and so were the students. The teacher spoke to us like we were in kindergarten. I was outside smoking a cigarette during our break. I gave up weed and everything else. My grandmother called me and said that my test scores had come. I told her to read them to me.

"It says out of a possible one hundred you scored a seventy-nine," Mom-Mom said.

"A seventy-nine? I don't think that is passing. Mom-Mom, give me that number off the refrigerator, it has the number to the program." She gave me the number and I called the program. The people there said I needed an overall 75 to pass. I had a 79, so that meant I passed.

"Thank you," I told the lady as I hung up the telephone. I had gotten my GED now. I just had to wait for my nursing assistant program to start. I didn't return to class.

Chapter Sixty-six

Natalie

Anthony asked me to take him to the airport. He was going to Houston.

"I have to go to work," I said.

"What time do you have to be at work?" he asked.

"Nine."

"I have to be to the airport at seven A.M.," he said.

"Okay, I'll take you to the airport."

"Is it okay if I spend the night there, so I can help you get the baby ready? Because I can't miss my flight. Plus, I want to spend the evening with him before I leave."

"I don't know about that, Anthony."

"I'll sleep on the sofa. I just want to spend some time with my son because I don't know how long I'll be gone for," he said begging.

"Fine, Anthony, just come to the house."

I said goodbye. Then I hurried to work. Ms. Jerri has been riding me ever since I called out on her. I would quit but she pays every week.

I dropped Anthony off at the airport. Then I rushed baby Anthony to day care and then went to work. Anthony called me from Houston and said he had made it. He told me to think about us getting back together. I told him we weren't getting back together and once he got over Ms. Renee he would be able to see it.

I called Troy. I hadn't talked to him in weeks. He was so glad to hear from me.

"Hey, stranger."

"Hi, Troy."

"How you been?"

"It's been hard, but I'm doing okay under the circumstances," I said.

"How is your son doing?" he asked.

"He's fine," I said.

"And his father?"

"My ex is okay. He is in Houston." I laughed.

"Why are you laughing? I really want to know how he is doing."

"He is okay. I don't want to talk about him," I said.

"I miss you, Natalie."

"I miss you too!" I mumbled. I couldn't believe what I was saying.

"Okay, then when can I see you?"

"I don't know. I'll call you and let you know. Bye, Troy."

Chapter Sixty-seven

Natalie

Troy was on his way over. He asked me could he see me. I said when and he said now. I gave him my address. I couldn't wait to see him and put everything else behind me. I arrived home and straightened the place up a little. I lit a candle and turned on my Kindred CD. I washed the baby and put his nightclothes on him and put him in the playpen. I baked chicken and made stuffing and broccoli.

Troy arrived minutes later. We gave each other a quick hug. He said the food smelled good.

"Thanks, everything is almost ready. I'm going to make our plates. I'll be right back," I said. The baby started crying the minute I walked out of the living room. Troy grabbed the baby out of the playpen for me.

"I got him. We're okay," he said as I walked into the living room.

Anthony stopped crying and I began making our plates. I pulled two glasses out of the cabinet. I needed ice, and was grabbing the ice trays out of the freezer when I heard a deep, strong voice say, "Nigga, what the fuck you doing with my son?" I dropped the glass. If I didn't know better I swore I heard Anthony's voice, but he was in Houston. I know because I had put him on the plane and he had called me. I heard the voice say again, "What the fuck you think you doing holding my son?"

I ran into the living room. Troy had placed the baby on the sofa. He stood up and said, "Man, take it easy." Anthony was standing in the living room yelling at Troy.

"What are you doing here? You are supposed to be in Houston!" I screamed.

"Don't worry about why I'm here. Who is he and what is he doing holding my son? Soon as I leave town you got this nigga playing daddy to my son. I should fuck you up," he said as he walked up on me. I tried to back away and reason with him.

"Anthony, listen! We are divorced. You cannot walk up in here asking me questions about anything going on in my home. Leave, now! Before I call the cops," I said.

"I'm not going anywhere, this is my house," he said as he mugged my face.

"Don't touch her," Troy said. That upset Anthony so he hit him with a jab right to the face, knocking him down to the floor.

"Mind your own business! That's my wife," Anthony said as he took off his jacket, rolled up his sleeves, and waited for Troy's next move. Troy got up and hit him back. They both put their hands up in a fighting position. They swung punches back and forth at each other.

"Anthony! Stop! Please stop!" I begged as he lunged at Troy.

Troy punched Anthony in the face. They were circling each other like they were in a boxing ring. They started wrestling and knocked down my lamp. I grabbed my son, picked up the telephone, and called 911. "Please, come quick, my ex-husband has broken into my house and is fighting my friend," I said.

I hung up the phone and held on to the baby tightly. I couldn't believe what was going on. Blood was coming out of Anthony's mouth. Troy was on top of him. Then they let each other go. While they were apart I stepped between them and asked them to please stop. Anthony pushed me and ran to get his jacket. He pulled out a silver object. The silver object was his gun. I stepped back and so did Troy. Anthony aimed the gun at Troy and started firing. *Pow! Pow! Pow!* I ducked behind the sofa. Baby Anthony was clinging to me. The gunshots were loud, they were scaring him. He was crying. Anthony just kept shooting. One bullet hit the wall and another hit the banister.

I looked over at Troy. He had been shot in the arm and leg, and he looked like he was about to pass out. His mouth was open and he was moaning. One of the bullets hit me in the leg. It was like a hot piece of metal tearing through my skin. I fell and I dropped the baby. Anthony came over to me and reloaded his gun. He put each bullet in slowly and said, "I loved you, Natalie. I loved you so much! You just don't know. I lost my mother. I wanted to kill myself today. I didn't want to live anymore. Then I said I couldn't kill myself without saying good-bye to my son. Or saying good-bye to you. So I got on a plane and came back home. That's all I wanted to do is say good-bye to you Natalie, I didn't want to be by myself with the holidays approaching."

"Anthony, I love you too!" I said, trying to appease him.

"No, you don't. You must love this nigga," he said as he walked back over to Troy and shot him again. I crawled to grab the baby. His sleeper was soaked with blood. He was looking up at me with a frightened look.

"My God, Anthony! You shot the baby. You shot our son!" I screamed. "Get him some help!" I yelled.

Anthony saw the baby's bloody nightclothes and dropped the gun. Troy managed to get up and stumble out the door. Anthony kneeled on the floor and began to cry. "I'm a failure! I shot my own son."

"We got to get him some help, Anthony." I picked up the baby. He wasn't crying. I couldn't tell where the blood was coming from. It was all over the place. Police sirens were approaching.

I went to the door and there were about a half dozen cops

in front of my door with their guns drawn. A paramedic ran up to me and took the baby. Then a cop grabbed me and put my arms behind my back. I yelled, "I didn't shoot him. It was my ex-husband."

Anthony stood in the door. He was on his way out. Then one of the cops shot at him. He went back into the house and shut the door. They pushed me into the car. They were going to kill Anthony.

"No, no. Don't shoot him!" I screamed.

After I answered a few questions they let me get in the ambulance with the baby. I was so concerned with my son I couldn't think about Anthony. The cops told me not to worry about him. I had to think about myself and my child. I called my mother and told her Anthony shot me and the baby. All I heard her say was, "Lord, are y'all okay? What hospital are you at?"

Once we reached the hospital I found I only had a graze wound. But my baby had a gunshot wound to his arm. The bullet had just missed his shoulder. He had lost so much blood and was lucky to have made it to the hospital. I couldn't think straight. They were going to transfer him to Children's Hospital when he was stabilized. They wanted to evaluate him first to make sure nothing else was wrong.

My parents had just made it to the hospital. I had blood everywhere. My mother was crying. My dad was crying too! A police officer came over to us and said that Anthony was still in the house and they were trying to get him out. The cop said, "Your husband said he is going to kill himself if he doesn't speak with you."

"What? She doesn't want to talk to him," my mother said.

"You don't want them to shoot him, do you?" my father asked.

"Right now I don't care. Look what he has done to me and my son," I said.

"You don't mean that, Natalie," he said.

"I do mean it, Daddy. I don't want to talk to him."

"If you don't talk to him he is going to be killed. Do you want that, Natalie?"

"No." I didn't want Anthony to be killed but he was so damn stupid. He didn't have to do all this.

"Then just tell him to come out."

"Okay, I will talk to him." I wept.

My mother stayed with the baby, and he was going to be okay. My father and an officer escorted me home.

We pulled up to my house. All my neighbors were outside staring and news vans and reporters were setting up. They brought over a telephone and called my house. My dad told me to talk to him nicely. I was going to try. I wanted to cuss him out. Anthony picked up the phone. He was sobbing. He was crying hard like the night his mom passed on.

"Anthony, it's me, you can't stay in there, you got to come out."

"Natalie. Is he okay? I need to die. I hurt my son. I should die, it's too late, I'm going to die."

"Anthony, it's not too late. You are not going to die. Please come out."

"Is our son okay?" he asked.

"Yes, he is fine. Now, Anthony, you have to come out. You can't stay in there." My dad and the other officers were telling me what to say. I was so nervous. I could hear it in his voice that he was shaken.

"Our son is fine? He is not dead?"

"No, he is not dead. So please come out."

"Natalie, you are a good woman. I was wrong. You should be able to go out with your girlfriends. Baby, I love you," he said over the police telephone.

"Anthony, please just come outside with your hands up. Right now. They promised me if you come out they won't hurt you. They will help you. If you don't they are going to kill you."

"I'm sorry I messed up our family. You're a good woman. I should have treated you right."

"Please come out." I asked again.

"Are you mad at me? If you are I don't want to live anymore. And I'll kill myself. Right now. I got the gun against my head now."

"Don't kill yourself. You have so much to live for, Anthony. You have me and the baby. Just come out. Put the gun down. You have to be here for baby Anthony. You're his daddy and I'm his mommy and I do love you," I said.

The phone went dead and I thought the worst. But then the front door opened and Anthony walked out with his hands up above his head. He walked slowly like they told him. The police ran up to him and put him in handcuffs and placed him in the wagon. Me and my dad went back to the hospital. Tanya was there with my mom. She ran up and hugged me. I hugged her back and the nurse came over to us and said they were ready to transfer Anthony over to Children's Hospital.

"What happened, Natalie?" Tanya asked.

"I don't know. Anthony just came in and started fighting my friend Troy and then he pulled out a gun and started shooting."

"How did he get in?"

"He used his key. I never changed the locks. I know, I know it's all my fault. I was so stupid. I shouldn't have never let him come over."

"It's not your fault," Tanya said.

I don't care what anyone said, she couldn't convince me otherwise. "I got to check on him," I said. I called upstairs to the nurses' station on Troy's floor. I asked her about the condition of the patient Troy Sloan.

"What's your relationship to the patient?" she asked.

"A good friend," I said.

"Ma'am, I'm sorry, we can't give any information to anyone without the consent of the patient."

"Can you just answer one question?"

"What's that?" she asked.

"Is he going to make it?"

"That information is confidential, but it doesn't look good."

I couldn't believe what had happened. My family was together six months ago, and now this. I felt like it was all my fault. I couldn't stop the tears. They were flowing and flowing down my face. A man in a blue trench coat approached me and said his name was Detective Lattison.

"Hi, Mrs. Grant, I have a few questions I need to ask you."

I wiped away my tears and said, "Okay."

"Your husband is in custody right now for attempted murder. Mr. Sloan might not make it. If he doesn't, your husband is going to prison for a very long time. So tell me what happened."

I told him the long, tired story. I started at my trip and how I had come back and met Troy online. How we went out on a few dates. How me and Anthony were no longer married and had signed divorce papers.

"Thanks for your time. We just had to find out exactly why your husband was so upset with Mr. Sloan. Does you husband have a history of mental illness?" he asked.

"No, not to my knowledge. Is that all? I have to get back to my baby," I said. I called back to Troy's room. I told the operator I was his wife then they patched me right into his room. Troy's brother answered the phone. I told him who I was and he gave me minimal information. He said he didn't blame me for the shooting, but didn't think it was a good idea for me to come to his brother's room. He said all of Troy's family was there, including his daughter and ex-wife.

Chapter Sixty-eight

Tanya

I was watching the preview for the six o'clock news. Deja and Davon were doing their homework. And out of the corner of my eye I saw a reporter standing in front of a house that looked like Natalie's saying live at six we'll tell you more about a police standoff in progress in southwest Philadelphia. I jumped up and called Natalie's cell phone; it kept ringing. Her house phone was busy. I dialed her mom's house, no answer. I ran into Mom-Mom's room and told her I thought I had just seen Natalie's house on television with a police standoff.

"Mom-Mom, can I hold your car?"

"Go ahead girl. Be careful. Call me when you find out what is going on," she said as she turned on her television.

I drove to Natalie's street. I was right. It was Natalie's house and there were cops everywhere. Oh my god, what is going on. I hadn't talked to Natalie in weeks, I thought. I saw a lady standing in her doorway. I asked her did she know what was going on. She told me the husband had tried to shoot the wife.

"Is the wife okay, I asked."

"I think so, I saw her walk to the ambulance," the lady said. I thanked the woman and got back in the car. I knew they had to be at Mercy Hospital because it was the closest hospital, so I drove there.

"Is there a Natalie Martin here?" I asked the man at patient information. He looked in his computer. He was taking too long so I just walked back to the emergency room while he was still searching. I saw Aunt Sharon. I called her name and she turned around.

"Aunt Sharon, what's going on?" I asked as I approached her.

"Anthony went crazy and tried to shoot Natalie. But instead he shot the baby in the arm and some guy Natalie was dating," she said as she hugged me.

"Is baby Anthony okay?" I asked.

"Yes, they're about to transfer him over to Children's Hospital."

"Where is Natalie?"

"She had to go back to the house with the police because Anthony threatened to kill himself."

"Oh God," I said. Aunt Sharon was wiping tears herself but she tried to console me. I calmed down and walked her back to the baby's room. I felt so relieved. I couldn't take another death, or tragedy. I don't know.

Chapter Sixty-nine

Janelle

Damon had a big interview with *Sports Illustrated*. They were doing an article on second chances in the NFL. He said he wanted me to go, but I didn't feel like it.

"I don't feel like talking to this reporter by myself. I want you to go with me. Wear something dressy because they might try to take your picture."

"Damon, I don't feel like it. I don't feel well."

Just as I said that my phone rang. My mother called me and said, "Janelle, get down here now. That dumb-ass fool shot Natalie and the baby."

"No," I said as I dropped the phone. "What makes somebody do that, the dumb shit?"

"What's going on?" Damon asked.

"My cousin's ex-husband shot her. I have to get home now," I said as I put my clothes on.

"I'll go with you," he said

"What about your interview?"

"This is more important."

We got in the car and got on the turnpike. I couldn't believe Anthony would go off like that. You see it on the news all the time, but you never actually think somebody you know would do something so stupid. I couldn't stop crying. I feared losing my cousin. If something happened to Nat or the baby I wouldn't be right. My phone was ringing, but I refused to answer it. I didn't want any more bad news. Damon answered it. He tried to soothe me by rubbing my back.

"Baby, calm down. Calm down. Your mom is on the phone. Natalie and the baby are okay. Her husband is in jail. Natalie's friend is the one that is hurt."

I calmed down a little.

We went to the hospital and Natalie was going crazy. Tanya was trying to calm her down. She was walking back and forth. Her friend Troy was in critical condition. She thought it was her fault. I stayed at the hospital with Nat and Aunt Sharon until they upgraded the baby's condition to fair and transferred him to Children's Hospital.

Damon was too tired to drive home and I was too shaken up. There wasn't enough room at my mom's apartment. Damon suggested we stay over and get a hotel room. All I wanted to do was get some sleep, so much had happened. I was thankful to God that my cousins were okay. We got a room downtown at the Embassy Suites.

The lights were out and I was beginning to feel calm. We were both lying in bed and Damon went to the bathroom and told me to come here.

"What? I'm tired," I said.

"Just come here," he said. I reluctantly got out of the bed. My eyes were barely open and I was shunning the light coming from the bathroom. "What's up, Dame? I'm tired."

"Go into the bathroom."

"For what?" I asked.

"Just go." I walked into the bathroom and on the mirror written in soap was *Will you marry me?* A red velvet box was in the sink. Damon was standing in the doorway. I didn't even think about it.

"Yes, of course I'll marry you!" I said as I turned and went to hug Damon.

"I know it wasn't the most romantic way of proposing. I had a big elaborate plan. Then all this happened. I hope you don't mind."

"Damon, this is perfect," I said.

Damon took the ring out of the box and placed it on my finger and got on his knees and said, "Janelle, since you came into my life you haven't left my side. You were in my corner when nobody else was. When I didn't have a contract you were right there. My baby even returned her stuff to the store for me. That meant a lot, Janelle. I know my men's girls wouldn't do that for them. I love you, baby."

"I love you too!" I said. "How long have you been planning this?"

"Since we got to New Jersey. I made up the *Sports Illustrated* interview."

"Really? I was feeling so bad that you missed the interview. Damon, you want me to be your wife?"

"Yes, I want to spend the rest of my life with you. We can get married as soon as we get back to New Jersey. You can go get a dress and we can fly our parents in. It can be something small."

"I think we need to take our time, baby. I'm not in a rush. We have the rest of our lives," I said as I kissed him.

Epilogue

Natalie

Troy is still recuperating from his gunshot injuries. He did survive thanks to God. I have decided not to stay in touch with him. It's too much guilt. It's time for me to get on with my life. Anthony's court date has been postponed several times. He is in jail awaiting trial. He signed the house over to me, and I sold it and put the money in the bank for him. His lawyer's fees are eating away at the insurance money his mother left him. There was no way I would ever live in that house again. I moved back in with my parents for awhile until I get everything in order. I quit catering for Ms. Jerri 'cause I didn't feel like dealing with her anymore. I can't wait until the spring. Until then I'll work with my mom. I'm thinking about moving to North Carolina or maybe Atlanta. Anywhere I could get a fresh start. I often think about what would've happened if I never went to Miami. Would Anthony and me still be together? Would I be happy? That's a question I'll never be able to answer. If I had a chance to do it again, I wouldn't go—I would stay home. And that is the honest to God truth. I'm just happy to be alive. I can't even watch the news because I start wondering about what would have happened if Anthony had succeeded. Every night I hear about murder–suicides or some woman getting beaten to death by her boyfriend and it scares me. I just think it could have been me and I had never seen it coming. I'm just happy to be able to see my son and live another day. I don't think I should have started a new relationship so soon after my divorce. I should have waited. I shouldn't ever have gone to Miami.

Tanya

I started my nursing program and I graduate in April. My mother is doing good. She and I are okay. She's taking her meds and taking care of herself. For now, she is off that shit. I have stopped smoking weed and only smoke a cigarette here and there. Monica got five years probation. Lil' Ron is facing seven to ten years. The cops had been watching him for awhile, so they knew Monica wasn't a major part of his operation. They just wanted to see if she knew anything. My grandmother is taking it easy. She has a job at Wal-Mart and is taking trips and vacations. She told me that she felt incomplete when Saundra was gone. Now that she is home, she feels like she could live again. I still keep in touch with Buc. He is a good friend. There is nothing romantic going on between us. Right now I'm trying to get out of school, get me and my kids a place, and then maybe I'll start thinking about a man. Until then I'm cool.

Janelle

Who knew that one weekend trip would change my life forever. I'm planning my wedding with a coordinator. Natalie is going to be my bridesmaid and Kelly is flying in. We are getting married in Los Cabos, Mexico. All of our family is coming. I'm paying for my uncle, mom and brothers, and Damon is paying for his family. My mom and brothers moved out of my apartment and are living in a house in

Germantown. Damon is a good man. He is going to a 12-step program and I go to the meetings with him. I'm so happy that I stayed with him. He is what so many women are searching for. Even though he isn't perfect, I love him. Women think that if they find a man with money, it is going to be the end of all their worries. It might be, sometimes, but not always. Everybody is doing okay. I finally found a job as a buyer's assistant for a boutique.